PILLARS

of SALT

PILLARS
of SALT

A NOVEL

J. A. Adams

atmosphere press

For my husband, Joe; my son, Matt; my brother, John;
and in memory of my son, John

PROLOGUE

November 20, 1980
Lake Chevreuil, Louisiana

Auguste Savois lifted his tackle box into the back of his *bateau*, the flat-bottomed river boat tied to his makeshift dock of weathered cypress boards on stump pilings. Toward the east, along the horizon, the moonless sky was already beginning to fade to the same iron-ore gray as the pier and the canal. Auguste trudged back to the unpainted cypress shack built on stilts by his father, where Auguste had lived all his seventy-four years. His wife of the last fifty of those years, Angelle, was pouring milk in Jamie's jelly glass as Auguste walked into the kitchen for the metal ice chest.

"I put you some boudin in there," she said, smiling at the husband she had spent her entire adult life waiting on.

"Ah, you're a good woman," the old man replied, patting Angelle gingerly on the bottom that seemed to fill up a good portion of the kitchen. "You put us plenty to drink in there, I know."

"I put you some water."

"And some beer?"

"Of course, *cher*. I put in two Cokes for Jamie and two beers for you. You don't need no more than two beers when you've got your grandson along," she said, her crinkly smile reminding Jamie of the dried apple doll he had seen at the Stuckey's where his father had stopped on the trip from Opelousas yesterday afternoon.

"Finish up that egg, boy," Auguste said in the sternest voice he could feign, taking a noisy slurp of his Community coffee. "We've got us some sac-a-lait to catch, and it's almost sunup." Auguste grabbed two slickers from the hook by the door, slid the ice chest off the counter, and headed back out to the *bateau*, letting the screen door smack against the jamb. A few crows squawked their discontent and flew off.

Auguste arranged the ice chest and the cane poles, then folded the slickers and stuffed them under the seat, just in case. He pulled up the net filled with bait fish and sloshed them into the shiner bucket, then shoved the bucket next to the tackle box. He heard the screen door slam again in the distance, heard Jamie thumping across the overturned soft drink crates Auguste had confiscated from Bergeron's General Store to provide a walkway through the muddy *batture,* the land between the levee and the canal.

"Hah, you finally finished?" Auguste laughed when Jamie arrived breathless, carrying his last piece of toast, his brown wavy hair still standing on end. Jamie was only eight, but Auguste was proud of Léon for raising such a strong, independent boy. Léon's wife Jeanine had left them when Jamie was only four, insisting that she couldn't care for such a precocious child and running instead to the arms of the palm tree salesman who had passed through Opelousas from Pensacola more often than necessary ever since he had sold a tree to Jeanine one lonely Monday morning.

"*Allons*, Jamie," Auguste said, pulling the *bateau* close to the dock as Jamie stepped in and found his seat. Auguste shoved off and stepped in as easily as a much younger man, finding his seat in front of the Evinrude and easing the *bateau* away from the dock. "Here, put on this life vest, boy. You know what your MaMaw made me promise," Auguste said as he shoved the orange vest at Jamie. "I think we'll pass by Lake Chevreuil this morning." Jamie grinned, buckling his vest as he chewed on his last bite of toast, then held both sides of the *bateau* that chugged slowly with the current of the Delcambre Canal.

Within the hour, they found a spot in the *cyprière*, the cypress grove that bordered Lake Chevreuil near Oka Chito Island. In the distance, they could see the eerie silhouette of the jack-up oil rig rising from the placid lake against a sky that was beginning to lighten. Closer to shore, the tower of the salt mine rose above the salt dome that formed Oka Chito Island. Jamie baited the hook on his cane pole and swung his line among the cypress knees while Auguste tied up to a cypress tree.

Before long, the two anglers had strung a dozen sac-a-lait, bream, and catfish onto the stringer. Jamie was glad his father had been called to Houston on oilfield business. Otherwise, Jamie would be sitting at his desk with the other third graders right now, no doubt beginning the Pledge of Allegiance. He thought about 'Tee Jack as he watched his peaceful cork bobbing on the water's surface. Too bad his best friend couldn't have escaped school three days before Thanksgiving break as Jamie had. 'Tee Jack would have liked the feel of pulling five or six sac-a-lait every hour out of the shallow lake.

But while Jamie was staring absently at his cork, suddenly it flopped on its side and began racing toward the distant rig. "Paw Paw, look! It must be a big one!" he exclaimed. "I can't hold my pole!"

Auguste, who had just landed a sac-a-lait and was re-baiting his own hook, dropped his pole to reach for Jamie's. "Here, boy. Hand me that pole. You'll drop it if you ain't careful." As Jamie turned to hand it to Auguste, the pole slipped from his hands and sped toward the open water, following the cork. "*Aye Yee!*" Auguste yelled. "That ain't no fish, no! Look here, boy! All those limbs and debris ain't supposed to be racing like that! What the hell's going on?"

A rapid current had begun hurtling everything on the lake's surface toward the oil rig. Leaves and chunks of driftwood raced past the *bateau*. Cranes and gulls, herons and mallards, all began flying in the opposite direction, shrieking their warnings. "Is it the end of the world, Paw Paw?" Jamie shrieked, wide-eyed with fear.

"Hell, I don't know, me. What the hell! Say your Hail Mary's, boy. Something is bad wrong here!"

Auguste's *bateau* was straining against the rope tied to the tree. "We got to get out of here, boy," Auguste yelled over the roar as he started the motor so he could put enough slack in the line to untie it. Once free of the stump, he revved the motor at full throttle out of the *cyprière* and back toward Delcambre Canal, passing the limbs and driftwood that sped in the opposite direction. He noticed that the debris seemed to have slowed down until he realized that the limbs hadn't slowed down at all; instead, the *bateau*, even at full throttle, was sliding backward!

"We'll have to try to make the island," he hollered over the roar of the water. As Auguste fought the current, Jamie, holding the sides of the *bateau* with a death grip, watched as the distant jack-up rig listed to one side. Jamie saw a lifeboat fleeing the tangled rig and heard what sounded like screams audible above the roar of water.

A ten-foot swell heaved Auguste's *bateau* high but mercifully left it upright. The jack-up rig in the distance screeched a last gasp as it finished its descent, landing on top of the lifeboat, and plunging its passengers into a watery grave beneath tons of twisted metal. As the derrick disappeared beneath the surface, Jamie saw only a remnant marking the tomb, the mast from the top of the boom crane, which slipped into the hole moments later. The massive whirlpool plunged the remnants of the lifeboat and twisted metal down what had become a 150-foot waterfall, the largest ever in Louisiana, swirling the flotsam out of sight beneath the surface of the lake that was known to be only 11 feet deep.

"I got to bail out, Jamie," Auguste screamed over the roar, "and try to get us to that solid land over yonder. You stay in the *bateau*, or you'll sink in this mud, sure!" With strength he didn't think he had, he was able to push the little boat a foot or two ahead, then drag his body horizontally after it. When he became unable to continue pushing against the weight of the sliding mud, Auguste hoisted Jamie into the mud, where the pair were able to pull their way slowly on their bellies the last ten feet to solid ground.

After a grueling several minutes, Auguste and Jamie heaved themselves onto dry land, drenched in black slime, Auguste's beard crusted with thick, dripping mud, Jamie's tears streaming little canals through the mud on his cheeks. Auguste would swear that a merciful God wanted them to survive, even though one of his doctors later attributed his burst of strength to adrenalin, along with his younger years of physical labor as a derrickman in the Gulf.

Shortly after the pair had reached the island, sirens and lights from emergency vehicles out of Delcambre and New Iberia began arriving on the scene. Rubberneckers in piper cubs from New Iberia airport began circling to view the destruction they heard about on police band radios.

Besides the oil rig, barges, and tugboats, most of the buildings of the salt mine on the shore were also sucked into the hole. Cars, a mobile home, ancient giant live oak trees, even some houses were being pulled into the widening cavern. Auguste and Jamie saw the land slide from beneath one of the largest homes on the island and leave it dangling on the edge, its screened sunroom hanging six feet out over the churning foam. A chopper descended and hovered directly over the house to get a closer look, then rose again as the house and the land it rested on plunged into the chasm.

A police car appeared on the road behind Auguste and Jamie, its flashing lights ironic against such disaster. Spotting the mud-drenched pair, the officer stopped, grabbed blankets from his trunk, and hurried over to wrap them up against the November chill. Amidst the horror,

Jamie had failed to notice his teeth chattering and his body shivering convulsively, possibly from being wet on a chilly morning, possibly from shock, most likely from a combination of the two. When he felt the warmth of the blanket around his shoulders and noticed the strong arm of the policeman that guided him to the car, his knees became weak, and his tears began anew.

~

Earlier that morning in New Iberia, Marlisa Daigrepont woke with a start and sat bolt upright. She had begun having the nightmares shortly after the wedding, and no amount of Charles's reassurance placated her. Charles held her close, caressed her silky nightgown and reached one hand into her thick auburn hair, cradling her scalp and coaxing her cheek close to his chest. The trembling subsided and Marlisa slumped onto Charles's shoulder.

"Stay home with me today, Charles," she pleaded.

"*Bébé*, you know I can't do that, no. There ain't nothing I'd like better than to curl up in bed with my bride all day," he said. "But you know I got no choice. Brad can't handle it alone. You know they cut our crew to the bone. Come on, *ma chère*. Don't make it harder than it already is to leave you."

Charles Daigrepont, a rough-hewn Cajun with hair the color of the strong coffee he drank, becoming flecked now with salt at the temples, was master electrician at the Oka Chito Island Salt Mine. He understood why Marlisa, having lost her father in a gas pipeline explosion fifteen years ago in St. Francisville, was petrified at the notion now of her husband being 1300 feet beneath Lake Chevreuil. That's one reason he never told her how run-down the new owner had allowed the mine to become.

Charles had often tried to persuade her to come with him on visiting day to ride the cage down the shaft to the vast underworld, invisible to the residents overhead who lived their own lives and visited their neighbors for coffee in the early evenings. He argued that upper layers of the mine boasted galleries fit for Goliath, 65 feet wide and 100 feet high, separated by 75-foot salt pillars, the workers like ants scurrying in their underground colony. Both gallery and pillar sizes were even greater at lower depths. Charles thought Marlisa would lose her claustrophobia if she would enter the mine one time and see the immensity and strength of it. So far, Marlisa had refused, complaining that the cage "hung by a thread" from the head frame, and Charles had no response.

Sometimes he questioned his choice of a bride twenty years his junior just two years after his divorce. Jack Brouillette, his one-time best friend, and the burly foreman on the 1500-foot level had warned him of the dangers of marrying a twenty-three-year-old, but Charles had followed his heart instead of his brain. If he felt he was rearing another daughter at times, his confidence in his choice was renewed during their frequent passionate intervals of lovemaking unlike anything he had ever experienced.

Charles pulled Marlisa down on the bed beside him to hold her close. She was pliable in his arms, yielding to his caresses, as he kneaded her arms, her hair, her back. It was moments like this that Charles knew, Jack Brouillette be damned, his marriage to Marlisa was anything but a mistake. It was during these moments of lovemaking that he felt alive, that he felt young again, that the nose bleeds from the perpetual salt contamination didn't frighten him.

An hour later, Charles creaked down the shaft with Brouillette, whose bulk dwarfed the cage, the smell of Marlboros clinging to his muskrat-brown Oshkosh jumper and unkempt hair of the same color. Jack was not an educated man. During the thirty years that he had served in the "bowels of hell," as he called the mine, he had clawed his way up through the ranks from laborer, to driller, to powderman. He survived the layoffs four years ago and achieved his current position as foreman at the 1500-foot level.

"*Yie Yee*. Back to the old salt mines, eh, Daigrepont?" Jack chuckled in his rasping morning cigarette voice, using the cliché literally as only salt miners could.

"Yeah, yeah. Another day," Charles said, still wearing the contented grin of a man tingling from the lingering warmth of the firm body next to his just sixty minutes earlier.

"Mable and I are going to the honky-tonk tonight. You and Marlisa come along with us."

"Nah, Jack, can't do it on a work night. You go tomorrow night, we'd probably meet y'all."

"I hear ya, *sha. Les nouveaux mariés se coûcher tôt*," Jack teased, slapping Charles on the back.

Charles bristled at the allusion to his conjugal activities, aware that Jack Brouillette disapproved of his April-November marriage. Or perhaps it was Mable, twice Marlisa's age, fifty pounds overweight, and prone to jealousy.

When Charles didn't respond, Jack broke the silence. "So, my friend, how's Marlisa making out?"

"Oh, Marlisa's fine, Jack. In fact, she's about the finest woman I ever met."

"Yeah, brother! I hear ya!" Jack laughed as the cage jerked to a stop at the 1300-foot level and Charles stepped out.

"Y'all have fun tonight, Jack," Charles called as the cage rumbled on down the shaft.

Jack's bass voice boomed back up through the shaft as the cage groaned out of sight. "Gonna pass a good time, us!"

Charles clocked in, poured a cup of coffee, and began leafing through the log from the previous night. Bradley Dubois, the only electrician on Charles's crew, sat down beside him and lit a cigarette.

"What's it look like today, Charlie?" Bradley asked through a cloud of exhaled smoke.

"Looks like they're having a few problems with that main conveyor belt. We need to take a look this morning," Charles said, not raising his eyes from the logbook.

Before Charles had his second sip of coffee, his two-way radio beeped. The conveyor tender was on the other end.

"Yeah, Frank. What ya got?"

"Hey, mon, the breaker feeding number 3 conveyor tripped. Got somebody to take a look?"

"Bradley's right here. I'll send him over to check it out." He hung up and turned to Bradley.

"Yeah, yeah, I'm going, I'm going," Bradley said, partially snuffing his cigarette so that it smoldered in the overflowing ashtray.

Charles poured some of his coffee on the smoldering pile, grumbling under his breath that since the mine had been sold, all they had time for was repairing old worn-out equipment.

After a few minutes, Frank called again. "Charlie, I got a ground on B phase winding on 3B drive motor."

"OK, Frank. Be there in fifteen." Charles dumped what was left of his coffee, walked to the supply depot, and handed his list to Pierre Brossette, the supply manager.

"Morning, Chaz," Pierre said. "What'll it be?"

"Oh, we got a damned ground to check into. Probably have to send 3B drive motor out for rewinding."

"Always some shit, ay, man? We'll get this stuff out in a few minutes." Pierre handed the list to Paul, his assistant, and the two scattered to find the requisitioned wire, insulators, and connectors.

Whistling "The Lover's Waltz," Marlisa's favorite Cajun waltz, Charles walked back into the gallery and bent to grab his tool pouch from the tool crib. Startled by a banging noise that shattered the silence in the gallery, he jerked upright and wheeled toward the racket. Directly behind him poured a salt miner's worst nightmare: a calf-deep river of root-beer-colored saltwater pouring through the gallery. Even a small water leak into a salt dome meant disaster. Charles recognized this massive intrusion as imminent inundation. The noise that had first alerted him had come from empty fuel drums floating and banging together on the saltwater river.

"MAYDAY! Mine flooding!" Charles screamed, his heart pounding as he raced to the power disconnect switch for the 1500-foot level. He flashed the switch three times, the Mayday signal. He phoned the hoistman upstairs.

"INUNDATION! Get the cage down fast!"

Then he phoned Jack on the 1500-foot level. "Mine flooding, Jack! Not a drill! You OK down there?"

"What the hell's goin' on? No water down here!" Jack said, indicating that the leak must have started at the 1300-foot level.

"You'll be flooding any second! Get 'em up here fast, and we'll load from here!" Charles bellowed before slamming the receiver down and dashing toward the ramp.

Fortunately, only around twenty-five men manned the mine this morning. Following evacuation procedure, the men met at a designated point so Jack could count noses, then pounded up the incline like stampeding cattle, their usual aplomb replaced by terror. Charles stood at the top of the ramp directing traffic, as the inadequate cage, squeezed to capacity, hauled load after load of men to the surface.

Charles, in water to his hips, loaded the cage with the last man. Not enough room to squeeze himself on safely, he hammered the cage to signal the hoistman to lift.

Nervously awaiting the cage's return one last time, water now swirling to his waist, Charles glanced in the direction of the flow just in time to see a thirty-foot swell fill the gallery, tossing drums, heavy equipment, and machinery like so many Tonka toys. Before the cage could make its return, an angry wall of saltwater engulfed Charles as massive pillars of salt crumbled into the stew. As the last load of men to make it to the top ran for the safety of the center of the island, they heard one final piercing scream escape the shaft: "Oh, God! Marlisaaa!!"

~

The disaster in the salt mine was caused by the emergency unfolding earlier above the lake. Having reached a depth of 900 feet, the drill pumps on the jack-up oil rig were operating smoothly. Night derrickman Sid Ardoin was solely responsible for the night shift drill mud operation since Dallas Matherne, the night driller, had called in sick. But Sid could handle it. Not a tall man, Sid was built like a scrappy bantam rooster, muscular without an ounce of fat, his thighs bigger around than his waist, his arms like rock from his years working the heavy drill pumps. On the log sheet at 0145 hours, he had reported that both mud pumps were running normally.

Sid knew that circulation could be smooth one minute and turn to crap with no apparent provocation: Murphy's Law. So, he wasn't unduly surprised when, shortly after 0300 hours, number one pump screeched to a halt and sent the hovering gulls squawking into the night.

Sid called Eric Arcenaux, tool pusher and foreman. "Hey, Arcenaux. We burned a damn clutch up here on number one. We're going to need a mechanic up here, STAT."

"OK, Sid. I'll send Dauzat up."

Drilling rates under a salt dome were higher than normal, but there wasn't much Sid hadn't seen or couldn't handle. He didn't have a lot to be proud of, ever since Louisa, his wife of four years, had a fling with one of the Doucet boys, the spoiled one. Their marriage now felt like walking on eggshells, ever since she had come to him begging after Victor Doucet slammed her on the discard pile with the rest of his women. Something about an unfaithful wife rips a man's balls off, Sid thought, remembering how he beat the ever-loving crap out of Victor one morning when he got home from the rig a little early and found Victor half-dressed, hopping on one foot as he tried to pull on his other shoe. And how Victor rounded up three of his druggie friends to come back to the house later, drag Sid out of bed, and land enough blows to send Sid to ER, where he got twelve stitches sewn into his right eyebrow. Sid remembered old man Doucet damn near firing him until Sid convinced him that his precious Victor was no angel.

Old Harvey Doucet probably realized he couldn't replace Sid all that easily, so Sid stayed on. The job paid well, twelve on and twenty-four off, leaving plenty of nights for him and Louisa to go to the honky-tonk and work at putting their marriage back on track. Besides dancing the zydeco better than anyone in the bar, except for maybe Charlie Daigrepont, Sid was the hardest worker old man Doucet had, and the old man knew it. Victor Doucet might inherit all his daddy's money one day, but at least Sid still had his wife and his dignity.

"Hey, man, I hear ya got problems up here," Robert Dauzat called when he and a couple of roughnecks arrived with a rolling tool chest.

"Yeah. Damn clutch burned out on number one."

Dauzat straightened his hardhat. "We'll have her up in a flash," he said.

But by 0400 hours, while the men struggled with number one drill pump, number two pump got stuck, halting what was left of mud circulation. Unable to restart the pump, Sid whistled down to Ted Romero, night driller. "Hey, Romero, I need a hand with a stuck pump up here.

Dauzat 'n them is still finishing up the clutch on number one."

"Be right there, Sid," Ted called back, heading for the stairs.

Even together, Ted and Sid were unable to raise or lower the drill string or to restart the pump.

The men were still struggling a couple of hours later when the crew boat with the day crew docked. Sid's replacement, Big Joe Langlois, jolly as always, lumbered up and whacked Sid on the back. "Hey, man, I hear you guys have had it. Take a break. I'll take it from here."

"Naw, man, we'll stay," Sid replied over his shoulder. "This is going to take a few hands."

Ted Romero's replacement, Jack Tullier, joined Ted in the fight. Working together, the four men got load indicators down and held them down briefly. But then indicators shot up to an unprecedented 400,000 pounds, as one side of the rig leaned, with a groan that echoed through the morning, sending noisy gulls flapping again. Eric Arcenaux called the Calco Oil office in New Iberia on the marine radio.

A slight lean was not all that unusual, as supporting pilings sometimes gave a little when the rig settled. Unruffled, the Calco official said, "OK, Arcenaux, we'll get a contractor out there to take a look."

"Oh, well, man. Let's hope she's just settling," Dauzat said when Eric reported what he'd been told.

But as Sid and Ted glanced at each other skeptically, one corner of the rig platform dropped another three feet.

"MAYDAY! This ain't no piling problem!" Sid hollered to no one in particular.

"Untie the barges!" Eric screamed over at Carl, captain

of the tug. "Ted! Go help Carl get all that equipment the hell away from the rig!"

Meanwhile, Sid hollered to the group scattering around the drill pipe, "MAYDAY! Man the lifeboat! You guys from the night shift, head to the crew boat!" He ran over to pull the master shut-down switch and sound the platform evacuation alarm. The crew followed orders quickly, as they had practiced routinely. This time, though, their eyes revealed that this was no ordinary drill.

Carl shot down to the lowest level of the rig and boarded the tug to move the supply barges away from the platform. Ted, close at his heels, began untying the barges. Starting the tug motor, Carl watched in disbelief as the rig dropped another foot.

The night crew piled onboard the crew boat to head toward the safety of the island. The day crew grabbed life vests from the bin and tumbled noisily aboard the lifeboat. Finally, the last man climbed on board, counted heads, and pressed the lever to lower the lifeboat into the shallow lake.

But while the crew boat headed toward the safety of the island, the men on board heard the platform shriek, then watched as all 166 pilings crashed into the lake below. The twisting metal caught the lifeboat on its way down, dragging the day crew with it into a widening whirlpool. Incredibly, the shallow lake had swallowed the rig and the lifeboat, crew and all, as if Lake Chevreuil had become a bottomless, ravenous pit.

The crew boat captain, going at full power and speed, was barely able to creep slowly and safely ashore against the force of a tidal wave pulling them backwards. Manning the tugboat, Carl was not so fortunate. The retiring crew watched helplessly as the tugboat and the supply barge it was towing were sucked into the pit. Sid vomited. Burly oil rig workers, heads bowed, wiped tears away with greasy black hands.

It was amid this scene of terror that two Calco assistant district superintendents arrived by helicopter, able now only to stand on the shore as the multimillion-dollar rig disappeared, only the top of the derrick remaining above water briefly before it too sank into the chasm.

By this time, private pilots with ham radios had arrived and circled the scene. A helicopter arrived from Lafayette carrying Harvey Doucet, owner of Doucet Drilling Corporation, who, along with his bodyguard Placide, gaped at this scene straight out of Hell. Becoming suddenly nauseated, Harvey grabbed the barf bag from the seat pocket in front of him. Witnessing the deaths of valued employees and, yes, perhaps some could be called friends, though he was never known as the friendly sort, the 230-pound multimillionaire of cold, tough steel, speechless now, gazed from the small plane's window, holding a barf bag with a death grip.

First responders sped to the scene in flashing squad cars, ambulances, fire trucks, and choppers. Officers began securing the area and scrambling to the houses on the island to evacuate residents. Families were wrested from their homes, some women hysterical, others taking the stoic role of protector, piling whimpering children, frightened dogs, and a few hastily grabbed favorite toys and important papers into trunks and backseats, as an exodus proceeded at a snail's pace along the bumper-to-bumper lone road from the island that officials had just arrived on.

According to protocol, a mine emergency team from the Federal Mine Safety and Health Administration, the MSHA, was summoned to the scene, their first grim order of business to make sure the island had stabilized, begin identifying casualties, and notifying loved ones. At daybreak on November 20, 1980, twelve men, one from the salt mine, one from the tugboat, and ten from the rig's lifeboat, had been sucked into the hole in the earth, now over a quarter-mile in diameter and 150 feet deep. As the crater sucked the water backwards up the Delcambre Canal from the Gulf, shrimp boats far away in the canal found themselves resting on the muddy bottom like beached whales.

More officials arrived that afternoon from both the salt mine and the oil and drilling companies, dressed in dark business suits and talking in guarded, confidential tones. Henry Gorman, a Calco Oil official, quietly began plotting the drill site on the map placed on an easel in the storage *qua* meeting room that had been set up in one of the surviving salt company buildings. Harvey Doucet's Executive Officer of domestic drilling, Marc LeBlanc, solemnly carried files of the men reportedly drowned and handed them over to officials.

The MSHA officials watched the proceedings somberly, as did officials from the Louisiana Department of Natural Resources who had provided the original permit to drill.

Jeffrey Allen, sent by the Sapphire Salt Company, shuffled over to the map and drew a large blue X with his felt tip pen. Interrupting Henry's proceedings, Jeffrey said in soft but ominous tones, "With all due respect, Mr. Gorman, this spot here, this drilling site you've so kindly just shown us, would have inserted your drill directly into the far southwest corner of the salt mine, right here at the 1300-foot level, an area Sapphire has already mined out. Who in hell, excuse my French, gave you orders to drill right *there*? Or did anyone ever really check? Hell, sir, what we had here was an onrush of water that simply dissolved the entire southwest corner of the salt dome. Clearly, Calco Oil did an improper survey and is entirely to blame for this travesty."

Nine days after the inundation, Sapphire Salt Company filed suit against Calco Oil and Doucet Drilling for an unspecified amount of damages. Calco Oil followed with a countersuit against Doucet Drilling for an estimated ten million dollars' worth of equipment plus a settlement of a million dollars to the family of each of the deceased. Sapphire Salt Company mineworkers followed up with a separate class-action suit for the loss of their jobs.

To top it off, Harvey Doucet, owner of Doucet Drilling Company, was found dead in his Lafayette condo, an apparent suicide, after discovery of a stomach full of enough sleeping medicine to put down a rhino.

Chapter 1
WAKE-UP CALL

I lay staring at the yellowed ceiling, streaked by decades of nicotine from previous down-on-their-luck tenants. The haze from my Camel desert dog softened the stains, like the lenses used to hide the creases of aging actresses. Flickering neon lights in front of the newsstand downstairs cast flashing pink and green stripes through the Venetian blinds onto the walls.

I had been existing in this fleabag hotel for a week, after having escaped what turned out to be a parasitic relationship. Six years ago, I gave up my base single housing when, against all common sense, I had moved in with Midge in the modest home she purchased after finding her dream job as a physician's assistant at a Charlotte clinic. Midge had run off a few college suitors since our neighborhood touch football games and our steamy high school romance. She had always complained that none of her squeezes worked out because of neuroses that her twelve hours of college psychology had enabled her to diagnose. Missing all the red flags, I jumped in with both feet. Then a week ago, I got my diagnosis: "Flat affect, an emotionless cynic," she said the night she threw me out. Who knows, maybe she was right. Or maybe she just hadn't elicited much emotion. I'd have to ponder that one. Certainly, something was missing in her or in me that prevented the lasting emotional bond we've all come to expect in romance, and few of us ever find.

The phone ringing on the nightstand jangled me back to reality. I debated whether to answer it, fearing it would be Midge again, spouting more evidence of my neuroses. Instead, I ignored it and took a drag on my Camel, but its persistence outlasted me. After the seventh or eighth ring, I gave in and grabbed the receiver.

"Major Doucet?" said the voice on the other end. "Lieutenant Massey here. We just got an emergency message for you to call your Aunt Ethel, ASAP. She doesn't have your new number, and Midge told her you had moved."

Oh, crap, I thought. I had meant to call Aunt Ethel with the news I knew would cheer her up: Midge and I are history. I just hadn't gotten around to it, preoccupied as I was with my own self-pity.

"Thanks, Lieutenant. Any idea what's up?"

"No, Sir. I just got a note to tell you it's an emergency."

Aunt Ethel and Uncle Louis had raised me and my brother Victor since I was three, Vic was two. Along with my baby sister who never saw the light of day, the mother I barely recollect died of complications during childbirth. I was too young at the time to hear the details, and no one had shared them with me since. All I know is that my father, grief-stricken, had what the relatives whispered was a "breakdown" and refused even to name his stillborn offspring. Ethel sat Vic and me down, and we agreed on christening the baby Faith. It only seemed right.

Father's breakdown wasn't the type that hospitalizes its victims or leaves them incapacitated. Instead, my father's emotional collapse caused him to immerse himself in the multinational oil drilling company he eventually came to own and sacrifice Vic and me in the bargain. Aunt Ethel and Uncle Louis oversaw the operation of the old family farm, what was to become the agricultural branch of Father's corporation. Unfortunately, Ethel and Louis were never able to have children, so they just raised Vic and me as their own. Father made periodic "business" visits to the farm, but he rarely spoke to me, lavishing his sporadic attention on Victor instead. When he did speak to me, it was usually to correct me for some mischief I was never as good at pulling off as Victor. "Why can't you be more like your brother?" I can still hear Father scold, as Vic, usually the instigator, grimaced at me from behind his back.

I never remember a hug or a kind word from Father. Looking back, I would have to guess now that I reminded him of Mother, while Vic took after Father's side of the family, the tall muscular frame, wavy black hair, and Roman nose that generally made the women swoon. I was always told, somewhat condescendingly, that I looked just like my mother's side, having fuller lips, lighter coloring, and a less muscular, wirier build. After all, Mother had no French ancestry, and Father was a proud Frenchman.

Or maybe Father just expected more from his first-born son. He always expected little from Victor and got little in return. Whatever the reason, Father and I have always had a strained relationship, no less strained since I opted not to join Doucet Drilling.

Instead, I joined the Air Force Reserves, got a civil engineering degree at LSU, and was commissioned as second lieutenant in the Air Force. Now, as a Major currently stationed at Seymour Johnson airbase in North Carolina, I oversaw a squadron of engineers in airfield construction and maintenance.

Not that I disrespected my father, though that's not how he saw it. In his view, I had abandoned him. Above all, he wanted loyalty, and he felt my departure showed disloyalty to him. Father was a hard man, emotionless, suffered fools badly, and shot straight from the hip. Hell, maybe that's the man Midge saw in me.

I finally picked up the receiver and dialed Aunt Ethel, dreading the questions that were sure to follow. It took her about five rings to make it to the hall phone from the kitchen.

"Aitchie?" she said when she picked up. My family called me H, since I was named after my father, Harvey Willard Doucet, and I guess it was too confusing to call me Harvey. Only my Aunt Ethel still called me Aitchie, my childhood nickname. Or sometimes she called me 'Tee Harvey, short for petit Harvey, the affectionate Cajun name for junior. Or just 'Tee. Somehow 'Tee Harvey didn't stick.

"Yes, Aunt Ethel, it's your long-lost nephew. What's the emergency?" I asked, concerned that something might have befallen Uncle Louis, a hard-living, hard-playing old Cajun of dubious health.

"Oh, Aitchie, *cher*. I have terrible news! I'm afraid your daddy has passed on. I'm so sorry, 'Tee," she said in a thin voice. I could tell she'd been crying. At age 65, Father was as robust, muscular, and healthy as any man half his age. I was dumbstruck, and my heart raced.

"Oh, no! What happened, Ethel?"

I could hear her sniffling for a few seconds before she continued, barely audible, "They say by his own hand, 'Tee. Suicide, *cher*... After the inundation....that salt mine where the company had the jack-up, over at Oka Chito Island... Earlene's the one who found his body in his bed!" I heard Ethel blow her nose.

I pulled myself out of the alcohol fog I'd been using as a crutch the last couple of days on liberty. I needed to think fast, but my brain was still in slow-mo. "Listen, Ethel. I have some business to attend to here tonight, but I'll try to hop a plane and shoot out there first thing in the morning."

"Oh, Aitchie, I'm glad to hear that. Louis and me need you here, *cher*!

Trying hard to digest all the implications of suicide, I added, "Listen, Aunt Ethel. I'm going to need to stay at the farm for several days at least. That OK with you?"

"Of course, *cher*. I was hoping you could stay!" she said. "This is your home! Uncle Louis ain't doing so good, and me and Earlene have been making arrangements for the funeral. The wake's tomorrow evening, then the funeral's on Tuesday. I expect a lot of kinfolk will come to town."

Earlene was the office manager of Doucet Drilling and one of Father's most valued employees. She'd been with the company from the beginning.

"OK. Try to relax, Ethel. I'll be there to help. After the funeral, I'd like to stay awhile to look into a few things," I said, not wanting to upset her with the doubts that had immediately surfaced about the cause of death. No point in putting a bug in her ear until I had some facts.

"Stay as long as you can, *cher*. But don't you have to get right back to the base?"

"I can get an emergency leave." Though I didn't mention it, I hoped to be able to use up some of the extensive leave time I had been saving up over a few years so that Midge and I could have an extended honeymoon in Bermuda or Cabo, if I had ever gotten around to proposing. Looked like that wouldn't be happening now.

"Wonderful, *cher*. I'll call Placide right away to have him pick you up at the airport. Poor Placide. *Il voit du bleu!*"

"Yeah, I figured it would hit Placide hard, inseparable as they were. Tell him I'll get the flight details to you in the morning."

Placide had been my father's devoted driver and bodyguard. People had always rumored that Placide was a killer, that Father had saved him from a life sentence for second-degree murder. I knew Father's story, though. I remember Father explaining it to Vic and me when we were in our teens.

"Placide saved my life," he had told us, "but in the process, he killed a judge's drug-addict son and winged the other low-life thug. Those two bums attacked me in the parking lot at L'Auberge in Lake Charles after I won a couple grand in a poker game. Always remember, boys, Placide is a godsend to our family. Treat him like family, hear?" After Father hired Placide, he provided one wing of his condo for Placide to live with him and protect him 24/7.

Father and I had been estranged for so long that it wasn't a matter of my missing him, not as Placide must miss him. How can you miss what you've never really had? Still, something was unsettling about his death. Suicide? Never! Not my father. As I sat on the edge of my bed and smoked what was to be my last desert dog, I decided it was time to stop feeling sorry for myself, clean up my act, and get to the bottom of this alleged suicide! Hell, I knew Victor, with all his bravado, would not have the balls for the job. I set down the glass, plopped my suitcase on the bed, and dragged over my trunk *qua* end table. I packed up, then rang Lieutenant Massey back.

"Lieutenant? Major Doucet here. Listen, my father just died, so I need some arrangements to get over to Louisiana. I'm going to need to take an emergency leave, at least two weeks, maybe four. How about getting the paperwork together and setting me up some flight arrangements for tomorrow morning? I'll be over there at 0700 hours."

"Yes sir, Major. Very sorry, Sir," Massey said. "I'll have the paperwork sitting on your desk when you get here, Sir."

"Thanks, Lieutenant."

I moved my bag over to the chair, threw back the covers, plumped the pillow, and putting everything on hold, I drifted into a fitful sleep.

~

I groaned as I lifted my head from the pillow a few hours later and felt a throbbing pain in my temples. No woman is worth this, I thought, lying back down and shutting my eyes to the world.

The memory of last night's phone call seeped through the haze. "Suicide, my ass!" I heard a voice deeper than mine spit out of my parched throat. I dragged myself out of bed, stumbled to the bathroom, and swung open the medicine chest to grab the aspirin. When I closed the door, I growled at the stranger with bloodshot eyes peering back at me from the mirror.

I made a strong cup of joe to clear my head, but the half-empty fifth on the counter beside an overflowing ashtray damn near made me blow chow, so I dumped it down the drain and slam-dunked the empty bottle into the trashcan. I told the pack of Camels staring at me from beside the reeking pile of butts, "You've had it too!" I crushed the smokes remaining in the pack and flung them on top of the broken glass. Time to get my ass in gear, I told myself, and headed for the shower.

I had heard about the inundation and the loss of lives near New Iberia. Hell, everybody had. But I hadn't kept up with Father's dealings for years, let alone the corporation. I didn't even know he had been the drilling contractor at Oka Chito, and truth be known, cared less.

After a shower, I headed downstairs to the newsstand. They carried damn near every major paper, so I picked up a copy of the Sunday *Times-Picayune*. I paid Sam, the old codger who had probably run this smoke-filled neighborhood store in Goldsboro for the last fifty years. I skimmed the front-page article. November 30, 1980. Ten days after the inundation, one day after Father's death. Still headline news, of course:

Harvey Doucet, owner of Doucet Drilling, apparently committed suicide in the early morning hours yesterday, after his company was served with several lawsuits from both Calco Oil and Sapphire Salt, for allegedly miscalculating directional drilling in Lake Chevreuil.

Just bloody hell, I thought, as I called over my shoulder, "Later, Sam," and carried the paper outside.

I checked out of what had been my base of operations during my wait to get back into base housing. Midge may have me down for the count, but she sure as hell wasn't going to keep me on the mat.

Chapter 2
THE OLD HOMEPLACE

"Placide," I said when I walked into New Orleans International, embracing him with one arm, clapping him on the shoulder with the other.

"H." I could read the grief in his eyes. I knew what Placide and Father had meant to each other. One hardly took a breath without the other there to watch him exhale. Everyone joked that Placide was Father's shadow.

Though I was six feet tall, Placide dwarfed me. Rumor had it that his mother was black with some French Creole blood thrown in for good measure, probably added before the Civil War when slave women were free game to wealthy Creole plantation owners. Earlene always said Placide's grandfather had been full-blooded Atakapa, though Placide never spoke of his family. Always a man of few words, Placide stood tall, 6'7", and proud enough to be Atakapa, his arms the circumference of small trees, his black eyes, intense and piercing. One of those giants whose neck started at his ears and extended outward toward massive shoulders, like the trunk of a live oak meeting the ground. Today, though, the proud giant stared glumly at the ground, looking more like a deflated parade balloon than an oak.

After I grabbed the bag and he effortlessly hoisted the trunk that I pointed to on the conveyor, we walked silently to the parking garage and to Father's nondescript black Ford LTD. So typical of Father. Here he was driving an old car, albeit a polished one, when he could easily afford a new one every year. Nothing pretentious for Father, just something to get him back and forth to job sites, run errands, and get around town. That was about all he would have cared about. He would much rather hop in the company helicopter for longer trips.

I knew that a replica of that old LTD was located in Houston. The same security code fit both vehicles, just as one security code accessed the house in New Iberia, the one in Houston, the condo in Lafayette, and even the cabin on Toledo Bend. Father preferred an uncomplicated lifestyle. I could still hear him grumble, "Anything beyond necessity is Pure-D waste." And aside from having several well-stocked residences for "convenience" during his numerous business trips, and an occasional getaway for fishing, his lifestyle had reflected his frugal philosophy.

"Well, Placide. You getting along OK?" I finally asked, beginning to feel awkward in the suffocating silence.

"Yessir. I'm making it, me."

"You still staying in Lafayette?" I knew he had been staying in his wing of Father's condo in Lafayette before the tragedy.

"I moved into an apartment in New Iberia. I want to be close to Ethel and Louis, give them a hand sometimes."

"Good. I'm glad you'll be close by."

"Oh, I'm never too far away, sir," he said, glancing briefly in my direction for the first time since I'd arrived.

Within the hour, we reached the old home place outside New Iberia, the farm where I grew up. This was the house my great-grandfather had built along Bayou Teche in the late 1890s. The front yard was at least an acre, the same acre where I remembered playing touch football and Hide the Flag with Vic, Midge, and a couple of other ragged, nondescript kids, black and white, who showed up now and then from somewhere nearby. I also remembered days spent mowing that yard, perched atop Father's old Ideal tractor, since Vic was always "too young" to mow, even though he was only fifteen months my junior. Probably still too young to mow, I thought sardonically.

Flanked by fields on both sides, the house sat on a rise overlooking the winding shell road that approached it from the front and sloped down to the bayou in back. Ethel and Louis didn't need a security system: The mixed-breed dogs, always plentiful and vocal, sounded an alarm as soon as a car ventured up the winding shell driveway, ensuring that no one, friend or foe, would drop in unannounced. Placide followed the drive through the main gate, which always stayed open. No one had ever seen the need to close it, at least as far back as I could remember. On our right was the pecan orchard, and ripe pecans crunched under our tires as we approached.

Aunt Ethel and Uncle Louis greeted us out front. Aunt Ethel was twelve years older than Father and nearly as tall, but I noticed she had stooped and grayed a good bit since I saw her several months ago. Louis had also aged since my last visit. Still lean, he had begun to look gaunt and sinewy, his few remaining strands of gray hair ruffling in the light breeze off the bayou. He was a few inches shorter than Aunt Ethel but made up for it by being feisty and tough as nails all his life, until his old heart began to tire, possibly because, like most Cajuns, he had always played as hard as he worked.

Father was the sixth and last of Mamaw Doucet's children. Back then, childbirth at midlife was not uncommon, especially in a good Catholic family like ours. "It's a wonder Harvey wasn't named Oops!" Ethel used to joke. Surely Mamaw would not have wanted a baby at age forty-four. But Father would grow up to be the most successful member of the bunch and the one who helped all the others stay afloat.

Aunt Ethel had eventually demanded indoor plumbing. Father, already reasonably successful by the late '60s, had sent his workmen over to upgrade her to the relatively lavish lifestyle she enjoyed today. A screened-in porch added on the side, indoor plumbing throughout the house. Ethel only regretted that Mamaw Doucet never had the opportunity to experience the luxury of an indoor toilet on a brisk January morning.

Father had wanted Ethel and Louis to move into a newer, more modern house closer to town. He even offered to build them something better instead of simply connecting the old farmhouse to the water main. But no one could drag Ethel, kicking and screaming, out of the house she was born in. She swore she would die here, just as her mother and her grandmother before her.

The homestead had grown over the last generation. Along with renovating the façade back to its original spindles and railings, Father had the kitchen connected to the main house, updating it to classic 60's modern, with all the latest and greatest appliances of the day.

The gallery along the front and one side was as inviting as ever. The same pair of swings, a little more worn but recently varnished by the looks, still hung invitingly on both ends. Uncle Louis, or probably Father, had obviously had the old house repainted within the last couple of months. It was the same basic white, but bright and fresh, with the same gray gallery floor and steps, the same forest green shutters, and the same traditional sky-blue gallery ceiling. Some things never change, I thought with a rare pang of nostalgia that I brushed off as quickly as I would have brushed a spider off my arm.

"Good to have you home, boy," Louis said.

"Oh, yes, Aitchie. We're so glad to see you, *cher*," Ethel said, practically squeezing the breath out of me with a hug. She looked sadder than I ever remembered seeing her, but then she had just lost her baby brother.

"Good to see you both looking well," I said.

After the obligatory hugs and handshakes, Ethel went straight for the jugular and asked the question I was expecting. "Midge told me you wasn't staying there anymore?"

I knew it was coming, so I had prepared. "Midge and I are finished, Aunt Ethel," I responded, relieved to have it behind me. No comment. Just a wide-eyed stare from both of them. "This time, there won't be any going back," I added, hoping for some response. I was reasonably certain that Ethel would have trouble concealing her elation at the news.

"Well, Aitchie," she said after recovering from her

initial shock, "I'm sorry to hear that." At least she was making a valiant effort not to reveal her relief. Not that she hadn't always liked Midge. She had just become skeptical after our sixth or seventh breakup.

To call our relationship volatile would have been like calling the sinking of the Titanic an unfortunate mishap. Carefree and seductive in her youth, Midge as an adult had become as judgmental and controlling as her mother had always been with her. Of course, admittedly, that was from my perspective. She had far more complaints about me from her point of view, none unjustified, I'm pretty sure. But to me, it was always sad to see a young daughter who was rebellious against her mother as a teen turn into her mother as an adult, just like the old wives' tale warned. In our case, it had finally become a transition I couldn't overcome. Lord knows I tried. Several times.

Interrupting the silence of the uncomfortable moment that followed my announcement, the dogs came to life again and sounded their alarm. Through a dust cloud ascending over the rise, I caught sight of a fire-engine red BMW M1, one of those luxury sports cars that Father so disdained, speeding up the shell drive at a speed normally reserved for four-lane highways, and rudely scattering a shower of shells into the yard when it skidded to a stop in front of us.

Before Louis and Ethel could tell me who owned this wheeled projectile, my brother Victor emerged and walked around the car, red-faced and grinning, leaving his curvaceous bleach blonde passenger peering out from under heavily mascaraed eyelashes. Vic had become vain and shallow over the years, everything Father despised in a man. Sadly, Father was no doubt complicit in the creation. There Vic stood, regally, with his greased-back black hair that still waved on top despite his efforts to tame it, his mirrored shades, his muscular body tanned beneath the open shirt, heavy gold chains encircling both wrist and neck. Placide turned and walked back several paces to distance himself. I contemplated turning away myself. I had not seen Vic in several months, and I was not prepared for this spectacle.

Vic glanced from Placide to me. "That redbone better check himself," he said, then turned back toward Placide and hollered, "Update your résumé boy. After what you let happen to Daddy, I ought to have you locked up. I'd like to finish you off myself."

Placide glared in Vic's direction, fists clenched, intense black eyes shining. At a different time and place, things might have ended violently. But whatever Vic was, he wasn't stupid. He probably figured Placide wouldn't show disrespect today, so soon after Father's passing. But since there was always that outside chance, he opted not to push his luck. Instead of pursuing an argument with Placide, he looked back at me, his lopsided Elvis smile resembling a sneer, and said, "Hey, big brother, it's been a long time. I heard you were getting in this afternoon. How's Uncle Sam treating you?"

Not nearly long enough, I thought. But forcing a smile, I said, "Hello Vic. Can't complain. Looks like life has been kind to you in the meantime." I nodded toward the exorbitantly expensive vehicle, wondering how Vic was able to finagle Father into springing for what must have been a sizable down payment.

"Yeah, big brother. A few good speculations," he said, nodding proudly toward what appeared to me to be an overpriced phallic symbol. We shook hands cordially enough but chose not to comfort each other about the tragedy that brought us together unexpectedly. Rumor had it that Father had recently become displeased with Vic's absolute dissolution but had continued to make excuses for him. Father must have realized Vic's behavior resulted from being spoiled his entire life, but he would never have admitted it, even to himself. The gossip mill teemed with rumors that Vic stayed in trouble, what with his gambling and with the thugs he hung out with who counted on their winnings to live lavishly. Father had a recent history of bailing Vic out. At least that was what I had overheard Earlene tell Aunt Ethel the last time I was home.

"Always something with that boy," Earlene had said to Ethel. "I hate to say it, but your brother spoiled him, Ethel. Vic knows it, too. Lord, I hate to see him taking your brother for all he has." Earlene was maybe five feet tall with her Red Cross shoes on, while Vic and Father towered over six feet, but Earlene never took any guff from Victor.

Earlene was probably the only other person Father had trusted as much as he trusted Placide. She had stuck by him at least as long as Placide had. Some people rumored they were lovers, though Earlene and Father always denied any suggestion of it, and I saw no reason not to believe them. Father would not have made the fatal mistake of mixing business with pleasure. But I knew they were devoted friends and colleagues all the same.

Earlene and Placide had been in the inner circle of Father's life, one probably as important as the other: Earlene to oversee the business and the employees, and Placide to ensure Father's well-being. Father believed simplicity was the best route, and the philosophy had served him well: a good cigar, a single malt, and a few trusted employees to share it all with.

Father had other circles of trusted colleagues. Of course, nepotism and business favors ran rampant, but as far as he was concerned, every family had its difficulties, so his own problems with Vic—or me—would not have been unexpected—or advertised. And of course, he had given up on me years ago. Father's philosophy was that families need not share their troubles with him, and in return, he would not saddle them with his. But now Father's passing would ripple through all the circles as all his trusted employees jockeyed for position.

Vic sniffed and rubbed his nose impatiently. The platinum blonde bombshell sitting in his car whined in a high-pitched, nasal voice, "Vic, shut the door. You're letting all the dust in! It's going up my nose."

Vic turned to admonish her briefly under his breath. He kept his arm on top of the car, not bothering to introduce the young woman, though no one really cared. She was here today, but we all realized that if she lasted until evening, it was a long-term relationship for Vic.

"I guess we need to talk, Bubba," Vic began, turning back to us.

"Talk about what, Vic?" I asked naively, even though I already knew exactly what was on his mind.

"Well, time is money, Bubba, as Father always said, and since you chose to be absent all these years," Vic said, straightening a little, "you should know that Father has been grooming me to replace him as President and CEO of the company."

"Victor, this is not the time nor the place. A day or two

surely won't cause the corporation to fold. Besides, I imagine Earlene has all the essential paperwork and contingency plans." I knew Father must have prepared for just such a circumstance.

"Yeah, that sawed-off kiss-ass has been trying to get her name in that will for years. When I take over, she's going to get something all right. Her ass is going to hit the gate like a smooth slick river rock skipping across still water," he said, pantomiming skipping stones. "I've had enough of her gold-digging."

I knew better than to bother arguing in her defense. "Well, regardless, Vic, out of respect for Father, let's at least wait until he's buried."

"No problem, Bubba. I'll give ya your time," he said, sweeping it aside with a grand wave of his arm, a deep bow, and a sneer, just so we'd be sure to note his sacrifice. "See y'all in town at the church later. What time is the soirée, Ethel?"

"The wake is at seven," Ethel replied flatly.

"Try to leave that redbone here," he added, glaring at Placide as he slid into the car and slammed the door. He sped back down the drive, carrying the same chip on his shoulder that he had brought with him. If Placide heard him, he did not acknowledge it, but that was Placide's way. Neither did Aunt Ethel nor Uncle Louis say a word. They just looked away from me, probably to hide their shame and grief over what Vic had become.

Chapter 3
THE WAKE

By 1750 hours, Aunt Ethel had managed to get Uncle Louis and me presentable and herded toward the LTD, where Earlene and Placide waited. The evening's proceedings wouldn't be easy for any of us, especially for Aunt Ethel and Earlene, the women in Father's life. At least the ones I knew about. It wouldn't be a picnic for Placide, either. I knew Aunt Ethel hadn't had much rest since the morning the Iberia Parish Sheriff's Department came knocking on her door. It didn't look like either she or Earlene would get much rest for some time, what with out-of-town relatives to entertain and sundry business and legal affairs to tend to. As for Placide, I had plans to keep him busy. While the women in front talked about what lay ahead, I spent my time staring out the side window and planning my strategy for after these obligations were behind us.

I knew a few people of interest would attend the wake in Lafayette: Business associates, suppliers, executives from the oil, drilling, and salt companies, all wanting to pay their last respects, some with lawsuits pending. This would be a good chance to meet some of Father's business acquaintances, friends and foes alike, maybe excavate a few buried resentments or deals gone awry. I had no idea how to get to the bottom of the alleged suicide, but I remembered Father's adage: "How do you eat an elephant? One bite at a time." That philosophy had brought him untold millions, often against litigious foes. That's not a man who would take his own life, *ever*! Suicide is a mortal sin in the Catholic faith, and I vowed to follow Father's philosophy to save his name and reveal the truth, one bitter bite at a time.

A large crowd of friends, relatives, neighbors, company people, and a host of people I had never seen, began filing in to view the body shortly after those of us in the family had paid our last respects. Ethel stayed beside the coffin longer than the rest of us, saying her Rosary, red-eyed and head bowed, while Placide waited at the chapel door and kept people out until she had her time alone with her baby brother.

Cynic that I am, I guess I wasn't as pious as I should have been. But I was onto the ulterior motives that lure some people to such somber occasions, with their subtle nods of sympathy, their voices hushed in feigned respect for the departed. I've always believed that the purpose of a wake is for family and close friends to share fellowship, show respect for the departed, and reach some kind of closure. Instead, I feared the passing of one of the wealthiest men in Louisiana had morphed into a self-serving social gathering of unfamiliar faces quietly discussing business deals while awaiting their turn to console. To complete the tableau, Father's passing corresponded with a state election runoff. I think every politician in south Louisiana showed up to shake hands, along with various strata of humanity, including those ne'er-do-wells who came just to associate with members of the upper crust so they could drop names later, back in their home parishes.

The sleazy politicians were the most irritating, of course, pressing palms, kissing squirming little ones, and telling each other and anyone else in earshot how they were dedicated to improving things so that this sort of travesty would never happen under their watch. Hell, Father had undoubtedly voted for most of them, and they hadn't managed to keep him above ground.

Next were the contractors, auto salesmen, and insurance representatives, all attempting to tap the vast wealth present today. And of course, the bottom-feeding lawyers, the sleazy kind, who chased ambulances and obituaries for a living. My eyes searched individual small gatherings for someone who might shed light on the incident. I pasted on a smile so as not to reveal my cynicism, while I shook hands with the sleaziest, pocketing their cards.

"H. Doucet," I said, joining one likely-looking group. "Did you folks work with my father?"

"*Mais, non.* We never knew your daddy, son. But we're sorry for your loss," a gravelly-voiced bull of a man said. "We was in the salt mine. Name's Jack Brouillette," he told me, leaving his heavy-set middle-aged female companion looking on as he walked over to a real looker in her twenties and put his arm around her waist. "Lost my best friend down there. This here's his widow, Marlisa

Daigrepont."

This was the Sapphire group with the class-action against Calco Oil and Doucet Drilling, I realized, probably here just to scare up evidence of negligence. Still, it could be beneficial to hear their side of the story.

"I'm sorry for your loss, Ma'am," I said as I took her hand in both my own. "Looks like we both lost loved ones."

Before she could respond, Brouilette butted in. "Y'all ought to meet and compare notes." I couldn't figure out his motivation for that suggestion, but I knew I wouldn't be averse to it.

She looked questioningly at Brouillette before she replied, "No, I don't believe Charles would want..."

Brouillette pulled her aside. "Hell, girl. Give you a chance to get on the inside," he whispered to her, but loud enough for all to hear.

I deduced that the middle-aged woman glaring arrows his way must be Jack's wife, so I looked at her and asked, "Ma'am, did you know the man they lost down there?"

"Yes. I knowed him awright. Almost my age," she said, raising her eyebrows and her chin toward Marlisa as if to point out the age of the young widow in comparison to her deceased husband.

I could still hear Brouilette's gruff whisper. "Go ahead on, girl. Give the man your number," he urged as Marlisa still seemed to hold back. "He's big bucks, you hear me?"

Marlisa finally nodded reluctantly and wrote her number on the back of a business card Jack shoved in her hand. That gave me his contact and hers for future reference. Couldn't hurt, I thought. I thanked them, repeated my sympathy to her, and pocketed the card. Then, nodding my "Good evening," I made my escape and continued milling through the feeding-frenzied crowd.

I saw Earlene in a serious conversation with a sleazebag I vaguely recognized. He was one of Father's business contacts I remembered meeting once years ago. Even in my twenties, I had figured him for a shyster, and the memory stuck. Deslatte, I think his name was. He was giving her some song and dance, but I trusted her to recognize a bullshitter when she saw one. She'd had a good teacher. Father could smell BS a mile away. Rubberneckers who thought they could circumvent her were in for a harsh awakening. As I kept my distance and watched Earlene in action, the old Jim Croce lyrics came to mind: "You don't pull the mask off the old Lone Ranger/And you sure don't mess around with Earlene." I'll ask her about that meeting later, I thought, as I moved on.

I walked over to an older couple looking ill-at-ease against the wall. I wondered what could have brought them. The heavily bearded old Cajun, done up in a suit that had probably not seen the light in the last decade, introduced himself and his wife as Auguste and Angelle Savois. He told me the story of how he and his young grandson had been fishing in the lake that morning. His wife told me the story of how Auguste and Jamie had narrowly escaped being dragged into the enormous pit, weeping now as she said, "Auguste pushed that ole *bateau* as far as he could through the mud…" Auguste took over and said, "I didn't do it for me. I done lived my life. But I couldn't let nothin' happen to my little grandson, no." I patted him on the back, and we shared condolences, while Angelle took his hand and looked up at him adoringly through teary eyes. I scribbled down the old man's number for future reference, thanked them for coming, and excused myself.

By that time, Deslatte had walked away from Earlene, and another man I didn't recognize had approached, so I walked over to find out who he was. "H," Earlene said, "This is Marc LeBlanc, our Executive Officer of domestic drilling. Marc, this is Major H. Doucet, Harvey's son. Marc is one of our most valuable employees, and he's agreed to take over in Harvey's place for now."

"Oh, that's wonderful news! I've wondered if there were any contingency plans for the company. If you have Earlene's vote of confidence, that's good enough for me, Marc. I plan to be in close contact with Earlene, so we can stay in touch through her."

"Nice to meet you, H. I'm so sorry for your loss. Harvey's death is a great blow to Doucet Drilling. His shoes will be hard to fill, but rest assured, I'll do my best. I should be in the Lafayette office a good bit, so I'm sure I'll see you there. And I welcome any advice on taking the reins."

"I can vouch for Marc in the highest possible terms," Earlene interjected. "And your father had already set up this contingency, in case anything happened to him, precisely because of his faith in Marc. I've been filling him in on recent events, so he's already up to speed."

"That's a great load off my mind, especially since I have a few more years to give to Uncle Sam. Thanks for agreeing to take over, Marc. And thanks for coming today." We shook hands and I moved on, feeling better about the future of the company.

I approached two men I didn't recognize in dark business suits and slick comb-overs standing near Auguste and Angelle against the wall, talking seriously between themselves and looking official. Either Feds or New Orleans mob, I figured. Hard to tell. They stopped talking abruptly when I approached them, offering me superficial condolences. Whatever their discussion was about, they weren't sharing, so I thanked them for coming, excused myself, and moved on to a particularly talkative bunch of various races and hues, clearly blue-collar workers, speaking in Creole. They began filling in some of the missing pieces about the tragedy. Along with the salt miner, eleven of their fellow drilling workers had also met their tragic end in the disaster at Oka Chito Island.

The most vocal of the group introduced himself as Sid Ardoin, a stocky Cajun wearing a suit with sleeves stretched to capacity over the muscles in his arms. He explained that he had been the derrickman responsible for the drill mud operation. "That night," he said, "...or early morning, I should say, ...a clutch burned plumb up. Then, number two pump got stuck, and the load indicator kept on climbing, over four times capacity." He rolled his head from side to side and looked at the floor.

One of the others took over. Said his name was Eric Arcenaux. "Yep, she started going down, so we got the hell out. But it was too late. Lost us some good men down there. Lord, Lord." Then he too shook his head and looked down.

A third guy stepped up, called himself Big Joe. "Our crew boat barely made it back to the island against the pull. The current in the canal reversed! Sucked the water right out from under them shrimp boats in the canal and left 'em settin' in the mud. I ain't never seen nothin' like it."

Pretty soon the others all started cutting in at one time

to add their versions of events, just as Victor made a late entrance with his entourage. I was glad Father wasn't able to see the painted women surrounding Vic, some in spandex low-cut blouses, looking more like pole dancers than mourners. The men, with slicked-back hair, sporting kilos of gold chains, looked like the cool mafia type, any one of whom could have passed for a hit man. The bile backed up in my throat at the spectacle. Vic interrupted the discussion with the drilling crew and began introducing me to his entourage. Thankfully, Earlene tapped me on the shoulder just then and beckoned me to the front of the chapel. "It's time to seat everyone for the Rosary, H," she said quietly. Father was still in charge, I thought with no little satisfaction. I excused myself and followed her to the chapel door.

Earlene and Ethel had chosen an informal service for the wake, fortunately, just some prayers and the reading of a few scriptures. Earlene had specified the small chapel for this service, so that seating could be limited to family and close friends only. No room was set aside for Victor's friends or the rubberneckers. They could leave or remain in the fellowship hall. Earlene assigned Placide to stand at the door and direct traffic.

A Chopin nocturne played by a local young prodigy tempered the gloom as I found my seat next to Ethel. Few flower arrangements adorned the front of the chapel since Earlene had asked that contributions be made instead to the homeless shelter in Lafayette, Father's favorite charity. "There but for the grace of God..." I recalled him saying when he spoke of that shelter, where he had always personally bought and helped serve meals over the Thanksgiving and Christmas holidays. And whenever he could, he hired someone out of that shelter for his crew. Some of the men that I had just talked to had undoubtedly come from there. Much as he had ignored me growing up, at least he wasn't stingy with his money when it came to people in need. A lot of men in his position would just have bought another yacht, but Father never had any use for anything beyond a sturdy bass boat. And he never forgot his own humble roots.

Although the chapel looked barren with those few arrangements and the lone spray of ivory roses Aunt Ethel had chosen for the coffin, Father would have been pleased. Someone had sent two yellow roses in a bud vase that sat next to a picture of Father, its simplicity causing it to stand out over the one or two elaborate arrangements. I made a mental note to find out who had sent it.

Aunt Ethel's priest from New Iberia conducted the rosary, after which he added a few personal words about how cherished Harvey Doucet had been by all who knew him. I was relieved for Father's sake that the priest didn't mention suicide. Next, to everyone's genuine amazement, or chagrin, Victor got up and delivered a eulogy, a few tears sliding down his cheek as he concluded, "...the most generous and loving father a person could hope for." *Boy, can he turn it on*, I thought. A final hymn, a prayer, and *fait accompli.*

As abruptly as the wake had begun, it was over. But before we made our escape to the car, Victor confronted me and began to broach the subject of the will again. A touching little afterward to his eulogy, I thought. "Look here, big brother, the wake's over. We need to talk about..."

"I said we would discuss it later," I interrupted

through clenched teeth, then immediately sensed Placide directly behind me. Maybe he had always been there. Had I adopted father's shadow? I walked with Placide to Father's car, and Victor turned abruptly to join his unseemly entourage.

Chapter 4
THE MOURNING AFTER

Mourners queued like ants to make their appearance in the vestibule of the cathedral for the funeral mass on Tuesday. Cousins I hadn't seen in a decade or two had arrived from homes scattered across the South, some with grown children and grandchildren I'd never seen. Business friends and foes alike filed in, many I had seen last evening, some I had not seen in years, all looking as pious and contrite as they thought befitted the occasion.

The parade to the graveside service at the family mausoleum must have stretched five miles south along Highway 90 and managed to span the bulk of the afternoon, followed by several of Ethel's nieces and nephews joining us for an early evening potluck meal provided by neighbors and friends. Several planned to stay over in a couple of spare rooms upstairs and head out after breakfast. Ethel was visibly exhausted, but she managed a stoic front, though her face looked drawn and pale. As for me, I endured the camaraderie, joined in the reminiscences with cousins as I ate my way through the chicken casserole, the three-bean salad, the chocolate cake.

Relieved when the ritual was in my rear view, I crashed early, slept soundly, and woke with the chickens. Literally. Ethel's rooster jarred me out of a dream about thugs speeding after me in a James Bond-style car chase hours before dawn and just moments before I would have flown off a cliff at 70 miles an hour. Once I figured out where I was, I was wide-eyed, so I dragged myself out of bed onto the chilly wood floor and found my slippers.

Leaving my bedside lamp on and the door ajar so I could see to walk down the stairs, I felt my way along the hallway to the kitchen at the rear of the house to start the coffee. To my surprise, behind the swinging door, the kitchen was lit up like a shopping mall, while a local AM station spouted off the early farm report. Squinting in the glare, I saw Aunt Ethel at her usual post hovering over the stove. I would have thought, since she no longer had to feed breakfast to ten hired hands, she would have broken the habit of pre-dawn culinary feats.

"My land, Aitchie. You startled me!" she exclaimed when she saw me.

"I'm sorry. What time is it, anyway?" I grumbled, rubbing my eyes in the blinding light as I followed my nose to the coffee pot and found a cup in the cupboard.

"It's only 5 AM, *cher*."

"Good God, Aunt Ethel! You still get up this early?"

"Oh, I'm an early riser." She turned her attention back to whatever simmered in the pot. "I'm used to gathering eggs and fixing the farm hands biscuits, gravy, boudin, and grits to go with them eggs. I never could break the habit of getting up early. Besides, we still got folks rattling around in the house. No telling what time they'll be pokin' their heads in here, ready for some chow before lighting out for home. But you're sure the last person I expected to see this early!"

"That damn rooster woke me up," I complained, carrying my cup to the table. "I can sleep fine through F-15 take-offs, but I'm not used to squalling damn roosters."

"Better get used to 'em if you're going to stay around here awhile." Ethel turned down the flame, then poured herself a cuppa and joined me at the table.

Her coffee tasted a damn sight better than that instant rot gut I'd been choking down lately. "Ethel, let me ask you something," I said after my first few slurps. "Did you see Father at all after the inundation?"

"Placide carried him over here the next evening around two, while I was folding clothes right here at this table. Come here looking ghostly white. Why, 'Tee?"

"Did either of them discuss the inundation at any length?"

"Not a word... Mostly they just set still, right there where you're settin' now, Aitchie, staring into space, ya know? Didn't talk to nobody. Your daddy didn't even touch the coffee I poured him." She pointed to the door leading to the dining room. "But then he got on the phone out there in the hall... There was one thing I overheard on my way to the stairs. Now, mind you, *cher*, I wasn't eavesdropping. Just happened to hear as I passed by with the laundry. I think he said something like, 'OK, Mr. Gremillion. I'll see you then.' I ain't positive I got that name right. Why, Aitchie?" She paused and looked me in the eye. "What are you driving at, *cher*?"

"Oh, nothing, really, Aunt Ethel. I was just wondering how Father was feeling after the accident." I didn't want to let her in on my suspicions of foul play, at least until I had some solid evidence. There were plenty of Gremillions in South Louisiana, so the name didn't help narrow it down much.

"Placide was in the kitchen drinking his coffee while your daddy was on the phone," she said. "I asked him, 'Placide what's the matter?' but he just shook his head. Didn't say nothin', just stared at the floor. I knew they was broken up about the inundation, so I didn't ask anymore."

After a few sips of coffee, she went back over to the counter, humming "Amazing Grace" as she began putting together a peach cobbler for Uncle Louis and the cousins still upstairs.

"Listen, Ethel, I need to borrow your car, just for today, if it's OK. I'll rent a car, then get it back to you. Will that be OK?"

"Sure thing, Aitchie," she answered, turning toward me. "Your Uncle Louis and me don't hardly ever drive it. Only once a week, on Saturdays, to pass by New Iberia for a few groceries and go to mass at St. Pete's is all. You just borrow it as long as you like. No sense wasting money on a rental car."

"Well, we'll see how much I need it, then decide. Anyway, I'll use it today. Thanks, Ethel."

I refilled my cup and carried it upstairs to shower as the morning sky was beginning to show gray on the horizon. Then I grabbed the keys off the hook by the back door. Ethel said, "Land's sake, Aitchie. You didn't even eat any breakfast." I gave her a peck on the cheek and a hasty, "Later, Ethel," then headed out.

In the early morning haze, the lonely road to Oka Chito Island, the island that was not an island but a peninsula, looked ghostly. Eerie gray Spanish moss hung like hag's hair from the live oak and cypress. As I neared the island on the only road, a roadblock stopped me, manned by a lonely overweight Rent-a-Cop, his distended belly stretching the seams and buttons of the tan uniform shirt he had somehow squeezed into this morning. His bulk dwarfed the makeshift sawhorse barricade with its hand-painted sign that read, "Road Closed Indefinitely to All but Residents."

"Sir, we can't let no one enter!" he barked, red-faced and expressionless, as I eased Aunt Ethel's ten-year-old Grand Prix up to where he postured, fists planted on hips, his disdain revealing a general distaste for his mundane existence beside a barricade. He lifted one hand the heft of a T-bone to wipe away some sweat that trickled down his forehead, notwithstanding the chilly November morning.

I stuck my Air Force I.D. under his nose and said, "I'm Major Doucet. Now that Harvey Doucet is deceased, I'm in charge of Doucet Drilling. I have some information that I'm pretty sure investigators would like to get their hands on," I fibbed, holding up my pocket Day-Timer as flimsy proof of the urgency.

"Well, Sir, I...uh..." he stuttered. He took the I.D. and continued staring at it, then back at the Day-Timer, wheels obviously turning in a brain that hadn't had to form an original thought for a while. He scratched his head, handed the I.D. back to me, and said, "Yeah, yeah. I guess it'll be OK. Let's don't make a habit of it, though."

"Thanks, Chief," I said. I shoved the I.D. back in my

wallet, then eased around the sawhorse and onto the narrow road.

I expected to find havoc at the end of the road, but the total devastation I saw nauseated me. It looked like a bomb had hit. Houses, some split in two, sat at odd angles as though they had skidded to a sudden stop on their trip to Lake Chevreuil. Three-hundred-year-old live oak trees lay like giant fallen soldiers, their massive arms akimbo, their monstrous roots reaching in supplication to the heavens, dwarfing the out-of-kilter houses. The island was vacant of any living thing, save a few free-ranging peacocks strutting amid what looked like the ravages of war. By the looks, a Victorian mansion remained virtually untouched, but a couple of ancient oaks lying in the front yard had not been so fortunate.

Dotting another section of Oka Chito sat a few makeshift living quarters for investigators and officials, consisting of mildewed campers and government-issue motor homes. A few hastily constructed metal buildings looked as though they must be serving as storage units and meeting rooms. I parked, then walked over to one of the buildings that already had a couple of cars lined up out front. The air reeked of mildew and the rotting flesh of belly-up marine life. The hand-stenciled sign on the door read, "Mine Safety and Health Administration," so I walked on in.

Inside, a girl Friday, who might have been attractive if she had scrubbed off the top two layers of make-up, had just arrived and filled the room with the scent of her knockoff cologne. She looked up from the Mr. Coffee she was pouring water into to see what I was about.

"Good morning, Sir. May I help you?" she asked

through a bright red smile. Outsized dangling gold ear medallions continued to swing after she raised her head, like hypnotic trance inducements, daring me not to follow them with my eyes.

"I'm Major Doucet," I announced, showing her my I.D., "owner of Doucet Drilling Corporation. Is anyone here yet who could talk to me?" I asked, glancing around at the few closed doors that led off the cramped reception area.

"Mr. Morton is in, I believe. I seen his car outside when I come in a few minutes ago. Just a moment, please." She picked up her phone and hit a few buttons. "Mr. Morton? Yes, good morning. I have a Major Doucet out here, says he owns the drilling company. Uh huh...uh huh...yes, sir." She hung up and looked back at me through black-rimmed puppy eyes. "Mr. Morton says you can go on in," she said, pointing at the office door behind her, her eyes still fixed on me.

"Thank you, Miss..."

"Stewart. Babette Stewart. But you can call me Babette," she said as I walked past her to Morton's door.

"Major Doucet," said the squirrely man inside, his Cream of Wheat complexion indicating a man whose life must consist solely of sitting behind a desk or in front of a TV. He stood as though it were an effort and stretched out an anemic hand.

"Mr. Morton," I answered, grasping the hand across the desk and shaking it more firmly than he might have wished.

"You can call me Earl."

"All right, Earl, and you can call me H."

"So, H, what can I help you with this morning?" he asked, motioning for me to sit in the straight back chair facing his desk, while he continued shuffling a few papers.

"I'm trying to gather some facts about this tragedy," I said. "I'll be CEO of Doucet Drilling now that Father's gone," I fudged, not sure yet who would actually take the ropes, "and I need to build a report for my files. I thought maybe if I got out here to the island, I might find some kind soul willing to help me fill in some of the blanks."

"Wish I could help. So far, we are simply seeing a gross error on the part of Calco Oil and Doucet Drilling. We haven't concluded yet who's responsible for the miscalculation, but there is certainly negligence on someone's part. As you can see, it was a multi-million-dollar mistake, and that's not even counting the loss of a dozen men, plus your father, God rest their souls." He shook his head solemnly.

"Of course. You can appreciate my concerns and my hopes to clear my father's name, now that he is incapable of explaining. I'm not too familiar with the drilling business yet, but I do know enough to look into where the orders to drill at that specific angle and depth came from."

"Calco Oil says the map came from Louisiana DNR, but looking at their survey," he said, hoisting himself out of his seat and walking over to an easel at the side of the room, "you can see that the angle of drilling they ordered would have put the drill here, under the salt dome."

"I see. Well, Earl, can we not conclude that Calco Oil presented a flawed map here? And wouldn't that exonerate Doucet Drilling from any blame?" I inquired using what I believed was simple logic following his explanation.

"Not that simple, I'm afraid. According to Calco Oil, Doucet Drilling ordered a study to determine the accuracy of the map. Calco is accusing Doucet of altering the map sometime during that process."

"Well, who in hell did they order it from? Who did the surveys?"

"That leads us to another dead end. Doucet Drilling officials said they didn't order the study, pointing the finger instead at Calco Oil. Said they didn't arrive on the scene until Calco Oil merged with Aloco Oil and took over the rig, about two years ago. That's when Calco hired Doucet Drilling to take over drilling operations. So far, everyone is just trying to pass the buck, as you might expect. We're still digging through a paper trail, but I'll keep you posted when we learn anything. Of course, your father's death sort of put the brakes on finding a reliable source at Doucet." He sat back in his swivel chair, hands folded across his chest.

I hesitated to tell him Earlene was at least as reliable as Father, and probably Marc LeBlanc as well. Let them figure that out on their own. I wanted to put off his next step, which was the "We'll be in touch" step that I wasn't ready to accept yet. "I mean, aren't these wells all regulated on either a federal or state level?" I asked, thinking of the layers of regulation in any Air Force project I'd ever worked on.

"Yes, DNR would have granted Doucet the permit to drill, but the EPA oversees domestic waters, so they would have assisted in the survey and getting the permit. We still haven't been able to pinpoint who made the error. I'm sure in time it will all come out. And I'll be glad to call you when it does." His forced smile was inviting me not to let the door hit me in the ass.

Damn bureaucratic red tape, I thought, then took a

deep breath, remembering that this guy could eventually turn out to be an ally. "OK, thanks, Earl. I know you're doing everything you can. Please get in touch as soon as you find out anything. I'll be staying out at my aunt's, and extremely anxious to hear." I wrote my name and phone numbers for Ethel and the office on the notepad on his desk.

"Of course," Morton said, clearly relieved to be getting me out of his hair. He reached out to give me one more limp-dick handshake, and I was on my way, not knowing much more than when I walked in. I didn't get the sense from our first meeting that he was going to bother trying to get to the truth unless it happened to jump up and smack him in the face. Even then, I wouldn't put corruption out of his reach. A milquetoast who would do anything to save his own ass and smooth things over for the agency, even lie through his teeth.

Sliding under the wheel, I drove back out the deserted road toward civilization, swerving to miss one of the island peacocks from the plant nursery dragging his furled tail slowly down the pavement behind him in his own silent desperation. As I eased past the barricade, I waved at Rotunda Rent-a-Cop, whose response was a flushed, stone-faced glare.

One look at that gut made me realize I was getting hungry. It was still early, so I decided to head into New Iberia, stop at Maybelle's Diner for some eggs. Maybe I could nose around some while I was there.

Chapter 5
GRITS AND GRIT

The familiar greasy spoon hadn't changed a stick of flatware in the years since I'd lived here. Same smudged silver tiles on the wall behind the counter, same 60's booths, same Neptune blue vinyl on the benches and stools, now cracking and tearing in a few places. Same Formica countertop, with the same old specials board, prices scratched out and higher prices scribbled in with felt tip pen. Same odor of old grease and fried bacon. Looked like the same old men hanging butt cheeks off the occupied stools, though I realized it had to be a new crop of flesh-eaters.

A few booths were free, so I grabbed the one next to a couple of swinging dicks I remembered from Father's wake, the suits who had shut up when they saw me approach. This morning, they stood out like aliens from Mars in their dark suits and shellacked comb-overs among the blue-collar workmen in coveralls and bib overalls. Deep in conversation, the two suits lowered their voices when I sat down.

Someone had left the sports section on my table, so I feigned interest in Friday's Westgate Tigers football game while straining to hear the hushed conversation behind me. "Coffee, Suh?" the large black waitress boomed from beside my booth.

"Thank you, Chantelle," I said, reading her name tag as I turned over the cup that sat upside down in a saucer. "I'll have two eggs over easy, biscuits and grits, please."

She hollered over the counter to the short-order cook, "Two over easy, biscuits, grits." Then she stepped to the booth behind me to refill the two suits' cups, while I turned to the sports page to read about Terry Bradshaw's hopes to take the Steelers to Super Bowl XV in New Orleans.

"Yeah, bastard skipped that night," the suit with his back to me said just above a whisper after Chantelle left their table.

"Hell, that don't mean anything," the suit facing him murmured under his breath. "Guys miss work all the time."

"Not Matherne. Never missed a shift except when his daddy died three years ago."

"Don't worry. Nobody's going to pick up on that."

"I hope you're right. You ready?"

"Yeah. Here, I got the tip."

Turning my head toward the window, I watched peripherally as they paid at the register, then went out to their black late-model Chevy Blazer with a reinforced push bumper. I had parked Aunt Ethel's Grand Prix next to them. Oddly, they didn't recognize me from the wake, or at least it hadn't registered yet, maybe because I was dressed in cords, a Members Only jacket, and a ball cap, instead of my only sport coat and tie. When I finished my eggs, I'd head back to the island, see if I could find out anything about this Matherne guy.

When I edged up to the barricade for the second time, the security guard grumbled, "Hell, maybe you want a pass to come in here half a dozen times a day? These folks in here got better things to do than listen to you, ya know."

"It's just that I told Mr. Morton I'd get something right back to him. Had to go get it, is all." I smiled up at him innocently.

"Well, you could've given me a heads up when you left here an hour ago. All right, go on, go on," he scowled, as if I were interrupting his demanding job beside a roadblock.

Babette greeted me with the same painted-on red grin, her cologne sticking in the back of my throat.

"Sorry to interrupt again," I said. "I have one more question for Mr. Morton."

"Oh, no problem, Major Doucet. I don't often get a chance to play receptionist. It gets lonely around here at times," she said with a girlish pout.

"Glad I broke the routine, then."

"Feel free to break my routine anytime," she said. "Mr. Morton is in a meeting right now, but I'm sure it won't be long."

I flashed a benign smile and picked up a *Field and Stream* from the table between the two straight chairs in the corner. While I was skimming an article about the best crankbait for catching bass, a short Cajun with Popeye forearms bulging from the rolled sleeves of his navy-blue work jumper emerged from Morton's office and nodded toward me on his way to the door. I recognized him instantly as a guy I had spoken to at the wake, a guy from the rig. But I had spoken to so many, I couldn't recall his name. He might know Matherne, I thought, just as Babette signaled for me to go on in.

"Well, Doucet. We meet again," Morton said when I entered.

"Yes, Morton. Sorry to bother you again, but I've come up with a question."

"Earl," he corrected me, motioning me toward the chair.

"H," I responded. "I'm trying to find out what I can about a guy named Matherne. I don't have a first name. I believe he either worked on the rig or in the mine."

"Classified. You understand."

I didn't budge or respond. I just sat there, staring at him, trying to see if he had the balls to look back. He didn't.

"So, if that's all, Major," he said, shuffling some papers awkwardly.

"OK, then. I'll be back as soon as I get a subpoena," I threatened calmly as if I actually could. Then I stood and turned to leave.

He didn't call my bluff, not right away. When I reached for the door handle, though, he said, "All right, Doucet. I'll see what Miss Stewart can round up. Come by tomorrow morning."

"Thanks. Be glad to. Oh...that guy that just left. I believe I spoke to him at Father's wake, but I can't recall his name. I think he might have worked for my father. He may have known Matherne." I knew I was pushing my luck.

"Oh...uh...could be, H," he said, returning his gaze to something on his desk. "Tomorrow, then, say around eleven?"

"Eleven it is."

Morton's reaction when I mentioned Matherne's name convinced me he was hiding something. And he didn't want me knowing the name of the guy who just left, either. After I left his office, I decided to spend some time checking out some of the other folks I'd met at Father's wake, see what skeletons I could scare up. I grabbed my Day-Timer off the car seat and fished out Jack Brouillette's card. Bereaved widow, I thought as I turned to the number on the back. Might be willing to spill her guts to a sympathetic listener. I figured she lived in or near New Iberia, so I headed back that way.

Bourbon Hall on Main was already opening up by the time I got back to town. Only in Louisiana, I thought, but hell, I decided, it's 5 o'clock somewhere. Might as well stop in and see if any of the town drunks were getting talkative yet. I parked and walked in just as one old fella was settling in for the day, so I grabbed the second stool down from him.

"Morning," I said. He just grunted and lit up a desert dog with a cough that started at the bottom of his gut and worked its way up. The underage barmaid carried a draft beer to him without being asked, so I knew he was a regular. I figured I'd better give the old codger time to down some hair of the dog before I asked him any questions.

"Can I get you something?" the waitress asked me, looking far too young and innocent to end up in a place like this. Then she bent over to wash some glasses and I saw the name Josh tattooed on the top of her left breast.

Too late, I thought. Not innocent anymore.

"Have you got grapefruit juice?" I asked.

"Sure thing." She walked over to the cooler, her firm, ample hips rotating her paint-on blue jeans in all the right directions. She'd been around the block, all right. She returned with a quart bottle of juice and poured me a glass.

The old guy next to me sat silently for a while, slurping from his beer mug every minute or two, puffing on a second desert dog when he put the first one out, until the beer was half gone.

"Mornin'," he finally said in a gravel voice.

"You live around here?" I ventured after a strategic pause.

He grunted an affirmative-sounding grunt.

"Hear about the inundation?"

"Oh, hell, yeah. Everybody's yappin' about that. Me, I'm just glad they laid me off four years ago. Some shady dealings going on, y'ask me. Yep," he added, returning to his smoke.

"Shady how?" I prodded.

"Oh, well, I just rode down the cage every morning and up every night. Never asked no questions, me."

I sipped my grapefruit juice in silence as I waited through another coughing spell. After another long draw, he doused what was left of the butt and continued talking, smoke escaping from his nose and mouth as he spoke. "But when they hired that new boss," he said, "from up there in Tennessee somewheres, well, it hurt us all after that. Laid off a lot of key personnel, 'to save overhead during the recession,' they told us. Sent me on my way, a year before I was supposed to retire, so I didn't get my full thirty. And that's when it started getting worse for the guys still down in the mine, what they told me. Quotas went up, people was gettin' hurt. All I know, they sure screwed me." He ended with a flourish of his skeletal right arm, then resumed his beer. He pulled out another desert dog and tapped it on the pack.

"You happen to know the new boss's name?" I asked.

"Oh, hell, no. Not my business to know nothin'."

"How about a man named Matherne? Did he work with y'all?"

"Didn't know no Matherne in the mine. Done told you all I know." With that, the old codger lit his smoke and effectively ended the conversation. I decided it was time to move on.

It was nearly 1030 hours, so I walked to the pay phone in back, pulled out the card with the widow's number on the back, and plunked in some change. After three rings, Mrs. Daigrepont picked up.

"Hello?" came the breathless voice, as though she had run from somewhere to grab the phone.

"Mrs. Daigrepont?"

"Yes. Who's this?" She sounded impatient.

"This is Major Doucet. We met at my father's wake, day before yesterday. Do you remember me?"

"Yes, I remember you." She didn't sound glad I called.

"Well, Mrs. Daigrepont, again, I'm sorry for your loss, and I know you're still grieving. But after Jack Brouillette suggested we talk, I thought I'd see if you'd agree to see me. I have a couple things I'd like to ask you. And I might be able to help you figure some things out, too."

"Oh, Major Doucet, I don't know. I'm getting awfully tired of all the questions. I'm about to stop answering my phone. I honestly don't have anything more to say to anyone except my attorn..."

Hoping to keep her on the line, I interrupted, "See, Mrs. Daigrepont, I believe your husband and my father lost their lives needlessly. I can't prove anything yet, but I have a sneaking suspicion that something...uh...unsavory is going on, for lack of a better word. Maybe I'm paranoid, but so far, I don't trust anything any official tells me, and you shouldn't either. Any information you could give me might help us both get to the truth that they're not about to let us in on. I know it could be painful, but wouldn't you want Charles to do the same for you if the situation were reversed?"

"Well...I suppose I could at least listen to what you have to say," she agreed, her voice softening.

"Fantastic. Thank you. Could you meet me at Provost's Restaurant for lunch today, my treat? Say about one?"

"Um...I suppose, ...OK, Major Doucet."

"Great! Oh, and you can call me H."

"OK, H. I...I guess you can call me Marlisa, then."

"Thanks. See you at one, Marlisa."

I still had a couple of hours to kill, so I drove around New Iberia to see how some of my old haunts had disappeared or changed. I was pleased to see that East Main still had its integrity, an anachronistic village, surrounded by a sea of strip malls and big-box stores on its outskirts. Feeling a wave of nostalgia, I crossed the bridge and pulled into City Park, a favorite haunt of mine as a kid, where I had played Dixie Youth baseball, got beat at tennis a few times as a teen, got my indoctrination into the wonders of the female body with Midge on more than one occasion.

I parked under a canopy of live oaks facing Bayou Teche beneath some clouds that threatened rain. A couple of red-headed black and white Muscovy ducks waddled along the water's edge, while a few more graceful snow-white ducks skated by on the Teche. I rolled down my window to breathe in the fresh air that smelled like rain. I zipped my jacket but left the window down so I could hear the ducks squawking and the saw grass and elephant ears rustling in the breeze. I leaned my head back and shut my eyes to let the knot that had been building up in my gut subside.

In the past, these old oaks had temporarily replaced my adolescent angst with a sense of calm. I guess I was hoping for the same today. But today the park just brought back memories of Midge, the nubile seventeen-year-old, pliable in my awkward teenage arms half a lifetime ago, and more recently in our bungalow in North Carolina. These ageless trees had witnessed generations of other couples embrace and later part. Likely even see a few from the new crop of starry-eyed hopefuls tonight. These oaks would shade countless more unborn generations, witness more tragedy, more victory, more grief, and more joy. And somewhere in that conglomerate dwelt Midge and I, along with the nameless other souls, some possibly still together, most probably drifted apart, countless others buried now down near Father.

As it turned out, here I was, thirty-six years old, still wandering just as aimlessly through life as those two teenagers who used to grope feverishly under these oaks, still not knowing what next month or even next week had in store. But I was alone now, no woman to confide in, and yet, no woman quick to point out each one of my many shortcomings. Hell, maybe this was the perfect place in my life to be after all. At least until I figured some things out.

I cranked up Ethel's old car, drove back across Bridge Street, and drove down Old Spanish Trail to the cemetery, following an urge to pay my last respects to Father. I parked and walked over to the mausoleum, still adorned by a few wilting flowers from yesterday. I knew Earlene and Ethel would take turns coming out here regularly to replace the flowers with either real or silk ones, just as they had for Mother and baby Faith all these years.

The mausoleum, shaded by live oaks, held Mamaw and Papaw Doucet, with Father and Mother side by side under them, and Faith below Mother. I noticed the places reserved for what was left of our branch of the family, shuddering at the thought of spending eternity next to Vic.

Unlike Earlene and Ethel, I had never been one who understood visiting cemeteries, but here I was, gazing dumbly at where my father had been interred twenty-four hours ago, murdered, I felt certain, for God knows what motive. Somewhere in the recesses of my cynical gray matter, the word *greed* flashed like a billboard. I stood there feeling a twinge of guilt for being a disappointment to Father until the end. Hell, I was a disappointment to myself. Maybe one day I would be able to make amends the only way left at this point, by proving he didn't take his own life.

Glancing at my watch, I realized it was nearly time for my meeting with Marlisa. I said what I figured was my "last" last good-bye to Father, promised him I would clear his name, and trudged back to the car. For some reason, it was easier to say goodbye properly here, alone with

Father, than it had been at the resplendent cathedral and gravesite eulogy, surrounded by mourners.

Shaking off the reverie of the past hour, I headed back to town and parked in front of Provost's. The morning had deteriorated into a windy, drizzling December afternoon, and the air smelled like wet leaves and car exhaust. I picked up a copy of *The Daily Iberian* outside, then hurried to the warmth inside. The inundation was all the way back in section B now. Old news, I thought. Just a paragraph or two. Soon people not directly affected would forget about it, go on with their lives as if nothing had happened, adept as we all are at forgetting tragedy until it touches us personally. Not through callousness, I realized, but for our own self-preservation. No one can turn on the news without learning of another tragedy. If we held it all in, if we didn't let some of it go, we'd need a nation of military bases and mental hospitals, and not much else. We had to let go of other people's tragedies to make room for the next batch.

But people like Marlisa and the other family members who lost loved ones disturbed me. I knew those people wouldn't forget. The loss would live on in them, become a part of who they are.

Marlisa walked in right on time, closed her umbrella, and leaned it in a corner by the door. Spotting me, she glided over to my table, stunning, even in the black mourning dress and jacket she still wore, her auburn hair piled hastily on top of her head in a loose ponytail, her transparent green eyes looking deep into mine as she said, "Hello, H."

I fumbled to my feet clumsily, meeting her

outstretched hand with my own. "Thanks for coming, Marlisa. Please, have a seat," I said, pulling out the chair next to me. Her light hint of a musky jasmine perfume was intoxicating. I felt a twinge of pity for Charles's loss.

"Yes. Well, I don't have much to say," she responded coolly, taking a seat. "I was never even in the mine. You'd probably be better off talking to Jack Brouillette or one of the others. Why did you happen to call me, anyway?" Her inquisitive eyes never left mine.

"Oh, I intend to talk to Brouillette," I agreed, wondering myself why I had opted to call Marlisa first. Maybe it was because we had both just suffered losses. Maybe there was an ulterior motive, but I convinced myself that my motives were thoroughly honorable, logical even, and that it was no fault of mine that this woman was decidedly captivating.

"See, Marlisa, I feel that you and I have something in common. We both lost loved ones," I said, never having used the word love aloud in connection with my father before, except maybe as a young child. "So, I thought we might have even more motivation than someone like Jack Brouillette to dig deep enough to get at the truth. I'm convinced there's more to the inundation than an unfortunate drilling miscalculation. Have you ever felt that way?"

"To tell you the truth, I wonder how anyone could have made such a stupid mistake as drilling a hole in a salt mine," she blurted angrily. "Charles always used to reassure me that an accident in the mine was virtually impossible. I wanted to believe him....I..." She trailed off, looking down at the table as though she might begin crying. "I'm sorry. I shouldn't have come."

"I didn't mean to upset you, Marlisa. Let's just decide what to eat for lunch," I said, opening the menu. "Got any suggestions?" I continued, hoping to change the mood.

"I've always liked their redfish court bouillon."

"Sounds good to me," I said, signaling for the waitress and placing our order.

I turned my attention back to the inundation, even though I knew I was pushing my luck. I didn't know if she'd ever agree to speak to me again, so I soldiered on but kept it lighter, away from the topic of Charles. "I heard that Sapphire was being run by a relatively new CEO. Do you happen to know his name or where he came from?"

She took a deep breath and let out a sigh. Then she fiddled with her napkin awhile, unfolding it and smoothing it across her lap, clearly perturbed. Finally, still looking down at her lap to compose herself, she said, "Yes, Charles complained about him. He took over several years back. Charles and I were married just a little over a year ago." She paused and dabbed at her eyes with a Kleenex. "So I don't know much before that." Then she looked up at me again. "But Charles said things were a whole lot better before...oh, what was his name? ...anyway, before he took over."

"I heard there were some layoffs."

I knew I had hit a nerve when she suddenly got talkative. "Yes, they said they were 'restructuring.' Some of Charles's best friends got laid off," she said. "Some of them still haven't found work. The ones who were left were expected to take up the slack, with no pay increase, of course, and with two-thirds the work force. Naturally, the accident rate went up. Charles used to complain that they couldn't make quota anymore. Then they'd get chewed out, even get docked in pay sometimes.

"Charles was a master electrician," she continued after another pause for a sip of tea. "And the new boss never replaced any of the old equipment. Charles spent most of his time patching up old, broken-down machinery, trying to keep it running. I worried about him because he never slept well anyway, and the constant worry over quotas and outdated machines kept him awake lots of nights. He'd toss and turn, sometimes even talk in his sleep. Crazy stuff. Always about work."

"And you can't recall the new boss's name?"

"Warren something or other, I believe. Yeah, that's it. Warren...um...Warren Armstrong! That was it!"

"Any idea where he worked before Sapphire?" I asked.

"Charles never mentioned that, I don't think. Look, Major Doucet, I know you've got some conspiracy theory, but I don't want Charles's name dragged through the mud. All I know is he never did anything wrong. He was an honest man. Can't you just let him rest in peace?"

"I'm so sorry, Marlisa," I said, feeling like a cad. I jotted down my name and numbers on the notepad I carried in my Day-Timer. "Here are numbers to my Aunt Ethel's house and the office. Please, call me if you think of anything else that might help us get to the truth. It could bring you some peace."

At least she didn't crumple the paper and drop it on the table. Instead, she tucked it into the tiny black handbag that lay beside her plate. Then we focused on our steaming court bouillon without another word about Armstrong. After I paid and we got up to leave, she turned and said, "I'll call you if I think of anything."

Then, she just reeled and walked away.

Chapter 6
*LA CHE PAS LA PATATE**
(*Don't give up; literally, don't drop the potato)

"Restructuring": The euphemism for destroying people's lives, and in some cases, taking them. What company wasn't restructuring in this recession? Restructuring was the norm, not an anomaly, especially in Louisiana. Louisiana and Texas were probably hit hardest after the oil economy collapsed with the stock market in '79. The standing joke in Lafayette, a city that subsisted on oil profits, was, "Will the last one to leave, please turn out the lights?"

I ducked into the car quickly to escape the rain, steady and persistent now. When I checked my rearview before backing up, I recognized the black Chevy Blazer parked behind me. Those two guys from the diner this morning were hunkered inside the Blazer. Odd coincidence, it seemed to me. Opting not to let them know I had made them, I eased out of the parking space, keeping an eye on the rear view. The Blazer pulled out about three car lengths back. They had remembered who I was after all. But how could they know I was nosing around? Unless they had some connection to Morton, the only person I had spoken to besides Marlisa. I wouldn't put anything past Morton. And how did they happen to find me here? Not that anyone could successfully hide a vehicle in a parallel parking space on East Main Street in downtown New Iberia.

Well, no matter. I still had enough time to head up to Lafayette and go through Father's condo this afternoon, and I didn't have any afternoons to waste. I'd have to ditch these two jokers first. I headed around a few residential blocks and back to Center Street. I backed into a tight space between two cars in a strip mall and cut the engine. After several minutes with no sign of the Blazer, I eased out and drove to Highway 90, smugly proud of myself for losing those assholes, at least for the time being.

A few miles north, I relaxed as the hypnotic four-lane lulled me through the miles of wide, flat terrain, dotted on either side by oil field equipment sales and repair companies, pipeline companies, an occasional gentleman's club, numerous greasy spoons. Where would Louisiana be without big oil, I wondered? And how many businesses did it support? But to what lengths would big oil take Louisiana and its people? And what polluted ditch would big oil dump us all in once it had its way with us? And Father wondered why I avoided his business. Yet, irony of ironies, here I was relying on profits from Father's oil drilling business to investigate his death, which was a direct result, I was pretty sure, of that same oil drilling business.

Just past the Broussard city limits, traffic got heavier,

the usual work vehicles and oil equipment and repair trucks heading into and out of the big metropolis of Lafayette. I settled back in the right lane and switched on the radio, then grabbed the knob to tune out Ethel's zydeco station and see if I could find the Lafayette oldies station I remembered from years ago. But in the brief moment that I glanced at the dial, the jolt and crash of metal on metal, *my* metal, knocked my head into the door frame before my brain could even register that I'd just been rear-ended. Another harder smack to the driver's side, and my car careened out of control on the wet pavement and slid sideways across the shoulder as I pulled helplessly at the wheel and pumped the brakes with no positive result until Ethel's old Grand Prix sat in the shallow grassy drainage ditch facing back in the direction I had just come from. "You son of a bitch!" I said to the empty air. They had damn near rolled the car! If it hadn't had such a wide wheelbase, I was pretty sure they would have flipped me. These assholes meant business. I might not be so fortunate next time.

An oil field equipment repair truck pulled off into the grass and stopped beside me facing the opposite direction, so our driver's windows lined up. I finally had the presence of mind to roll down my window to see what this dude wanted. Tipping his cowboy hat to reveal a head as round and bald as a bowling ball, he smiled down at me and said, "Y'okay, *sha*?"

"Yeah, I think so. The jury's still out," I replied, holding my neck and rolling my head slowly from side to side, relieved that apparently, this guy was trying to help me rather than to finish off the job someone else had started.

"I seen the whole thing if you need a witness. That fool

sped up outa nowhere and run you right off the pavement. Smacked you twice, hard! On purpose, looked like to me. Looked like he wanted to flip your car over."

"Yeah, I noticed. Hey, you didn't happen to catch his plate number, did you?" I asked, still rubbing my neck.

"Nah. Happened too fast. He must have been doing ninety. I was several vehicles back. He come flyin' around me. Then he took off like a shot after he hit you. A shiny black Blazer. *Aieee*, that's some crazy fool driver!"

"Yep, crazy," I mumbled, brushing off my shirt absently and beginning to get my bearings. A black Blazer. They must've figured I'd be heading north. I guess it was no great mystery, after all. They were fully expecting me to snoop. Well, they'd get their expectations confirmed. "Hey, thanks for stopping, man. I think I'm OK, though."

"Sure thing, *sha*. Here, take my card. In case you change your mind about a witness," he said, handing me a crumpled business card that smelled of the oil field. "Jake Richard," I read.

"OK, Jake, I might just take you up on that. I'm H. Doucet, by the way. Doucet Drilling."

He clucked his tongue. "We sure hated what happened to the old man."

"Yeah, thanks," I said.

"A'ight. Call if you need me. *Lache pas la patate.*" He tapped his hat, then merged back onto the highway.

If those two goons thought they could discourage me, they had accomplished just the opposite. That stunt just made me all the more determined to get to the bottom of this, even if my life hung in the balance. And apparently, it did.

I jumped out to assess the damage to Aunt Ethel's rear

bumper and driver's side door, then ducked back in out of the rain. I'd need to replace the whole bumper and the door. I faced the car in the right direction, crawled out of the ditch, spinning mud and water, and merged back onto the highway.

I wondered why they didn't stop and finish off the job they had started. They clearly hoped to get me out of their hair once and for all. Whatever they were hiding ranked high on the priority list if they were willing to risk their own skins, even risk getting caught pulling a stupid stunt like that. I was pretty sure that little caper fell outside their professional purview.

I was still seething when I got to Father's condo on Jefferson at Vermilion, still cursing under my breath. I opted to park on the street instead of pushing my luck in the parking garage, imagining deadly garage car chases from watching too many action movies as a kid. Fortunately, the rain had slowed to a drizzle. I flashed my I.D. to Bobby, the doorman, who tipped his hat in recognition. "So sorry for your loss, H," he said as he pulled back the door to the garish mirrored and fresh-flower-strewn lobby of the posh condo complex. I rode the elevator to the top floor, Father's penthouse apartment. It was nothing like a New York penthouse, of course, but boasted a few amenities. At the door, I was rudely greeted by yellow crime scene tape. Maybe they just forgot to remove it. No one answered my knock, so I stepped over the tape, then used Father's security code that I still knew by heart to let myself in.

The condo felt eerie with Father gone. Somber and silent as a tomb, the ambient Muzak I was used to hearing no longer greeting me. A picture of Mother, still smiling her ageless smile, sat on the end table beside Father's L-shaped leather sofa. She was a beauty, immortalized at age 35. I paused and picked it up to peer into those eager hazel eyes, awaiting whatever the future held in store for her. Here she was, the picture of youth and naiveté, probably less than a year before her death, maybe already pregnant with my baby sister. I couldn't help wondering how things might have turned out if she hadn't lost her life in her prime. Father's life, my life, Victor's life would all have been different if we'd had some normal family ties. Father might have been less anal retentive. Hell, he might even still be alive. Victor and I might have ended up with less resentment and fewer neuroses. When Mother died, the family was no longer a family, and now the straggling remnants had been shattered again. I cringed at the thought that Victor and I were all that was left.

I set the picture back on the table, brushed off the lingering nostalgia, then walked into Father's makeshift office. No danger of finding any feminine touch here, I thought. Strictly utilitarian. The Commodore computer, his pride and joy, had been confiscated, along with all the floppies. The file cabinet was cleaned out except for a half dozen or so empty manila folders scattered in the drawers and strewn across the floor. I shuffled through the few loose papers left on his desk: Nothing but some random copies of old invoices tossed around. Nothing related to Oka Chito Island or anyone involved. I opened the top desk drawer: just a few pencils, paper clips, a blank legal pad, the usual. Clearly, the cops had confiscated anything remotely useful. But useful for what purpose? To get to the bottom of Father's death? Or to cover their own asses? It must have taken a concerted effort to wipe out Father's entire existence.

Still hopeful that Father had outsmarted them, I walked into his bedroom. The bed was stripped. I stood there imagining how Earlene must have felt when she found Father's body. I'd have to find out why Earlene and not Placide had walked into his bedroom that morning. I opened the drawer of Father's bedside table: a TV remote and a box of condoms. Leave it to Father to be prepared, I thought, wondering why the cops hadn't confiscated the condoms along with everything else. I checked the dresser drawers. His clothes had been rifled through, some of his socks and T-shirts scattered on the floor around the dresser. I even lifted the mattress and checked underneath. Nothing. Father was no fool though. I'd still bet he left a clue somewhere that the cops had overlooked.

I walked out to the kitchen, which he had used solely for heating up a TV dinner or a can of Chef Boyardee Ravioli. His go-to place instead was always the wet bar in the living room, to pour himself a shot of single malt Aberlour Scotch before he went to Café Vermilionville for dinner.

I pulled open the "forbidden" junk drawer in the utility room off the kitchen, where he kept a few screwdrivers, pliers, and nails for minor repairs. He used to call the drawer his "personal business drawer," and Victor and I were permanently denied access. He was probably afraid we would impale each other in one of our sibling "battles." Of course, that just insured that Vic and I would rifle through it every chance we got, which now I realized could have been the reason for the ban. He just let us think we were pulling something off.

The drawer looked neatly intact, so I was reasonably sure the cops had either overlooked it or determined it was benign. I searched through every one of the plastic containers Father had painstakingly filled with screws, picture hangers, and electrical connectors. Nothing out of the ordinary. But feeling around in the back of the drawer, I latched onto one of those little magnetic key caddies designed to hide a spare under a fender. Inside, I found a folded slip of paper with the name "Gremillion," a phone number, and an extension number scribbled in pencil. I was pretty sure that was the name Aunt Ethel had mentioned, the guy Father had called from the hall phone. I tucked the scrap in my change pocket, satisfied that I was onto something, however insignificant.

Walking back through the living room, I grabbed Mother's picture on the way past the sofa. Before leaving, I peeked through two slats in the vertical blinds that covered the sliding door to the side terrace. Parked about two car lengths behind Ethel's Grand Prix sat the black Chevy Blazer. Damn them! They must have figured out exactly where I was heading. What were they concocting, anyway? Did they just hope somehow to scare me off the trail? Fat chance that would happen.

Devising a plan to elude them, I stepped back over the tape and into the hall. But at the moment my shoe touched the floor, a hand grabbed the neck of my jacket and yanked me around to face a side of beef with a shoulder holster under the jacket of his raised arm. A second hulking ape stood at his elbow.

"This here's off-limits. I suppose you can't read," said the one who had grabbed me, his face squeezed at the neck by the collar on the dress shirt that he'd outgrown. He pulled out the badge of a local police detective, which gave me an ironic sense of relief at this point.

"I apologize, sir," I said. "I'm Major Doucet, Harvey's son. I drove all the way up here from New Iberia just to pick up this picture of my mother. My Aunt Ethel told me she had her heart set on getting it," I lied, playing for sympathy.

"Look, Doucet, I don't care if you drove up here to meet the King of Spain," the beefiest one snarled. "This crime tape specifically means stay the hell out. That means you! You'll get your daddy's stuff once the investigation is over, hear?"

"Do you suspect foul play?" I asked innocently.

"If we did, we wouldn't need no one messing anything up now, would we?" he growled as he jerked my mother's picture from my hand. I was glad I had picked it up, warding off suspicion of a deeper motive for my visit. "Don't let us catch you nosing around here again until we notify you, got that?"

"Yes, sir," I agreed, straightening my jacket after he let go. Not wanting to get in deeper or waste time getting questioned at the station, I opted not to tell them about the two goons waiting outside. For all I knew, they could all be working together.

"See that you don't." Chests puffed, they stepped over the tape and into Father's condo.

"Macho assholes," I muttered under my breath.

But I still had those two thugs outside to think about, and I really didn't want another run-in with them. Father's office was located in a building across Jefferson and a block down, so I used the door facing Jefferson. I didn't see anyone but the security guard at the parking garage entrance on the next corner, so I hurried toward him, greeted him as I passed, then crossed over to the office building. Several employees milling around the suite greeted me and offered their condolences when I walked in. Marc Leblanc waved from his office. I stuck my head in his door and asked how he was getting along.

"We're trying to get reorganized after the inundation," he said. "Lots to sort out, a lawsuit to fight, and one to file. Earlene keeps me informed about what's going on. But be sure to let me know if you need anything."

"Will do. Let me know if I can help you in any way, too."

"Of course, H. Thanks."

"Good morning, Earlene," I said when she walked up front. "I might have found some new information. Can we go to your office? Or to the lunchroom?"

"Sure thing, H. Let's go to the lunchroom. I haven't had time for lunch yet. They should still have some coffee down there. Strong as Mississippi mud by now, though."

"Put hair on my chest. Thanks, Earlene."

The lunchroom was vacant now, between lunch hour and afternoon coffee breaks. Placide followed us and found a seat just outside in the hall. Earlene told him, "Tell anyone who passes by that we're in a private meeting," then closed the lunchroom door behind us.

I sat at the '60's Formica table, which I remembered from Ethel's kitchen as a child, and where now I sipped on a cup of joe long past palatability. Earlene sat down and slurped spoonsful of the gumbo she heated in the microwave.

"Earlene," I said, unsure where to start, "I guess you could say I've had a rather eventful morning." I told her about my meeting with Morton and about the two guys who smacked my car and were still on my ass. "Keep that part about Ethel's car under your hat, though. I don't want to worry her."

"H, boy," she said, *sotto voce*. "I'm pretty sure your daddy didn't commit suicide. Do you understand what I'm saying?"

"No shit!"

"H, language!"

"Father wouldn't have taken his own life, Earlene. He was a devout Catholic, despite some of his more questionable practices."

"Don't elaborate."

"Don't worry. But Father sure didn't want to spend eternity in hell!"

"I agree. But we don't have proof. As the police keep reminding me, he was depressed after the inundation."

"Yeah, yeah, that's the snow job they're pushing." I fished the slip of paper out of my pocket and handed it to her. "This anyone you know? I think Father called this guy from Aunt Ethel's house after the inundation to set up a meeting."

She looked at it for a few seconds. "Your daddy made an appointment with someone for the Monday after Thanksgiving. He asked me to put a file together on the inundation for him to pick up Monday morning. But he died Sunday night. I figure he knew how much danger he was in. Otherwise, he would have had me put the appointment on his calendar like I always did. As it was, he left me with nowhere to turn."

"I'm pretty sure he wasn't planning to bite the big one. But he had this number well-hidden for some reason. I was wondering, Earlene, how did you happen to wander into Father's bedroom and find him?"

"Placide called me Sunday evening. He told me your daddy was sending him on an errand in Jackson, Mississippi. I thought at the time, it wasn't like your daddy to send Placide off alone like that. When Harvey was late to work the next morning, I called his apartment. No answer, so when he still hadn't shown up a while later, I headed over there. You can imagine my shock!"

"I'm so sorry you're the one who got stuck with it," I said, placing my hand on her forearm. "Did you find out why Placide had to go to Jackson?"

"Placide said your daddy told him a guy with alligator cowboy boots would meet him outside the Big Boy Drive-In on Commerce Street to give him some important information regarding the inundation. That's all any of us knew. It was a long trip, so your daddy reserved him a room up there for the night."

"What did Placide pick up?"

"Placide wouldn't open anything of your daddy's unless he was told to. But I believe the meeting was in Jackson just to keep Placide out of the way long enough to pump those sleeping pills into your daddy. The murderers knew he wouldn't be alive to read it. And of course, that envelope was confiscated like everything else. I'm guessing it was just a trick to get Placide out of town for the night. Anyway, the police were convinced enough to let him off the hook."

"So, the police must have had an interest in that envelope. That could implicate them, too."

"One other thing, H. Your daddy has a safety deposit box. I have a key to it, and he gave me power of attorney.

He told me years ago only to open it for you if anything ever happened to him. I was waiting to tell you until all this family stuff settled down. I'm sure he wasn't expecting anything like this at that time, though. You ask me, he just didn't want your brother getting his paws on it."

"After seeing Vic, I understand Father's concerns! Of course, Vic informed me he'll be running the company. No complaints here, but I wonder if Father really wants Vic holding the reins."

"H, your daddy went to his attorney just a few months ago and changed his will. I suspect he wrote Vic out of it, or at least gave him a smaller cut. But CEO of Doucet Drilling? Oh, *mais, non!* Your daddy would've never put it in that boy's hands. Your daddy was a shrewd businessman, and Vic's gambling has gotten much worse, H. Your daddy has bailed him out on the QT several times I know of. Who knows how many times I don't know about."

"I can't say I'm surprised."

"Far as I know, you, Ethel, Louis, and Victor all have joint ownership in Doucet Drilling, though Vic might even be written completely out. Your father's attorney has delayed sending the will to probate until they've ruled out foul play. Vic's scared, but he would never hurt his daddy, though a lot of folks have speculated that he did. My guess is he's just in an all-fire hurry to get his hands on the business to cover his gambling debts, especially since his papa won't be helping him anymore. Don't you worry, H, the Board of Directors isn't fixin' to let Vic take over! But we do need to get the contents of that safety deposit box, see what that's all about. Right now, you, Placide, and me are the only three that know about it."

"Can we get to it today? I'm on a tight schedule. But my car is indisposed at the moment, with a couple of thugs surveilling it."

"Let's go right now," Earlene said, getting up to rinse her bowl and spoon. "We'll get Placide to carry us over there."

"Great! Let's take two cars, though. I don't want to put you in any more danger than you're already in. As far as we know, they're just gunning for me."

"Aren't you the suspicious one!" she said. "OK, I'll meet you over there in fifteen minutes. Placide can drive you. I'll take an alternate route."

I rinsed the dregs out of my cup while Earlene stepped out to speak to Placide. A few minutes later, he stuck his head in and signaled me to follow him. In the parking garage, he had me wait until he rooted around under the frame of Father's car and under the dash for any random explosive devices. After he cranked the engine, he motioned, and I slid in the passenger side.

Earlene was already finishing the paperwork when we got to the bank. The guard checked my I.D., then unlocked the gate and led us toward the safety deposit boxes, Earlene's heavy Red Cross shoes clacking decisively on the marble floor ahead of me. She unlocked the box and removed a thick manila folder.

"We'll carry these to the office to make copies," she said, handing me the folder while she locked the box. "See you back there in a few minutes."

Placide pointed out the Blazer still parked behind Ethel's car when we passed Vermilion. "Placide," I said, "after we finish this, how about driving me to New Iberia? I'm not up for tangling with those two assholes again."

"Sure thing, H," he said.

When we got back, Earlene began copying the large stack of files. I walked out front to Marc's office to keep him abreast of the latest while I waited.

"Come on in, H," he said.

I helped myself to a chair. "Marc, things are happening so fast it's hard to keep up. I just wanted to let you know two goons damn near flipped my car this morning. They were at the wake, and they've been following me ever since they learned who I am." I told him about the Blazer and the business suits they wore. "Let Earlene or me know if you hear anything from them."

"Of course, H. I noticed two serious-looking businessmen at the wake, but no one seemed to know who they were."

"Yeah, I wish I'd taken them more seriously at the time. I'm going to ask Placide to be my bodyguard now that this happened. If they know anything about his marksmanship, they might think twice before sending me off to meet Father."

"Good idea, H. By the way, we just landed a new drilling contract in the gulf, so we'll be getting more men back to work. I'm working on a couple other possible contracts."

"That's great news! I know some of these fellows are hurting now."

When Earlene finished making copies, she brought one set to me in Marc's office.

"Thanks, Earlene. My car is still being surveilled, so I'm going to borrow Placide to drive me back to New Iberia. Then I'm going to ask him to be my bodyguard. Can you do without having him here all the time?"

"Of course, H. Placide's been wandering around here like he's lost his last friend. He'll be glad to have a purpose again."

"Great. Those thugs will think twice before they mess with him. I'll be talking to you, Marc," I said as I carried the files out to where Placide waited in the hall.

"Ready to drive me home?"

Placide nodded.

"I need to make a couple of stops on the way. First, I want to drop by the police station. After that, I'd like to see the best body man in town. Know who that might be?"

"Robert Dumont fixed plenty of dents for your daddy, mostly on Victor's cars. And your daddy was not an easy man to please."

"So I've heard," I laughed. "OK, let's go."

~

I introduced myself to the patrolman at the front desk and asked to speak to someone familiar with Oka Chito. A few minutes after he buzzed someone, a middle-aged man with a flat-top and a rumpled brown suit came to the front, looking impatient.

"Major H. Doucet," I said, sticking out my hand to shake his. "Harvey Doucet's son. Could we talk for a minute about the investigation?"

"Captain Broussard," he said meeting my handshake, but with no softening of his countenance. "This way, Major." He led me down the hall to a cluttered office with papers strewn across the desk and on every flat surface. He moved a thick manila folder off the chair so I could sit.

"I'm trying to learn what I can about the investigation," I began. "I happen to know my father would never have taken his own life."

"I believe that investigation has been closed. We found no evidence of foul play. Suicide, pure and simple."

"I don't buy it, Captain," I blurted. "I'm just as sure he didn't kill himself. He believed suicide was a mortal sin."

"O.K., look, Major Doucet, I'm sorry for your loss," he said, looking up at me for the first time. "We just don't have the evidence to reopen the case. We've already moved on to some more recent and pressing cases. I'm sure you've kept up with the local crime news. More than enough crime goes on around here every night to keep us occupied. Of course, if any new evidence turned up, we'd probably take a look. But I don't see that happening, frankly."

"No, I suppose you don't," I said indignantly. "But I haven't moved on. This is my father you're being dismissive of! And a powerful leader in the community, in case you hadn't noticed. I'm still going to be digging a little deeper than your department thinks necessary." I started to rise.

"With all due respect, Major Doucet, I'd advise you to stay out of police business. I already got word that you broke into the scene earlier. Don't make the mistake of opening yourself up to possible arrest. If those detectives hadn't been in a good mood, you'd be sharing a cell with Big Bubba right now."

"Yeah, well, I'd hate to see those two in a *bad* mood. And if it's still a 'scene,' why are you saying the case is closed? Somehow, they didn't act to me like the case was closed. And if it *is* closed like you say, then why can't I get my mother's picture, for chrissakes?"

"Watch yourself, Doucet, you're on thin ice. That Doucet name don't buy you any more privilege than the average poor ole widow who gets robbed. And I'm not obliged to fill you in on every little piece of police business. I meant what I said about arresting you if you continue to take things into your own hands. You can bank on it."

I was aware that it had not been in my best interest to lose my temper or let him know I was snooping. So, I just bit my tongue, thanked him as politely as I could through clenched teeth, and returned to the front where Placide sat beside a couple of unsavory-looking characters on a straight wood bench slammed up against the wall.

"Any luck?" he asked when we got back in the vehicle.

"Well, I learned we can't rely on the police for help," I grumbled. "In fact, I think they're as much a threat as the thugs who ran me off the road. I haven't figured out why, yet, but I believe they're all covering something up."

"No surprise there," Placide said.

Next, we drove to Dumont's Paint and Body Shop, where a classic '67 Mustang was being spray-painted candy-apple red. The shop was in an old tin repurposed warehouse next to a fenced auto salvage yard that also bore the name Dumont on a crooked hand-painted sign out front.

"This here's Harvey Doucet's boy, Major Doucet," Placide said when the man in coveralls looked up at us through red-splattered goggles.

"Hello, Placide. Major," Dumont said, straightening up and sliding his goggles to the top of his paint-encrusted cap, but sparing me a handshake with his work glove.

"Sorry to hear about your father. Harvey was one of my best customers. Had lots of scrapes on his various vehicles. Damn shame what happened. What can I do ya for today?"

"Some yahoo decided my rear bumper needed some rearranging. Decided the same was true of my driver's side door. So I'm going to need some body work, and I'm hoping for a rush order because I need to get it back to my aunt ASAP."

"I hear ya," he said. Setting the sprayer on the floor, he hollered over to his assistant, "Right back, Dwayne." He pulled off his gloves and said, "Let's go talk in my office."

He took down the make and model on his desk organizer. "Doubt if I can find new ones for a car that age, but I have a few Grand Prix's out in the salvage yard that should work."

"Yeah, brand new would probably be more obvious anyway."

"I can have Dwayne start on it right away, and of course I'll do the final painting. And you'll probably need an alignment, too, after that jolt," he said.

"OK, I'll get the car over here first thing tomorrow morning. Thanks!"

While Placide drove back to New Iberia, I leafed through the copies from the safe that Earlene had given me. I stopped when I came upon Warren Armstrong's CV, previously CEO of Ideal Tractor in Memphis. I wondered how on God's earth Father ever managed to get this copy. Did he have a mole in Sapphire? Why was he suspicious in the first place? And what possessed Armstrong to want to move to Sapphire Salt in South Louisiana?

Thumbing through more pages, I came across a

geological map of the Oka Chito Island oil drilling operations. I made a note to compare it tomorrow morning with the one in Morton's office.

When Placide dropped me off, I told Aunt Ethel the partial truth about how her car needed an alignment and I was getting it serviced for her over the next few days. I wouldn't have minded telling her it had been in an accident; I just didn't want her to know someone wanted to make lunchmeat out of me.

"Can you get a ride to church with a friend, Ethel? In case we don't get it back in time?"

"Oh, sure, 'Tee. My friend Gladys will be happy to pick us up. We always sit with her and Harry anyway."

I hurried upstairs before she had a chance to ask too many questions and combed through the pages more closely in my room. I learned that Armstrong had unloaded his shares in both Ideal Tractor and Sapphire Salt shortly before the inundation. I felt as if Father were telling me that somewhere within these pages lay the motive for murder. Clearly, he had been going down the same path I was stumbling down now.

Chapter 7
DIGGING FOR CLUES

"Morning, sir," Placide said when I slid in shotgun the next morning.

"Let's ditch the formalities, Placide. Call me H from now on, OK?"

"OK, H."

"Much better. I need to stop at a pay phone before we head to Lafayette. I'm afraid Aunt Ethel's phone could be bugged."

"Your daddy and me developed a code after that rig accident," Placide said. "'Let's grab a cuppa' meant, I've got a tail. 'See you later' meant, pick me up at the condo right away. Course we never got a chance to use none before..."

"That confirms that he knew the inundation was no accident. Jot some of those down for me when you get a chance, Placide. We might be able to use them in emergencies."

He pulled into a 7/Eleven with a phone booth on the

perimeter. "You can get down here and call, sir."

"H," I corrected him, as I stepped out and dug the slip of paper and some loose change out of my pocket. I instinctively scanned the area, though I knew Placide was way ahead of me. Just a few old pickup trucks and a middle-aged woman getting into an Olds 88. I dialed Gremillion's number, a 504-number indicating the Baton Rouge-New Orleans area. I plunked in a handful of change, then dialed the extension at the prompt.

On the third ring, a sing-song voice came on the line: "Department of Natural Resources, Louisiana Gas and Oil Resources."

"This is Major Doucet, Harvey Doucet's son. I'd like to speak to Mr. Gremillion, please."

"Hold a moment, sir."

After a mind-numbing Muzak rendition of "Yellow Submarine," Gremillion picked up.

"Major Doucet? Maurice Gremillion, here," said the deep voice at the other end. "How can I help you?"

"Mr. Gremillion, I believe my father Harvey might have set up a meeting with you shortly before his death?"

"He did indeed. We were all shocked at the news. You have my sympathy, Major."

"Thank you. Look, the reason I'm calling is to ask if you'd consider keeping that meeting with me instead. I have some things I'd like to discuss with you."

"I'd be happy to meet with you. I have some things I'd like to share with you, too, but I'm tied up the rest of this week. Where are you located?"

"I'm in New Iberia, but I can come to your office. Or meet you anywhere you'd like."

"I have a meeting in Lake Charles next Thursday.

Could we meet, say 10 AM, at the Little Capitol there in Henderson? That's my usual rest stop."

"That's great, thanks. I'll be there." Damn, I thought. A whole week wasted, with no weeks to spare.

When Placide and I pulled in behind Aunt Ethel's Grand Prix outside Father's condo, no thugs were in sight. I wondered with no little satisfaction how long they had sat here waiting for me before they realized I wouldn't be back. And what had they planned if I showed up? Placide took the keys from me, then combed the car under the frame, under the hood, under the dash, before he started it up. "All clear, H. Follow me," he said when I took his place behind the wheel.

Dumont greeted us with a smile. "I found a decent rear bumper on a '70 Grand Prix that was in a head-on. Looks almost new. I got the guys to pull it and clean it up this morning. Another Grand Prix had a decent driver's side door. Come take a look." He walked us over to where the parts lay in the garage. "We'll match the color on that door and get it painted.

"Perfect," I said. "How long will it take to install them?"

"Well, for a Doucet, I can get right on it. Let's say a week from today, around lunch time. Will that work?"

"Sounds good. We'll be here."

I joined Placide in Father's car, and said, "Placide, I've been wondering if you'd consider being my driver and bodyguard? I know Father trusted you with his life, and I'd like to do the same if you'll agree, now that I need a bodyguard. Of course, Earlene will keep you on the same payroll. You interested?"

"Yessir, H. I'd be glad to," he said, grinning as though his life had been given renewed purpose. I knew he missed Father, but maybe teaming up with me would be second best. And I was getting used to having him and his piece next to me, especially now that the stakes had gone up. I had to qualify regularly with an M-16, so I could shoot with the best of them. But I never carried a gun. I might have to start, but I wasn't excited about the proposition. Gun battles were not in any of my immediate plans. I was pretty sure any thug would think twice before messing with Placide, though. His reputation as a marksman preceded him.

When we got to Oka Chito, I leaned across Placide to greet my favorite wannabe cop through the driver's window.

"Well, lookie here. If it ain't Doucet. Now what?"

"I have an appointment to see Mr. Morton at 1100 hours. This is my driver, Placide." I was beginning to enjoy getting under the guy's skin.

"Oh. So, is that a standing appointment, now?" he sneered through clenched teeth. He seemed to be enjoying our little *tête à têtes*, too.

"So far, it's just for today, but no guarantees. Who knows what tomorrow might bring?"

"Go on. Go on," he growled, waving me through the barrier. At least he was getting used to me, and no one had ordered him yet to keep me out. And I was getting used to being growled at.

It was already a few minutes after 1100 hours when I

grabbed the manila folder and hurried to the office door. Placide stayed behind in the vehicle.

"Good morning, Babette," I announced cheerfully when I entered the lobby.

"Mr. Morton has been expecting you," she said, smiling up at me. She buzzed his line, batting heavy black lashes in my direction. She must've missed class the day they taught subtlety, I thought. "He'll see you now," she said.

"Doucet," Morton said when I walked into his office.

"Morton, sorry I'm a couple minutes late. Been a hectic morning."

He didn't respond but motioned me to take a seat and buzzed Babette.

"I've got that information you requested. Matherne's first name is Dallas. He was a driller, one of your father's own," he said, looking self-satisfied. "Usually worked with Sid Ardoin, another driller, the guy you saw leaving last time you were here."

In paraded Babette in her paint-on mini dress, hips undulating with every step she took in three-inch spikes, while I marveled at the wonders of women maneuvering stilettos. I just couldn't understand how they did it. Or why, for that matter.

"Here you are, Sir," she said, lowering her cleavage into Morton's face to place a manila folder on his desk.

"Thank you, Babette. That'll be all," he replied, with a stomach-turning smirk. By God, that little lecher was "in lust" with her, I realized. Babette knew it, too, and used it to her advantage. Morton stuck his index finger into his shirt collar, as lightly clad hips gyrated back across the tile floor. His eyes never left her ass until the door closed behind her.

He turned his attention to me, not without some difficulty. "Ahem...yes. Here's Matherne's file. He's been a driller with Doucet Drilling for about two years. Nothing outstanding. I didn't see anything in there that could interest you."

"Does it say where he was before he came to Doucet?"

"I didn't notice. Any reason you singled Matherne out? Looks to me like an average employee."

"No reason, really. I just heard he missed work the night of the inundation."

"Hell, that don't mean nothing," he said. "Guys miss work all the time." That was what the suit at Maybelle's had said, word for word.

"Yeah, but from what I've heard, this was the only time except for his father's funeral. Not significant, I'm sure. I just wanted to take a look."

"Who'd you hear that from?"

"Oh, just two goons who'd rather I wasn't nosing around." No change of expression, but his blank affect convinced me he wasn't surprised. I realized I had begun to suspect virtually everyone I met. I heard Midge's voice in my head, saying, "Paranoid. You need help, H." She was probably right about needing help, but things were becoming a little too coincidental. And I thought Father could have realized that, gotten nosy, and paid the ultimate price. I was hoping to escape that same outcome.

"I haven't heard about any surveillance going on," he responded after a pregnant pause.

"This is not your standard surveillance, I assure you. These guys want to hurt me."

"Well, then, they aren't any of our people, you can be

sure." Morton shrugged, looking down at his desk as if to dismiss me.

"Somehow that doesn't make me feel any better, and I don't imagine it would make me any less dead."

"Anyway, Doucet," he continued. "You can have a look through that file, but I'm afraid I can't let it leave the building."

"Thanks. I'll just carry it out to the waiting room, if that's OK. Let you get back to work," I said. "One more question: Ever see a geological map of Oka Chito like this?" I plopped the map from Father's safety deposit box on the desk in front of Morton.

His jaw dropped noticeably when he saw it, but all he said was, "May I have this?"

"No. It was Father's. I'll let you make a copy, though."

"Yes, thanks. Babette will do that for you."

"What do you make of it?"

"It's obviously an erroneous map," he concluded too quickly.

"OK, then, Morton," I said, standing to leave, with Dallas Matherne's file in my hand.

"Just so you don't leave with that file," he said, placing his hands behind his head as he leaned his desk chair back.

I could feel Babette's eyes following me when I returned to the corner chair in the lobby. "Get you a cuppa, Major Doucet?"

"That would hit the spot, Babette, thanks. Just black, please."

I began leafing through the file as she sashayed over and placed the coffee cup beside me on the table. Didn't spill a drop, I marveled, as she managed to keep the cup perfectly level without missing a single hip rotation.

"Thank you, Babette. Just what the doctor ordered."

"Anytime, Major Doucet," she replied, stopping to face me and lowering her eyelids to half-mast. "You just let me know if the doctor orders anything else."

"As a matter of fact, Mr. Morton asked me to have you make a copy of this for your files," I said, avoiding eye contact as I handed her the map.

"That be all?"

"Yes, for now. Thank you." Looking quickly back down at the file on my lap, I avoided her gaze, until she finally turned and swayed her impressive ass over to the Xerox machine. I focused on the file of what appeared to be an impeccable employee.

Toward the back of the file, Dallas Matherne's résumé caught my eye. Glancing over it, I saw a mediocre career unfold. He joined Doucet Drilling in '78, two years after Warren Armstrong had joined Sapphire. But I also discovered that, after an earlier career on offshore oil rigs in Louisiana, Matherne's last employer was none other than Ideal Tractor in Memphis, the same company Armstrong came from. It was at least feasible to find out if they knew each other at Ideal and what their relationship was. If Morton hadn't noticed that coincidence, he wasn't looking, I reasoned. Had he just overlooked that tidbit, and what other pieces of the puzzle had he conveniently ignored?

"Here, Babette," I said, carrying the résumé to her desk. "Could you make one more copy for me, please? Then I'll get out of your hair."

"No problem, Major."

Back in New Iberia, I had Placide stop at the bookstore so I could grab a Mobil Travel Guide before he dropped me off at Ethel's. Then I headed upstairs to pore over the file and figure out my next move. Looked like my best hope to get to the bottom of this Matherne/Armstrong connection was a trip to Ideal Tractor in Memphis, so I went back downstairs to the hall phone. Placide picked up the car phone on the second ring.

"Placide, I've got a little picnic planned tomorrow," I said, our new code for "throw some clothes in a bag for a trip."

"Yessir, H."

"Come by around 0930 hours."

I headed back to the kitchen and hugged Ethel's waist. "What'cha cookin', *chère*?" I asked.

She giggled like a schoolgirl and replied, "Oh, me, I'm just fixin' your uncle some jambalaya for supper. Had some pork left over and andouille. Plenty for you to join us, 'Tee."

"Thanks, don't mind if I do," I said. "By the way, I'll be heading out with Placide for a few days tomorrow morning. I'll be around until then to give Louis a hand, though. And I'll be back soon, for more of that good cooking." I gave her waist another squeeze.

"Aitchie, you'll be the death of me. You never set still a minute, child."

"I'll be home before you have time to miss me. I can't stay away from your cooking too long," I teased.

"You need to slow down one day, Aitchie. Start thinking about your future. You ain't gettin' any younger, you know."

"Thanks for reminding me, Ethel."

The travel guide listed a Days Inn near the Memphis airport, which seemed as good a place to start as any. I called to reserve a room for a couple of days, then went out back to help Uncle Louis dig a post hole to fix his fence.

Placide was waiting in the driveway when I got downstairs the next morning, so I filled a couple of travel mugs and headed out the door. Following her maternal instincts, Ethel walked me to the car to send us off.

"Now you be careful, Placide," she admonished him, sticking her head in the passenger side door as I chunked my duffle bag in the back seat.

"Yes'm," he assured her.

"We lost one Doucet. I don't know what this boy's getting into, but you just keep your eye on him, keep him out of trouble, hear?" Then she turned to me. "Boy, you be careful. And don't go sticking your nose where it don't belong, hear?"

"Don't worry, Aunt Ethel. It's just a little trip to get the cobwebs out." I gave her a peck on the cheek before I slid in. Even I knew that lie wouldn't hold water, but I didn't know what else to say. I wasn't prepared to worry her with my suspicions, even though it sounded as though she was making up some of her own.

"Ready to go to Memphis?" I asked Placide as we rumbled out the drive.

"Yessir, H."

Chapter 8
BEALE STREET BLUES

Bald cypress and tupelo trees in the swamp below the Atchafalaya Basin Bridge reached for the sky beside us and between the four-lane. Spanish moss draped across the branches like tattered lace. A roseate spoonbill stood ankle-deep in the basin, then arched its neck and lifted lazily into flight beside the highway. A few *bateaus* and *pirogues* sat motionless in the shallow water, their lonely occupants bent optimistically over fishing rods. The primordial life-forms below had become accustomed to the constant thwack, thwack of tires overhead, oblivious to the threat big oil posed to their habitat atop the rich oil deposits.

Despite heavy truck traffic, we made decent time in the left lane until we neared the perpetual bottleneck that was Baton Rouge. Apparently, there had been an accident ahead on I-10, so we headed north to highway 61 instead of sitting in the vast interstate "parking lot" that wound like a serpent as far as we could see.

"Let me know if you want me to drive for a while," I offered after we had escaped the jam-up.

"Thanks, H. But I'm used to being in charge of the wheel after working for your daddy all those years."

"You won't get any complaints here!" Settling back to look through my notes, I wrote down a few questions I hoped to ferret out answers for over the next couple of weeks. What reason did Armstrong give for leaving Ideal? How about Matherne? Did they know each other? And what connection did either Armstrong or Gremillion have to Father? What about the map I found in the safety deposit box? How did Father happen to get his hands on that map, and was it the accurate one? And what did Matherne have to do with any of it, if anything?

Thirty miles north of Baton Rouge sat historic St. Francisville, a town that fortunately Union soldiers had once deemed too beautiful to burn. The town, with its renovated antebellum homes, recalled a place time forgot, one less complicated than our current one, yet one both made possible and permanently scarred by the tragic flaw of slavery.

Thirty minutes north of St. Francisville, just outside of Woodville, Mississippi, Placide pulled into a truck stop so we could fill up and take advantage of the facilities. I grabbed a couple bags of Doritos and two Styrofoam cups of joe to keep us alert. Then we hung around outside to stretch our legs for a few minutes. The air had gotten much cooler than back in New Iberia, so I zipped my jacket and turned my back to the north wind. Two or three vehicles pulled in while we stood there, Placide mentally noting each driver.

"Did Father ever mention the names Armstrong or

Matherne to you?" I asked. We started heading back in the direction of the car after a gust of wind whipped the tops of trees and sent a shiver up my spine.

Placide scratched his head. "No, H, those names don't ring no bell."

"What about Gremillion?"

"I know some Gremillions, me."

"This one works for the Department of Natural Resources."

"*Mais, non*," he said, rubbing his chin to help him think. "I don't recollect hearing nothing about him."

After we returned to the car, I continued, "Father was supposed to meet Gremillion the day after he died. I think he might have set up the meeting from Aunt Ethel's house while you were in the kitchen. Do you remember bringing Father to Ethel's house that day?"

"Oh, sure, I remember that day. He made a couple of calls while we was there. He was some upset that day, him. We all was."

"Did he tell you anything at all about the calls?"

"Your daddy had a policy. He always said, 'Listen here, Placide. What I don't tell you can't come back to bite you.' So he pretty much never told me nothing. Said it was to protect me. I usually didn't know where we was going till we got there. 'After all,' he told me, 'if you know too much, and someone comes back and hurts you, then how are you gonna protect me, henh?'"

"He must have had reason to believe someone wanted to hurt him. That's pretty good evidence of foul play, if you ask me."

"Your daddy was a cautious man, him. Always was. Even before the inundation."

"Yeah. Look where caution got him," I grumbled. "Placide, any idea who the man was that you met in Jackson the night Father died?"

"No, H, but he had Tennessee plates on his truck. I remembered that when you said we was going to Tennessee. Think there could be some connection?"

"I think there's a good chance, Placide. Did you happen to catch the numbers on the plate?"

"No, it was dark out, and I just seen his truck from a distance when he peeled out. He drove a light blue pickup, though, and I seen the Tennessee outline on his plate. He had on some fancy alligator boots. That's how I was supposed to recognize him. I remember noticing them fancy boots when he walked toward the car. Had a beer gut too."

Probably just a hired delivery driver, I figured. This guy didn't sound like your run-of-the-mill white-collar criminal. So far every road led to a dead end. I let my head flop back against the headrest and turned my focus to the landscape out the side window.

The highway snaked ahead of us through the rolling Mississippi hills, making me drowsy enough to nod off. I woke up as Placide slowed near Natchez, drowsy thoughts taking me back to a childhood trip here I hadn't thought about in a couple of decades. I couldn't remember how Father ended up in Natchez. He was never one to take vacations, at least not with family. Probably a business trip, maybe when Aunt Ethel had gone up to Shreveport to help out when her niece's granddaughter was born. I remembered riding through downtown Natchez in a horse-drawn carriage, like the ones for hire along North Peters in New Orleans. Victor and I, no better friends then than today, punched each other sporadically in the back seat of the carriage, fighting over who knows what now, or maybe just for the hell of it. I must have been around eight or nine at the time. I remember Father buying us ice cream cones and pinwheels on that trip. The ice cream cones kept our mouths occupied for a while and watching the pinwheels spin in the breeze in the back seat of the carriage kept our hands and minds occupied for a few minutes. Of course, it didn't take Victor long to figure out we could dive bomb each other's pinwheel while we made the screeches and explosions of war with our mouths, until Father reached back and took them from us for the remainder of the ride. I had kept that pinwheel for several years, stuck into the headboard of my bed, maybe as a memento of the father I rarely saw, until I got angry at him that time he missed the Dixie Youth game he'd promised to attend, smashed the pinwheel, and threw it in the trash.

It occurred to me that Father must have had a lonelier existence than I had ever considered. I began to feel closer to him here, where I had a few pleasant recollections of him, than I ever did when he was alive in New Iberia, the way we are sometimes visited by the dead, our own imperfections illuminated from our new vantage point. Unfortunately, my youthful resentments, instead of mellowing with time, had blossomed into angst and intolerance. But for all his flaws, I was beginning to realize that Father was basically an honest man, just trying to stay afloat in the corrupt world of big oil. While his was a world I had never wanted to inhabit, I could appreciate how his perseverance in the industry and his unfailing integrity had been key to his success.

I still wondered if it had ever occurred to him that,

while he had lost a beautiful young wife, Victor and I had lost both a father and a mother. I could see the toll it had taken on Victor, and I was finally beginning to see the toll it had taken on me. Midge was right. I was the carbon copy of Father, at least his cynicism if not his determination.

Once we got past Vicksburg, the Mississippi hills flattened into patient fields harrowed for spring plantings of corn, soy, millet, or cotton. We passed more tiny nondescript churches than houses in northern Mississippi, the heart of the Bible Belt. Apparently, anyone who could afford a cross, a square cinder block building, and a collection plate was in business. But it was a mystery where the congregations traveled from to get to these tiny churches that dotted the terrain like push pins. I pictured large families in modest farmhouses across the countryside washing faces and dressing in Sunday-best clothes for the long trip to church in the station wagon; little boys finally corralled, their hair painstakingly parted and slicked down; little girls proud to wear their black patent leather Mary Janes and socks with lace edges neatly folded over.

The sun was settling lower in the west, casting red and gold streaks across the western sky and signaling a clear day tomorrow, a cold one judging from the wind gusts that still tossed the trees along the edges of pastures. When we got as far as Memphis, the Atlas directed us to the motel, our base of operations for the next couple of days.

"Pull in up there on the right, Placide," I said, pointing out the lighted blue and yellow Days Inn sign. As it turned out, the motel was just across from Graceland, the whole area crawling with tourists, an inconvenience that had not occurred to me. When we got to our room, I grabbed the phone book and ordered a large pizza. Placide picked up the TV remote, and we settled in for the evening.

The next morning, we headed to Ideal Tractor. Placide stopped at a 7-Eleven for directions and a couple cups of joe.

"Follow Third up there to Carolina," the pimply teenager behind the counter told us. "Cain't miss it. Big building right on the corner."

We drove past block after block of run-down shotgun houses that signaled broken dreams, broken promises until Placide spotted the parking lot at Ideal Tractor. It looked as if it had seen better times, as did most of the city we had seen so far. Weeds grew out of the cracked pavement in the parking lot, a large portion of which was in disuse. The neighboring buildings were also run-down, some even boarded up.

An attractive middle-aged receptionist greeted us at the front desk, wearing subtle makeup and a headset over carefully coifed golden blonde hair. She brought Babette to mind strictly by contrast.

"May I he'p you gentlemen?" she asked in a slow Tennessee drawl.

"Yes, ma'am. My name is Major Doucet," I said, showing her my I.D. "I'd like to speak to someone who has information about a former employee."

"I see. And is this an emplo'ee you are considering hiring?"

"Um...yes, ma'am," I fibbed, thinking that might be the only way to get my foot in the door.

"Let's see. I believe Mr. Dawkins might have a moment. Excuse me, sir," she smiled, turning to the switchboard.

"Mr. Dawkins, two gentlemen are here to discuss the possible employment of a former Ideal emplo'ee," she said into the mouthpiece on her headset. "Mm Hmm. Mm Hmm. Yes, sir."

She turned back to us. "Mr. Dawkins will see you gentlemen now." She pointed to her right, "Down that hall, third door on your left."

We passed two vacant offices to where Dawkins's door stood slightly ajar. I rapped gently, then stuck my head around the door.

"Come in, gentlemen," Dawkins boomed. He was a large, round-faced man with beefy jowls and jet-black hair, graying at the temples and slicked tightly back with some sickeningly sweet pomade, possibly for a slimming effect that failed.

"My name is Major Doucet," I said, reaching out to shake his hand. "This is my assistant, Placide."

"Have a seat, gentlemen," Dawkins replied in the slow drawl of a southern land baron, motioning us to two leather chairs that faced his oversized walnut desk. Nothing shabby about his office, I thought.

"Mr. Dawkins," I began, not sure how to broach the subject without getting us thrown out on our asses. "I have a question about a former employee. In fact, I am wondering about two former employees."

"I'll help y'all if I can. We do have some confidentiality issues, of course. I understand you are considering hiring these former emplo'ees?"

"Actually, well, ...no."

Dawkins frowned at my reply, shaking his heavy jowls. "Well, then, I..."

"You see, the thing is," I continued, unwilling to let him stop me once I had got this far, "their names have come up during an investigation of my father's death. The cops are dragging their feet, so I've decided to try to hurry things up a little, see how I can help them. Placide and I drove up here from Louisiana, and I'm just not prepared to leave without some information."

"I do sympathize, Major Doucet, but you see, company policy and all, my hands are tied." He paused, continuing to look me in the eye as though he might want to add something, instead effectively ending the conversation.

"I see." My eyes never left his. After a silent moment, I added, "Well, here's where Placide and I are staying, in case you think of anything." I jotted the room number on the back of the business card I had picked up in the motel lobby. Somehow, I felt that if I could get this guy away from his desk, he just might spill his guts. It wasn't necessarily anything he said, but something about his unflinching gaze gave me the feeling he wanted to tell me something.

"Yes. All right, gentlemen," he said, glancing at Placide for a moment before his eyes met mine again. "By the way, what did you say the gentlemen's names were?"

"I didn't, but they're Warren Armstrong and Dallas Matherne. Coincidentally, they both left Ideal within the last four years."

"Well, not such a coincidence, really. We've had lots of turnover in the last few years. Times have been tough. Armstrong, you say?" he asked, raising his bushy eyebrows.

"Yes, sir. And Matherne." I paused another moment, staring, hopeful. Nothing. "All right, then. Thank you for your time."

"Sorry I couldn't be more help, gentlemen." He turned his attention to some papers on his desk.

As we walked back past the receptionist's desk, she asked, "Did you find what you were looking for, gentlemen?"

"No, ma'am. I'm afraid not."

"Well, maybe you'd like to check back in a couple of days?"

"We might just do that," I said, sensing a slight ray of hope in her voice.

"Looks like we have a day or two to kill," I said to Placide on the way to the car. "Let's go up toward town and see if we can find a place to grab a bite."

Placide drove north until we found Beale Street. It was a tourist attraction, but why not, I thought. We found a parking place a couple of blocks away, zipped up our jackets, and walked down Beale to Dyer's Burgers, a casual lunch spot. While Placide worked admirably at putting away his giant double combo and fries, I finished my single combo, sipped on a Bud, and began leafing through my notes again. I would have to go back out to Ideal in a day or two, see who else I could cozy up to. Or find out if the receptionist was hinting at something. We were here and we weren't leaving. Not yet, anyway.

Tourists and what looked like a few regulars had poured into Dyer's Burgers and were filling the room with chatter. Unable to hold my train of thought in the din, I gave up on my notes and raised my head just as one tall, self-important redneck with a cowboy hat, boots, and a beer gut bumped into our table rudely on the way past and muscled up to a stool at the counter.

"H, it's time to leave," Placide said quietly out of the blue, his combo unfinished. Without a word, I put enough cash on the table to cover more than the tab, and we walked out.

"What was that all about?" I asked after he had hurried me down the street, turning to look behind us.

"The man that give me that envelope the night your daddy died," he responded.

"Where?"

"The cowboy that just come in and set at the counter."

"You sure it was him?"

"Yep. I recognized them alligator boots right off. It was him all right. He seen us too."

"Damn. We've been spotted all the way up here in Memphis?" I exclaimed. We decided to head back to the motel and lay low for now. In the Graceland corridor, tour buses heading to the King's house and pedestrians heading to the souvenir shops slowed us down. Placide dropped me off at our room, then pulled around behind the building to park the car out of easy sight since that cowboy would have recognized the car from the meeting in Jackson.

"I could pass by that souvenir store yonder, see if they got some playing cards," Placide said when he let himself into the room.

"Good idea. Maybe I can beat you out of a few dollars while we're stuck here." I dug out my wallet and handed him a twenty.

When he let himself and a gust of cold air back in, he carried a bagful that he began emptying onto the counter by the sink. A few Cokes and Buds, some Tostitos and French onion dip, two decks of cards with Elvis photos on the backs, and a couple of *Motor Trend* magazines. Picking up the ice bucket, he headed back out the door, letting another chilly blast into the room.

After he put the Cokes and beer in the sink, he dumped the bucket of ice on them, then took a seat at the table by the window, popped open one of the Cokes, and just slipped the drape back a sliver so he could keep an eye on the parking lot. He took his piece out of his ankle holster and set it on the table by the window.

"How about some penny-ante five-card draw?" I asked.

Placide flashed a grin and began shuffling the cards. I splashed a little water on my face and popped open a Bud. In less than an hour, I was down three bucks and Placide was happier than I'd seen him. I could tell he'd had some practice at poker, probably all those years at the tables beside Father.

Our next hand was interrupted by the phone ringing, just as my pair of nines was about to get beat. Placide and I just looked at each other for a few seconds before I got up to answer it on the third ring. "Hello," I said, my eyes still on Placide.

"Major Doucet?" boomed the voice on the other end.

I recognized Dawkins's large voice. "Yes, Sir," I replied, trying not to show too much elation.

"Henry Dawkins. I wonder if y'all could meet me."

"Name the time and place."

"You see Brooks on your map? Drive east on Brooks about a mile, mile and a half, until you get to Airways. Turn left. In about, oh, two miles, you'll see the Shrimp

King on y'all's left. Giant neon shrimp out front. Park in back. Got that?"

"Got it. Where are you calling from?" I asked.

"I'm at a pay phone."

"OK, good. Yes, Airways. I see it on the map."

"It's a country place, if you get my drift, so if y'all have casual dress, y'all will fit right in."

"OK, I have some jeans."

"I plan to walk in around eight. Wait till 8:30; then find a table. I'll come to y'all."

"We'll be there."

I hung up and repeated the plans to Placide. "Go grab a couple baseball caps," I said, fishing my wallet out and handing him a couple more twenties. "Try to find a fishing or Skol cap, anything like that. No Elvis caps."

"Yessir, H," he replied, rising to take the money and pulling his jacket back on.

I changed into my jeans and flannel shirt while he was gone. In a few minutes, he let himself back in with two baseball caps, a washed black Skol cap, and a camo Ducks Unlimited hat.

"Perfect," I smiled, grabbing the camo one for myself. Placide tried to suppress a grin when I tried it on. He lengthened the strap on the Skol cap to fit his oversized head and tried it on. Now it was my turn to suppress a grin.

"Color-coordinated with your Dockers," I joked as he scowled at me from beneath the brim.

We still had the afternoon to kill, enough time for Placide to win another five bucks. Then we set off for the Shrimp King, no clue what we might learn, but with a glimmer of hope that we might finally learn something.

Chapter 9
THE SHRIMP KING

I spotted the giant anthropomorphic neon shrimp, balancing on its tail and decked in a gold crown and purple robe. Placide circled the building, meticulously scrutinizing every pickup truck until he found a secluded spot next to the dumpster in back. Half a dozen motley feral cats scattered as noiselessly and plentifully as roaches when he turned off the ignition and doused the lights, their attraction, the stench of yesterday's fish platters escaping the dumpster. These were well-fed cats.

We cowboy-sauntered around the building and in the front door like a couple of regulars. We didn't fool anyone. Several pairs of expressionless eyes fixed on the two strangers invading their turf, one a black giant. Pretty hard for anyone Placide's size to be inconspicuous anywhere.

A corner booth was open, so we slid in as inconspicuously as possible. Satisfied we weren't there to stir up trouble, the eyes quickly turned back to Monday

Night Football on the small screen above the bar, the intruders already forgotten or ruled benign.

"He'p y'all?" drawled the dour little waitress who approached us, exuding boredom with her job, her world, her life. She worked her jaw ferociously at a large wad of gum as she tapped her pencil stub on the order pad.

"I'll just have a Bud, for now."

"And you?" she asked, diverting half-closed eyes to Placide without further acknowledgement of me.

"Just coffee, please, Ma'am."

She wheeled around and shuffled back to the counter to round up our drinks, the flouncy magenta and black plaid uniform and matching nurse-style cap looking incongruous on the spare middle-aged frame, her orange-ish teased hair screwed up into something of a make-shift French twist in back.

I hadn't yet seen Dawkins, but I knew he was here somewhere, probably in the adjoining room watching our icy reception. The joint was crowded, a hangout for couples and single guys, though I didn't see any single women. Charlie Rich belted a cry-in-your beer song from the jukebox about the most beautiful girl. A young platinum blonde in skin-tight blue jeans swayed her hips to the music while she browsed the selections, her current squeeze keeping one hand on her ass while he looked over her shoulder at the song menu. A couple slow danced in the narrow space in front of the jukebox, fused so completely it was impossible to distinguish where one began and the other ended.

The smell of fried seafood and cigarette smoke hung in the air. Several young couples sat at tables and booths eating from obscenely heaped platters of fried shrimp, catfish, and scallops. The group of beer-drinking cowboys at the bar cheered raucously and slapped backs at some exceptional play on the screen.

I couldn't understand why Dawkins would pick this place to meet. Maybe he figured none of his colleagues would dream of showing up in a place like this. I was pretty sure he was right.

After I ordered a second beer, Dawkins, wearing jeans that needed suspenders in the interest of gravity, loomed beside me holding a beer mug. He asked to squeeze in beside me. He wasn't lying about squeezing; he had to slide his ponderous gut along the edge of the table to fit.

"Doucet," he nearly whispered, eyes shifting around the room.

"Dawkins," I followed suit.

"I could have some information for y'all," he said, wasting no time on small talk.

"I was hoping you'd say that."

"First off, Armstrong sold us out. Long story. Sit back."

"I'm ready."

"I guess y'all know the ag business took a tumble recently."

"I know what I've seen in the news for the past few years."

"Well, your man Armstrong figured out how to capitalize on the loss before he left us. To be honest with you, Doucet, I don't have all the particulars by any means, but I'll tell you what I do know...in strictest confidence, of course."

"Of course. I'll forget your name the minute I get up from this table."

"Make no mistake; this is risky business. I could be putting my career *and* my life on the line just by meeting you. Yours too, for that matter. You're dealing with ruthless folks, now. Understand what I'm saying?"

"Yes sir. I've noticed that."

"You see, Armstrong made his money when he inherited his father's tractor company. Armstrong is a personal friend of Sapphire Salt's last CEO, Arnold Huff."

"The name sounds familiar."

"It should. Arnold Huff is now US Secretary of the Treasury. While small family-owned farms were struggling to stay afloat, the large-scale factory farms were buying their equipment wholesale from the large tractor and equipment manufacturers and abandoning the small companies. As they gobbled up the small fish, Ideal Tractor was showing amazing profits, all phony, of course, thanks to Armstrong and his friend Huff, who was then Sapphire's CEO. They were scheming to save their asses under the guise of saving the two companies. Armstrong had his fancy account books that his personal New York City CPA had doctored up for him, so it looked like Ideal was thriving, when, in fact, Armstrong was stripping out whatever he could before selling out."

"So then how did Armstrong end up at Sapphire?"

"God knows how he managed it, but Armstrong sold Ideal Tractor for millions more than it was worth. Huff turns right around and hands Armstrong the job of CEO at Sapphire. Huff had just been appointed to President Stanton's Cabinet, so Huff was moving up. I don't know how many millions changed hands, but they both got mega-rich, and Ideal Tractor was essentially sacrificed in the bargain.

"Within thirty days, we all knew there'd been a fraud because Ideal stock prices dropped over $60 a share in a two-week period, right after some insider trading and massive stock selloff by Huff and Armstrong and a few of their 'business associates.' Long-term emplo'ees who were counting on those stock options for retirement were hung out to dry. And their pensions mysteriously disappeared. There's been some rumor of suicide as their only option, though I don't believe anyone has gone to that extreme...yet anyway." He paused for another swig of beer.

"It damn near ruined Sapphire Salt, too, from what I've heard," he continued, wiping his mouth with the back of his hand. "They use industrial salt to clean gas and oil wells, as well as to make some chemicals and plastics, so when the recession hurt the oil industry, it hurt the salt industry too. Armstrong let a large number of Sapphire emplo'ees go, sold off God knows how many company holdings, but ultimately saved the salt company, at least temporarily, for which he got a commendation and a cool two-million-dollar bonus, plus whatever he's siphoned off Sapphire. Meanwhile, Ideal Tractor ended up in Chapter 11 bankruptcy."

"Well, I see you've managed to keep your doors open."

"Hah! Barely! We had to completely restructure the company. We're down to a quarter of the emplo'ees we had before the crash, and no one is guaranteed a future. Benefits have been slashed, morale is at rock bottom. But it's tough to find work with everybody restructuring these days. The future with any company is just a stab in the dark since the recession, so the ones left don't have any choice but to hang on. But there's still some Ideal Tractor cronies on the force here, and they're watching the rest of us like hawks. Armstrong wants to save his own ass, make sure the whole truth about his phony books and insider trading doesn't go public."

"I noticed the place looked pretty vacant. Now I see why!"

"You just saw the one facility. The plant out in Frayser is under half capacity. Besides nearly half our manufacturing and clerical staff, we also laid off all but two of our maintenance crew of thirty. We would have had to close the doors except that Armstrong's replacement managed to outsource a few manufacturing jobs and get us some overseas contracts. Of course, that just left more of our own people without jobs or pensions."

"I can't say I'm surprised," I said. "Now I need to find out what all this had to do with my father. And what about Dallas Matherne? Any word on him?"

"I couldn't find much on Matherne. He was in maintenance. When the company was going down the tubes, he just quit before he got laid off. A lot of guys did the same. He knew his days with Ideal were numbered. Could easily have been a coincidence that he ended up back in Louisiana like Armstrong. Especially since he was from there."

"That coincidence story is pretty hard for me to swallow. I still think there's a connection."

"Well, Doucet, you're on your own there," Dawkins said. "But that's how Armstrong got to Sapphire. What he did once he got there is anybody's guess, but I can grant you, it wasn't anything good. Armstrong is bad news. Whether Ideal Tractor survives him remains to be seen. As for Matherne? Small potatoes. No great loss or gain to have him or lose him. But Armstrong? I wouldn't put anything past a greedy S.O.B. like that—as in, watch your back."

"I hear ya. Sounds like Sapphire's future is in jeopardy too."

"Hey, I didn't say that," he said. "Of course, that inundation..."

But he was cut off mid-sentence when the whole restaurant was rocked by a 100-decibel crash that felt like a 3.0 earthquake. Placide's cup rattled in its saucer, spilling most of his coffee. Women shrieked. People stared blankly at each other for a hint of how they were supposed to react.

My first impulse was that it must have been a kitchen explosion. Placide's eyes panned the room instinctively before he jumped up and headed to the front door. He hurried back to inform me, "A blue pickup just peeled out of the parking lot, H."

Dawkins's eyes widened as he looked questioningly at me.

"Someone must have followed us out of Ideal today," I explained. "We saw him at lunch. I guess he's tailing us now. Drives a blue pickup, if that rings a bell."

"No one I know of. Look, I've got to get out of here," Dawkins said nervously, sliding his gut back out of the booth. "This convinces me that there's a bug in my office. I'm afraid we could all be in grave danger."

He tucked his head down and headed for the back door, then surprised me by walking back to ask if we'd parked near the dumpster. I just stared up at him and nodded. By this time, patrons had begun to recover from their initial state of shock and had begun hovering around the back door to catch a glimpse, shrieking in disbelief. Someone behind the bar phoned the police.

"A car just exploded," Dawkins said quietly but urgently. "Right next to the dumpster. I was never here." Then he slipped out the front door amid the commotion and frenzied buzz and shrieks of the crowd.

Placide squeezed through the crowd to confirm that it was Father's LTD, nodding solemnly toward me over everyone's heads. I didn't even rise. I just sat dumbfounded as the sounds of sirens pierced the din of the restaurant.

"Major Doucet? Captain Gordon," said the officer who seated himself in the booth across from me. After he examined my North Carolina driver's license and Placide's Louisiana chauffeur's license, he paused thoughtfully, then said, "I'm afraid we've discovered evidence of foul play."

I just looked at him wondering why he bothered telling me that. Cars don't generally explode by spontaneous combustion, in my experience. "No shit," I finally replied.

"Any idea who might have wanted to blow up y'all's car? Or what's more likely, y'all *in* y'all's car?"

I felt weak, and my voice reflected it. "We've had someone following us today," I replied. "We haven't been able to get his plates, but he drives a light blue pickup truck. I suspect he either works at Ideal Tractor or was hired by someone who does."

"Why do y'all suppose someone from Ideal Tractor might have it in for you two fellas?" he asked, narrowing his beady eyes suspiciously.

"It's a long story. Ya got a couple hours?"

"I got all night. Why don't you and your sidekick here

ride with me down to the precinct and we'll get y'all's story on record."

"Yes, Sir," I agreed, rising weakly and nodding to Placide as Captain Gordon and I walked over to where he stood watch by the front door.

It was nearly midnight by the time I finished relating selective bits of what I knew, and I was exhausted from the ordeal. I left out Dawkins's name, as requested, so as not to implicate him. I told the officer that Placide and I had simply ventured out in search of a quiet place to drink a beer without being watched and had happened upon this place. I fibbed that we hadn't been able to find anyone yet to talk to at Ideal, but we had planned to go back out there tomorrow. Of course, I filled him in on the blue pickup truck, alligator boots, and beer gut. Now I just wanted to hit the sack and chalk it all up to a day from hell. An officer agreed to drive us back to the motel.

"Y'all going to be staying around a couple days?"

"Yeah, a day or two, probably. Not scared off yet," I assured him.

"Well, we'll let y'all know when we get a ballistics report back on that explosive device. Not that it makes much difference at this point."

"Yeah, sure," I replied half-heartedly.

The next morning, I called my insurance company, which directed me to their Memphis branch to fill out the necessary forms. Placide had the guy at the front desk of the motel set us up with a mid-size rental car to be delivered at 0930 hours. Now, at least until we were spotted around town, we felt as though we could travel incognito in the gray Chevy Malibu.

After we left the insurance office, we stopped at Helen's Home Cooking, a nondescript hole-in-the-wall a block away, for a late breakfast. I grabbed a newspaper from the machine out front when I saw Father's charred LTD on the front page. Inside the restaurant, crowds of Elvis fans buzzed like hornets over the story.

After we got our breakfasts, I spread the paper on the table. Just under the explosion article, an alarming headline leaped off the page:

"Henry Dawkins, COO of Ideal Tractor, found dead in his home. Apparent Suicide."

Reading the story, I learned that not long after Dawkins had left us, the woman next door heard a gunshot coming from his house and called the Memphis police. We would still have been at the station. Dawkins was found holding his pistol in his right hand, with a hole blasted at close range into his right temple. Police were investigating, but it looked like suicide. Suicide, my ass, I thought as I read on.

"Like many Ideal employees concerned about retirement, Dawkins had been despondent for the last three years, ever since Ideal Tractor had gone into Chapter 11 bankruptcy."

Depression and despondency, my ass: same lame-brained excuse they had used for my father. I handed the article to Placide. So far, I didn't think our rental car had been spotted, but I knew it was just a matter of time.

"I'm thinking we need to get out of Memphis ASAP," I said, with most of our eggs, grits, and ham still sitting in front of us. We downed the rest without further discussion, then I paid the tab and we headed back to the motel for our gear.

Crowds were just beginning to queue up for the Elvis tour buses as we crawled back through the congestion toward the interstate. We could contact the Memphis police from our home turf and tell them where they could reach us. I decided I'd better 'fess up about meeting with Dawkins, but I'd rather do it long-distance than back at the station. Dawkins wouldn't be giving us any more information, that much was certain. But now that Treasury Secretary Huff's name had been added to the mix, I was beginning to suspect this could go all the way to the White House.

Chapter 10
HENDERSON SWAMP

It had turned colder, and a piercing wind blew snow across the highway, so we wasted no time getting out of Dodge, stopping only for gas and a late lunch at a Burger King in McComb. Placide made much better time on I-55, while I spent the hours recording every detail I could remember, in case I was called on to testify in a future courtroom.

I walked in the house that evening, relieved to discover that Ethel and Louis had called it an early night, so I wouldn't have to come up with some cockamamie explanation about Father's car exploding until morning. I had decided during the trip that I'd move out of Aunt Ethel's before I put their lives in danger, too, and I wasn't excited about telling Ethel that bit, either. When I flicked off my bedroom lamp a little later, my mind stayed in high gear, with visions of exploding cars and overweight cowboys in $300 boots rattling around in my brain, both while I was still awake and in my dreams for a few restless hours of sleep.

"Aitchie!" Aunt Ethel exclaimed, startled when I came downstairs around 0800 hours. "I didn't even know you was home! You'll be the death of me yet, boy."

"Sorry," I said, hugging her on my way to the coffee pot. "It was late and I didn't want to wake you."

"No harm done I suppose. Next time, though, mind you," she scolded, shaking her index finger at me, recalling a lifetime of that wagging finger over some childish infraction, such as leaving the milk on the counter. Of course, Victor and I had figured out early that it was an empty gesture. Louis, now, that was a different story. If he said, "Next time," we knew there'd better not be one.

"OK, Ethel," I promised. I plopped down, elbows on the table. "Look, Ethel, I need to talk to you. Something has come up."

"Now what?!" Ethel turned off the flame and sat across from me, concern contorting her face.

I proceeded to tell her things I had never expected to have to tell anyone, least of all Aunt Ethel. Of course, I left out some of the messiest details, but it didn't soften the blow.

"I'm afraid some people are angry with me. I've discovered that foul play was responsible for Father's death. People would rather I not nose around."

Her expression changed from worried, to tears, to wide-eyed disbelief as I continued my grim saga. Sometimes she just shook her head and clucked her tongue. Occasionally she interjected, "Oh, Aitchie!" or "My lands!" As distressed as she was, I knew she was a tough old bird. Hell, hadn't she survived the Great Depression on this old farm, World War II with Uncle Louis in Italy, and the turbulent Civil Rights 60's in a small southern town? She'd take this in stride.

"Anyway, Aunt Ethel," I continued, "I've got to move out of here for a while. I've put your lives in danger, as well as my own. Once I'm gone, I'll feel a whole lot better about your safety."

"Oh, Aitchie, where will you go, *cher*? What will you do?"

"I spent a good part of last night mulling over that very question. I just don't have an answer yet. I won't be far off. Anyway, if I were to tell you my plans, it would keep you in danger. I'll lay low and contact you when I think we're all clear. I'm sorry, Aunt Ethel. I didn't want to have to worry you with all this."

"Aitchie, I wasn't just yakking when I said you need to settle down, hear? Now, I don't understand what you've gone and got yourself into, but mind you, I don't want no more Doucet funerals, you hear me, boy? It's time you found you a *good* woman, instead of running all over creation getting into God knows what kind of trouble," she scolded, as angry as I'd seen her since I got caught feeding my Brussels sprouts to the dogs when I was a kid.

"I understand, Aunt Ethel." The less said about the danger we might all be facing, the better. And that went for my decision never to get involved with women again as well. I ignored the implication of her emphasis on the word *good* woman.

Handkerchief in hand, Ethel followed me to the car when Placide pulled up. "Mind what I said, now, boy. And stay in touch. You know how I worry."

"If I know nothing else, I do know that! But this is something I have to do...for Father." I threw my bag in back, hugged her, then slid in the passenger seat. I didn't look back to see her tears. I just didn't have the heart.

"Placide, I spent most of the night thinking," I began once we got on the highway. "I'm afraid you and I will have to part company for a while. I need to disappear, and it's pretty tough to fit a giant bodyguard into the woodwork. I'm going to leave you and Earlene in charge of getting this rental returned and replacing Father's LTD. I'm also leaving you in charge of keeping an eye on Ethel and Louis."

"Yessir, H," he said side-eying me. He wasn't sold on the idea.

"That means you'll have to come up with an explanation to Earlene. I've already explained it to Ethel. I need to buy an inconspicuous used car, rent a room in another town, and lay low for a while."

"Fugitives been known to disappear in Henderson Swamp," Placide said.

That thought hadn't occurred to me. I recalled bass fishing with Uncle Louis, and of course Victor, when I was a boy. I knew every inlet and cove. Fish and bird species enough to keep Darwin busy for decades inhabited this forgotten paradise. My mind raced to the logistics of such a move.

"Good thinking, Placide! Let's start by getting me into a car."

"Best keep a piece with you if you plan on being alone out there," he said, sliding a .44 Magnum out from under the seat and handing it to me. "Don't worry, in Louisiana, you don't need a permit, unless you carry it concealed."

I sat turning the gun over in my hands reluctantly, wondering how the hell my life had devolved to this. Louis took Victor and me duck hunting when we were teenagers, but killing things never caught on with me. Handling guns in the Air Force was one thing, but a handgun against civilians in my own country was a new ballgame. I was beginning to feel like we were entering into our country's war against itself, and that whoever won would also lose.

By that afternoon, after promising Placide to stay in touch, I drove up the levee to the Turtle Docks Marina in a nondescript 1969 beige Ford Torino I had picked up for a song and 500 bucks. I walked up the wooden porch steps to the Turtle Bar. Inside, a couple of old Cajun fishermen sat over a beer gabbing in the local patois.

I ordered a Bud, opting to eavesdrop awhile before showing my hand.

"*Ma frien', vas tu en collines prés de I-10, te trouveras les sac-a-laits en patate.*"

"*Mais, yeah, mon ami, j'attrape les perches beau en cyprière ce matin, moi. En hameçon, juste des vers de terre.*"

They were just swapping fishing lies, oblivious to the newcomer in their midst. So, I quietly asked the middle-aged brunette washing glasses behind the bar, "Got any houseboats for rent?"

" 'Tee Jacques's the owner. He's down at the dock working right now. Tall, black-haired fella. You can go talk to him if you want. He might have you one to rent."

"Thanks," I said. "Be right back," I added, pointing toward the full beer I left sitting on the bar. She nodded her understanding as her hands continued pushing glasses up and down on the stationary brush in the soapy water.

I found 'Tee Jacques working on one of the houseboats tied to the slips along the basin. It looked as though most of the twenty or so boats tied there were used as weekend retreats, but the first few looked as if they might be vacant.

"Howdy, 'Tee Jacques. Name's Hank Lee," I lied, picking the name out of thin air as I held out my hand to shake his. "Your waitress told me you might have a houseboat to rent for a month or so."

"My old lady, you mean. Yep. You can rent either one of these first two," he said with a nod toward the two ramshackle boats.

"What's a boat like that cost a month?" I asked, looking at the first one, the one with the name Hermit Crab painted in black letters across the stern, appropriately enough, I thought.

"Can let you rent her for $300 a mont'," he said with a firm nod that indicated I might as well not haggle.

"Can I take a look inside?"

"*Mais*, yeah. Step aboard." He motioned toward the deck and followed me onboard. "Got a little refrigerator, cook top. Got your small appliances, pots 'n pans, a few utensils. Look around."

"Any chance you could give me a slip farther down the dock? I'm a writer," I fibbed again, "and sort of a hermit crab myself. Probably take her out some, but I might spend some time at the dock, too. I hate to be right beside this boat ramp, especially when the weekend crowd gets here."

"I hear ya," he said good-naturedly. "There's a couple of slips farther down there. We can set ya up yonder."

I made a mental note of what was aboard and what I

would need to buy for subsistence living, then shook hands on the deal and we went back up to the marina to settle the paperwork.

After scribbling my new alias, I handed him cash for a deposit and the first month's rent. Luckily, he didn't ask for any ID. I'd have to remedy that with Earlene later. I took another gulp of my beer, then headed back out the lone road to a marine supply and grocery store I had spotted on my way in.

Muscling a shopping cart with one stationary wheel through the narrow aisles, I grabbed everything I saw that I might need: a parka, rubber boots, and also some lace-up boots with rubber soles. On a whim, I grabbed a cowboy hat and a few modest fishing supplies to complete my new image; it couldn't hurt to catch myself an occasional dinner out of the swamp. I stocked up on survival supplies: canned goods and an opener, cooking oil, cornmeal, milk, eggs, Tony Chachere's, Community coffee, and a six-pack of Bud. By the time I got to the checkout, my basket was heaped to overflowing. Of course, most of it could be tossed or given to Father's favorite homeless shelter when I came out of hiding, hopefully in a couple of weeks. Aunt Ethel would make good use of any Tony's or coffee I had left over.

I grabbed a newspaper at the checkout and carried it with me into Deanie's Cajun Kitchen down the road for a plate of étouffée, so I wouldn't have to cook my first night there. By the time I left there, it was nearly sundown, so I drove back up the levee to settle into my new digs before dark. I'd worry about moving her tomorrow. I waved at 'Tee Jacques and carried two bags at a time down to the dock. If I couldn't lay low here, my name wasn't Hank Lee,

I thought, as I found cabinets and cubby holes to stash my quarry. But the realization that my own survival depended on laying low unsettled me.

My first night on the water was less than ideal, what with the screeching tree frogs and cicadas, the plaintive hoots of an owl or two, and the haunting thoughts of the deaths of Father and now Dawkins. I left the .44 on the bed beside me.

Feeling agitated the next morning, I walked up the levee to the payphone and called the Memphis cops to see what they'd found out about my would-be assassin. "This is Major Doucet," I told the dispatcher. "Is Major Gordon available?"

"I believe he just walked in. Hold, please."

"Doucet?" said the voice on the other end a few seconds later.

"Yes sir. Wondering if you found anything out about that explosion."

"I've been trying to contact you. We have an APB out on that pickup. Pretty hard to trace without the plate. It's probably another color or even out of the country by now. But we did figure out the explosion."

"Oh? What was it?"

"A homemade pipe bomb. We've seen 'em before. Not too often, luckily. They can make 'em easy out of a few odds and ends laying around the house. A piece of galvanized pipe, gunpowder, batteries, flashbulb, wire, and a string with a heavy weight on the end. The weight hangs on the ground, so that when the car moves, a little piece of plastic pulls out, setting off the flashbulb embedded in the gunpowder. Bam goes the car and anyone settin' in it."

"Well then, why did it go off before we got in?"

"We think one of them cats that hang around the dumpster there must have played with the string attached to the weight. No need to tell you about the cat entrails we found mixed up in the remnants of y'all's car. No doubt it was supposed to go off after ya'll got in. They were gunning for y'all, that's one thing we know for sure."

"Look, I have a confession. I didn't give you the full story that night. In fact, we did speak to Henry Dawkins earlier that day, out at Ideal Tractor, and again at the Shrimp King the night of the explosion."

"Withholding evidence. That's a pretty serious offense, Major."

"Yeah, well the only way he would talk to me was with the promise of complete confidentiality since he knew he was in imminent danger. I was just keeping my word. And of course, I had no idea he was meeting his maker as we spoke. After his death, I figured it was a little too late for confidentiality to do him any good. That was no suicide, Major, I'd be willing to stake my life on it. I just thought you should know in case you wanted to dig into a possible murder."

"If that's the case, we may be calling you back up here to testify at some point. I could just charge you for concealing information."

"Yes, Sir. You could choose to ignore the real crime here. But I figure you're too smart a guy for that. Especially with a killer still on the loose."

I was disconcerted if not surprised about the car bomb. Someone still at Ideal Tractor had to have a link to someone at Sapphire. I was reasonably sure the guy with the alligator boots and the old pickup wasn't the mastermind. Probably just a hired gun and errand boy earning some drug money. Or maybe just beer money, judging from the looks of that gut. But I was just as sure that whoever wanted me dead wasn't giving up easily, and that those two goons in the Chevy Blazer had their slimy hands in it somehow. I wondered what kind of wasp nest Father had stumbled into. Or that Placide and I had stumbled into now, in Father's place.

Chapter 11
LITTLE CAPITOL

The sundry old men looked like regulars, solving the world's problems at their usual tables and booths in the Little Capitol truck stop, where I was to meet Maurice Gremillion from DNR this morning. The younger men were no doubt scattered throughout the multitude of oil or seafood industries in the area at this hour or home asleep after the night shift. The women were likely puttering in gardens or kitchens much like Ethel's.

In my cowboy hat, jeans, and flannel shirt, crumpled now from a few days mucking around at the swamp's edge, I hoped to blend in with the regulars. I'd have to spot Gremillion because he'd never single me out of the crowd, so I found an obscure corner table by the window and kept my eyes on the parking lot. Nobody even slightly resembling a DNR official appeared. At about 1045 hours, I realized he probably wasn't going to show. I walked to the pay phone out front to call Placide.

"This is Hank," I told him. "Call Gremillion's office.

Find out what time he left and get right back to me here."
I read him the number off the phone.

"Yessir, Hank," he said, catching the cue to my new alias.

I paced impatiently until the pay phone rang a few minutes later. "Hank! Bad news. There was an accident on the Atchafalaya Basin Bridge. Gremillion's car ran through the guardrail and into the swamp. DNR got word he was DOA."

"My God!" I blurted. They were dropping like flies in my path. I wondered why they hadn't been successful yet in eliminating me. Worst of all, I didn't even know who "they" were! Maybe they just wanted to watch me flail around awhile, like a hunted deer, see what I could stir up that might be useful to them before it was my turn to fly off a bridge or take a bullet to the temple. I had to collect my thoughts for a few seconds before I continued. Could they have learned of Gremillion's meeting with me? How? I needed Placide back by my side ASAP. Striking out alone had been a huge mistake, and now was no time for mistakes.

"Um...OK, Placide, get some cash from Earlene. Buy, rent, or borrow a car, throw in enough clothes and fishing gear to stay awhile, and drive to Whiskey River Bar on the levee in Henderson."

Back in my car, I sat still for a few minutes, my head and both hands on the wheel, waiting for my pulse to slow down and the immediate shock to wear off. Did it have something to do with the map I was carrying? Was someone in Louisiana DNR involved in the scam? And if so, what could have been the motive? I didn't know where to turn anymore. Everyone I had contact with seemed to turn up dead. The police were mysteriously absent. Finally gathering impetus, I eased out of the parking lot and headed back out the two-lane to the levee road and my operating base, keeping one eye on the rearview.

While I waited at the table next to the window at Whiskey River Bar, I jotted a sketchy plan of action and made a copy on a separate sheet for Placide. It had been dangerous to try to go it alone. I needed him nearby.

I stifled a laugh when he drove up in an old turquoise Oldsmobile Vista Cruiser station wagon, faded fake wood grain slapped on the sides. He stomped through the dirt parking area and onto the rough plank floor of the bar. I didn't avert my eyes but kept staring out the window after Placide walked in. I heard him order a Bud, then take a table between me and the exit. I just kept looking out at the parking lot. When I finished my beer several minutes later, I walked past him and tipped my hat as I let a note drop on his table on my way out— "Rent a houseboat at the Turtle Docks."

Thirty minutes later, I was casting off the bow with a basic ledger rig when Placide carried a duffle bag to the other vacant houseboat up on the boat ramp end of the dock. Eyes straight ahead, I kept casting, occasionally pulling in a bream that I threw in the ice chest. Looked like I'd have company to eat my fish tonight.

After dark, I carried a mess of steaming bream I'd just pan-fried over to Placide's boat. I handed him the game plan I'd scribbled, and he glanced over it as he silently and single-handedly polished off several pounds of fried fish. I picked at a few myself, but my appetite had been off ever since the news of Gremillion. I knew I was also a pawn in someone's deadly game, and it would take some canny footwork to escape flying off the same bridge whenever they decided it was my turn. At least for the moment, I felt my whereabouts were unknown.

Placide nodded his tacit approval as he looked through my notes. I figured the map showing that the drill would have pierced the salt dome was the accurate one because that's exactly what happened. The price for a map indicating that the drill would not pierce the dome, simply deleting that section of the salt dome from the map, would have been steep, which meant the rewards would have to be astronomical. If that map came out of DNR, then someone in DNR must have been bought off. I didn't figure it was Gremillion, based on his willingness to meet Father and then me, followed by his untimely death. But there was someone else who didn't want him talking. That person had to have ties to whoever wanted those maps, so that was the first person I needed to locate. I was pretty sure Gremillion hadn't simply lost control of his vehicle on a clear, crisp Thursday morning on the Atchafalaya Basin Bridge without a little outside help. I wondered if that "help" drove a Chevy Blazer with a steel reinforced bumper.

Placide's first assignment on the list was to find out all he could about whether another vehicle was involved. If so, to see if he could find out who was driving or what kind of vehicle it was. His second assignment was to have Earlene get me a fake ID. I knew she had done it for Father on more than one occasion, so I didn't figure it would be too much trouble for me to become Hank Lee for a while. I gave Placide my driver's license so Earlene could copy the picture and other details.

I emerged from my cabin the next morning as Placide's old Vista Cruiser bounced like warm putty over the rough levee road and onto the *batture*. He nodded in my direction as he carried the newspaper to his houseboat. I walked over, ducking into the cabin, where he was seated at the table with the paper spread in front of him. He slid it to me when I sat down.

As I suspected, according to the only eyewitness with the balls to come forward, Gremillion had been run off the road by a hit and run in a black Chevy Blazer, which the cops were still trying to locate. Or so they'd have us believe. The witness was quoted saying he had been following those two vehicles from a distance on the bridge, staying far back because the Blazer was weaving in and out of Gremillion's lane. Thought he was drunk. Then the Blazer smacked the front corner of the white Ford Galaxy state vehicle so hard that the Galaxy jumped the curb, crashed right through the guard rail, and plunged over the side into the swamp below. The Blazer picked up speed and disappeared. The witness said he never got close enough to read the plate.

My suspicions were confirmed. I'd considered going to the police with what I knew, but I didn't trust anyone by this time. I was afraid now that anyone I talked to would either end up dead or make sure I did. It wasn't enough that the guys in the Blazer were looking for me; now I was looking for them, too. And there was no "olly olly oxen free" in this game.

Chapter 12
MORE PIECES TO THE PUZZLE

Calco Oil was in deep, with someone in DNR getting enough kickback to rationalize committing murder. Sapphire Salt, Armstrong, and Secretary Huff stunk like dead fish, too. No one in the widespread cabal would hesitate to snuff out the last minor snag in their plan, which would apparently be me. I told Placide to get ready for a trip to Father's office, then walked up the levee and called Earlene from the pay phone.

"Earlene, did Father have a backup file system? Have you got anything that the cops haven't confiscated?"

"I had a lot of his files backed up on paper copies, H, but they went through everything and hauled a lot out of here. Seized our floppies and reels of magnetic tape, too."

"I need you to dig out any files you still have concerning Oka Chito. Make copies, just to be on the safe side. I'll have Placide pick it up." I glanced at my watch. "Do you think you can have that ready by two?"

"Might be a tall order, H. Let's say three. Tell Placide

I'll have it ready. Also, H, I've had a meeting with our lawyers, and they've agreed to help in the investigation, so let me know if anything new comes up that I need to share with them. They're talking about some FOIA requests."

"Good thinking, Earlene. It just so happens that I do have some information for the attorneys. In Memphis, I learned that Warren Armstrong and Treasury Secretary Arnold Huff are in bed together. For some reason, they decided to sabotage both Sapphire Salt and Ideal Tractor in Memphis. We need to find out why and who all was involved. Give the lawyers a heads up. Also, keep LeBlanc in the loop on this."

"Good Lord, H. Well, that should keep the lawyers busy. I'll inform Marc right away."

Late that afternoon, Placide arrived at my cabin door and swung a box of papers onto the deck. I pulled on a hooded sweatshirt, poured myself a glass of iced tea, then sat cross-legged on the deck beside the box and began poring over stacks of paper while Placide picked up my pole and cast off the bow. Unfamiliar names and a few familiar ones shouted out at me from Father's records. Some of the familiar ones I knew to be shysters and con artists. Father would never have allowed himself to get sucked into a crime for money or any other motive for that matter, but he seemed to be acquainted with a lot of people who just might.

One unfamiliar name that popped out at me was Léon Savois with Calco Oil in the Lafayette office. Father had an appointment with him in his Houston office on November 19th, the day before the inundation. The name rang a bell. I remembered a Savois at Father's wake, the old man who damn near lost his life in a fishing boat the day of the inundation. I had the old man's number, but I never figured it would be any use to call him. Of course, Savois is a pretty common name in Louisiana, but there could be some connection. At least it was worth exploring.

Dallas Matherne's name appeared briefly too, but there were gaping holes in files concerning him. Clearly, the police had helped themselves to anything of use, but the sparsity of Matherne in the files incriminated them and him. My guess is that Father was looking into his background and dealings, too. I needed to have Earlene locate this Matherne guy, even though he could mean trouble. But first, I decided to find Savois, see if he could fill in any pieces of the puzzle. I wanted to have as much information in my pocket as possible before I confronted Matherne.

At dinnertime, while we shared the bream Placide had snagged off the bow, I told him to contact Earlene tomorrow morning and have her set up an appointment with Léon Savois. Placide appeared at my cabin door the next day with a small slip of paper that read: *Meet Savois 1 PM Friday at the office.*

Placide dropped me off for the meeting at the office a little early on Friday. At about ten after the hour, a tall young man entered and glanced around the office. I stood and thrust my hand out. "Léon Savois?"

"That's right."

"I'm H Doucet. Pleasure to meet you. Let's talk in the conference room. This way." A strikingly handsome forty-something Cajun, he probably looked more like Vic's brother than I did, minus the bravado. He had the same black wavy hair, the same Roman nose, except his smile was wide and sincere.

After we seated ourselves, I said, "I found a note that Father was to meet you a day before the inundation. Did you keep that meeting?"

"Yes, I did. I was at a meeting at our main Calco office in Houston when I got word Harvey Doucet was in town and wanted to talk to me. So, I called, then passed by his Houston office."

"Would you mind telling me what the meeting with Father was about? A few questions have come up regarding his death, and I just want to make sure I understand everything."

"What sort of questions, if you don't mind my asking?"

"You see, he was a passably good Catholic, if you get my drift. Suicide wouldn't even have been an option for him."

"I'm a good Catholic, too." His smile faded. "If you think I had..."

"Oh, no, no! I didn't mean to imply... No, I'm just hoping you can shed some light on things. First of all, does this look like the map Calco was using in the drilling operation?" I produced the flawed map from my folder.

He studied it for a minute, then nodded. "Yep, that's the map."

"Do you know where it came from? Who produced it?

"DNR sent it certified mail. Why? Isn't it accurate?"

"As a matter of fact, I'm pretty sure it's nowhere near accurate. Do you happen to remember whose office it came from at DNR?"

He thought a minute. "Man name of Joseph Haggerty, I believe, out of Louisiana's Gas and Oil Resources branch."

"Do you remember how long ago that was?"

"Year and a half, two years ago, when Calco was taking over the rig. Calco Oil had merged with Aloco Oil by then. Oka Chito was originally an Aloco Oil project before the merger. They let the ball drop at Oka Chito, though, and Calco picked it up. But I guess you know all that."

"I've been out of touch with the company the last few years," I said.

Actually, I had been aware of the merger. Lots of oil companies merged after the 1973 oil shortage. When OPEC members refused to sell oil to Israeli supporters of the US, oil was in short supply. Demand in the US was escalating, and winter in the North was on the way. Lots of the small fish got swallowed up by the big fish. Even gas stations were running out of gas. I just hadn't kept up with Father enough to know anything about his involvement in the Oka Chito project.

"Did Calco Oil keep any Aloco employees on at the Oka Chito site?" I asked.

"A handful. Nearly all the Aloco employees, the rig workers, anyway, were given a severance package, transferred to other sites, or flat laid off. Big shakeup in the main office, too. Everything was on hold for several months. The original drilling company was canned, and that's when Calco Oil brought Doucet Drilling into the picture."

"And you were with Calco Oil then?" I asked.

"Yeah, I came in with the new Calco group. My department is in charge of contracting and overseeing drilling operations, so we had pretty close ties with Doucet."

"Oh, I need to introduce you to Marc LeBlanc. He's taking over for Father and working on some contracts."

"I know Marc. We've worked together in the past. Is he here now?"

"Yes, I'll take you by his office when we're done here."

"I'd like that."

"When you and my father last met, did Father sound at all suspicious?"

"Your father was always suspicious of Calco Oil, especially after the merger. He wasn't too excited about the new CEO of Sapphire Salt, either. My job was to assure him of Calco Oil's integrity. And I do believe in the company. Or I did before the merger, anyway. I couldn't have stayed on with them if I didn't."

"I see your point," I said. "I wonder why you stayed on after the merger, then?"

The question seemed to take him aback. He thought for a moment before he said, "Well, H, it's pretty hard to find a better job in this financial climate. Pay's good, and I got a young son to raise and get educated. At least until someone convinces me Calco doesn't have at least as much integrity as any other oil company, I guess I'll stay on."

"Point taken. Can you think of anything else Father said when you met?"

"He might have seemed a little more suspicious than usual, I guess, looking back, but he always acted like it didn't faze him, no matter what happened."

"Yeah, he always was good at hiding his feelings."

"At least, I always respected him. Couldn't help him much, though. Calco Oil plays close to the vest. I just do my job, don't ask questions. Just try to stay employed, if you know what I mean."

"Yeah, I gotcha! I wonder why Father set up that last meeting with you? He must've already had the map for some time."

"Pretty routine, if you ask me. He said he was in Houston for a few days checking on some jobs he was doing for Calco. He checked in with me pretty regular, so it wasn't unusual for him to contact me when he learned I was in Houston too. He asked me a few questions about Oka Chito Island and some other jobs. Just technical business stuff, nothing out of the ordinary. He wasn't focused on Oka Chito, didn't seem to me."

"You mentioned your young son. Is Auguste your father, by any chance?"

"Yes! You know my father?"

"He and your mother came to my father's wake. He sure thinks the world of his grandson."

"Yes, sir. I carried Jamie down there when I had to go to Houston. He loves to go fishing with his Papaw. When the little *bateau* was getting sucked toward the whirlpool, his Papaw got the strength from God, is the only way I can figure it, to drag Jamie through the mud to the island. My daddy is a hero, in my view."

"That's quite a story. You're a fortunate man."

"Oh, I thank God, every day. If it hadn't been for my daddy's bravery, there's no telling."

After our meeting, I walked with Léon up to Marc's office and left them to catch up with each other, maybe even to come up with a Doucet contract.

If the inundation was planned, it was clear that Savois didn't know anything about it, or he wouldn't have allowed his son to go fishing. But I got a couple more crucial pieces to the puzzle from him. Oka Chito Island had originally been an Aloco operation, and the merger simply produced one much larger international conglomerate. Calco Oil could have paid someone off for that map before it began operations. Or Aloco could have ordered it for a selling point. But who would agree to produce such a false map? And why? And what about Joseph Haggerty in DNR? What was his involvement with that map?

I also needed to learn more about Sapphire Salt and its executives. I decided Jack Brouillette, the burly salt miner, would be my next contact. After Savois left, I dug out Jack's card and rang him.

Jack's wife Mable answered. "Nope. Jack's over at Oka Chito. They kept a few of 'em on to sift through what's left of the building. I expect him about four this evenin'."

I still had a couple hours to kill before I could contact him, so I decided to call Marlisa, Charles Daigrepont's widow, to see if she'd thought of anything. Or hell, maybe just to talk to a sympathetic soul.

"Marlisa? This is H. Doucet," I said when she answered, hoping she might be more receptive than at our last meeting. I wasn't disappointed.

"Oh, H. It's good to hear from you. How are you?"

"I was about to ask you the same thing. Is everything all right? You sound a little rattled."

"Everything's OK, I guess, except that people keep calling and asking me a million questions. I was glad it was you calling. It seems to me like everyone is trying to blame Charles for dying!"

"Oh, wouldn't they love to be able to put the blame on him somehow. Save themselves a lot of settlement money if they could prove negligence. We don't dare let that happen, Marlisa. That's a good reason for me to continue digging into this, for Charles's sake." I hoped she agreed with that reasoning.

"Have you learned anything new, H?"

"Nothing concrete, but I have some hints. Would you consider meeting me for some tea or coffee this afternoon? I've got a few hours to kill before I can meet Jack Brouillette, and I'd like to share what I've found and compare notes."

"Well, it would be good to talk to someone who's on my side, for a change," she agreed after a pause. "How about 3:00 at Provost's?"

"Perfect."

Placide dropped me off a little early, and I found an inconspicuous corner seat. Placide sat near the front window. Twenty minutes later, Marlisa walked in, still in mourning clothes, a black sweater over slender black pants that elongated her legs to model proportions. The sun behind her in the doorway as she walked in gave her thick auburn hair a momentary golden halo. She was a goddess, all right. She looked around the room but didn't recognize me until I stood and motioned for her.

"Marlisa," I said, holding my hand up. I guided her to the chair next to mine. "It's good to see you."

"Good to see you, too, H."

"Tell me how you're getting along."

"It's been tough." After the waitress took her order for iced tea, she continued, "Charles was my strength. I've had to learn how to handle all those little details he used to take care of: taxes, insurance, credit card bills. But the nights are the worst. I still find myself saying, 'I'll have to tell Charles when he calls,' or, 'I'll ask Charles when he gets home.' Then I catch myself." She glanced up at me. "Do you have experiences like that?"

"I'm sure there's no comparison. I only saw Father every couple of years. I want to get to the bottom of his death, but it's nothing like losing a lifetime companion. It's eerie, though, everywhere I go, I see reminders of him, almost as if he's speaking to me from the grave. And he's still alive in my dreams, too, urging me on in this investigation. I'd have to say, he seems more alive to me now. It's almost like I'm just now getting to know him."

"I still see Charles in my dreams, too. Then I cry when I wake up and find out he's not there. A few of the wives looked in on me at first. Not much anymore, though. I think some of them didn't like me, or at least didn't like the fact that Charles married me." She thanked the waitress for the tea, then sprinkled in a packet of sugar.

"Jealous, I imagine," I said. "Don't let it worry you, though, Marlisa. I think Charles was extremely fortunate."

"You're kind," she mumbled self-consciously. "I do have one close friend, though, Christie. Her husband is an accountant for Sapphire. They're around my age, so that makes a difference, I think. Most of the wives are older."

"I rest my case," I said, smiling at her.

"Christie stops by for coffee and to check in on me every few days. It helps a little to have someone to talk to now and then, someone besides attorneys and investigators. Anyway, what was it you wanted to talk to me about, H?" she asked, moving the subject in the direction I had hoped to move it.

"Partially, I have to admit, I just wanted to see how you were getting along," I said. "I know this has been devastating. I'm glad to hear that someone is looking in on you occasionally."

"Thanks. And the other reason?"

"Yeah, you got me. There was also an ulterior motive. I'm still digging into this disaster, of course. I suspect some nasty characters were at the root of it all. And they'd like to have me eliminated. I just can't quite put my finger on who or why yet."

"But I've told you everything I know."

"I know. But who knows what could turn up tomorrow? Any slightest incident could be a new piece to the puzzle. How has Sapphire dealt with your benefits, for example?"

"Oh, they've been dragging their feet, of course. Besides looking for some way to blame Charles for dying, Sapphire is arguing that the inundation is Calco Oil's and Doucet Drilling's joint responsibility. They'll go to any length to pass the buck and come out smelling like a rose, and I'm sure Calco and Doucet Drilling will do the same. The lawyers will be haggling over this one for a decade, I'm afraid."

"How are you doing financially? I could help you out if need be."

"Oh, no, H. Thank goodness, Charles was depositing part of his paycheck into a nice savings account since before we met. 'For a rainy day,' he always said. And he had bought a life insurance policy, too, so that's helped a lot."

"Well, don't be afraid to let me know if you need some help."

"Thanks, H. That's very kind, but I think I can manage. I'll keep hounding Sapphire for a while, see if we can't reach a settlement before too long."

"Well, OK. I wouldn't put anything past Sapphire, or Calco Oil for that matter, but I'd stake my reputation on my father's innocence," I said. "I know he'd want me to give you a hand. Despite all his flaws, and he had plenty, integrity and generosity were his greatest assets. If I didn't believe in his integrity, I don't know if I could go on with this.

"I believe he had begun to snoop into Sapphire and Calco Oil himself before the disaster," I continued. "I think if he hadn't suspected them, he'd be alive today."

"Oh, I didn't mean to imply that your father had any blame. I don't trust Sapphire, though," she said. "They've been extremely evasive. Have you learned anything more about the new boss?"

"Just that he moved here from Ideal Tractor in Memphis. And that someone up there wants me dead. I've got my ear to the ground, though. I've already learned a good deal about Armstrong's shady dealings at Ideal. There's no reason to think he cleaned up his act with Sapphire." I paused to let that sink in. "I wonder if you'd be willing to share any of the correspondence you've had with Sapphire?"

"Well...I suppose I could make copies," she replied. "You could also talk to some of Charles's working buddies. They're all waiting for settlements, now, too. Tempers are flaring."

"I imagine so! But I'd like to keep as few people in the loop as necessary right now. I'm hoping to meet Jack Brouilette in a little while, but other than Brouilette, you're my only source at Sapphire for now. I'd rather you didn't tell anyone else about our meetings, though. It's for your own safety as well as mine," I said. "I'd even be careful about saying too much to your friend, Christie. I hate to sound paranoid, but I'm beginning to wonder who we can trust."

"Well, you know you can trust me." She finished her last sip of tea, then looked at her watch and rose to leave. "OK, H, I'll make copies of any of the letters I get from Sapphire Salt." I rose, too, and laid enough on the table to cover our tea and a tip so I could walk her out.

What was that lump in my throat after we said goodbye and I closed her car door? Just sympathy for her loss, I told myself. Anyway, it was time to call Jack Brouillette. I walked over to the pay phone on the corner and fished out his card. Jack picked up on the first ring.

"Brouillette," his gravelly voice boomed over the phone.

"Mr. Brouillette? This is H. Doucet. Remember me?"

"Sure thing, Major Doucette. Call me Jack, *sha*. Mable told me you called. *Comment ça va?*"

"*Ça va bien.* And call me H. Look, do you suppose we can meet sometime? In fact, I'm in New Iberia for a little while today, if you're free."

"Be glad to. I can meet you soon as I shower. Where y'at?"

We met a half-hour later at Bourbon Hall, the same little dive where I had spoken to the disgruntled old drunk, who, as I suspected, was seated in a cloud of smoke on the same bar stool, undoubtedly his home away from home, poor fella.

"Thanks for coming out on short notice," I told Jack, extending my hand when he arrived.

He took the stool beside me and ordered a Bud.

"I'm trying to see what I can find out about Warren Armstrong," I began after he'd lit a Marlboro and taken a swig of the beer the waitress set in front of him. "Any chance you have any insights to share?"

"Oh, no, H. The only thing I know is he's a slave driver. He's fighting the settlements and our damn pensions. We're waiting on our class-action suit, but I expect that'll take years. And him, sittin' on his yacht down there in Corpus. A Pure-D bastard, if you ask me."

"Don't hold back," I laughed. "I heard he had cut your crew to emergency level. Was production off?"

"Yeah, Old Armstrong said times was hard, and sales were way down, what with the recession. He just pushed those of us left all the harder. Son of a bitch didn't bother keepin' up his business, far as I could tell. Equipment was wearing out, breaking down every day. Seemed like he wanted it to fall apart. I get pissed off every time I think of how hard we all worked just to keep that old bastard floating on that yacht. I never told Mable, and I know Charlie never told his wife, but it was gettin' damn dangerous down there. I figure it would've folded soon even without an inundation. That disaster just saved old Armstrong's ass, is all I can say."

"Yep, that's about what I was afraid of. Seems Armstrong had a vested interest in destroying the mine."

"Oh, I ain't saying he had anything to do with the inundation. Just a lucky day for him. Yep. A real lucky day. He can just set back on that yacht and wait for his lawsuit against Calco to add a few more millions to his coffers."

"Pretty sad when 'luck' means the death of over a dozen innocent people," I said. Jack raised his bushy eyebrows but just shrugged as he exhaled a cloud of smoke.

Odd, I thought. Why would Armstrong purposely let the mine deteriorate? And if he was in on the inundation, wasn't he responsible for Charles Daigrepont's and the others' deaths? "Thanks, Jack," I finally said. "Look, I may get back to you after I do some more digging around. That be OK?"

"Sure thing, H. Glad to help, anytime. You got my card." He took another drag on his Marlboro, then downed half a beer in a gulp. "Sorry I don't know no more than that."

While Jack finished his beer and ordered another, I went to the pay phone in back to call Earlene. Dallas Matherne must at least have known Armstrong back at Ideal Tractor, if not been his pawn. It was time to locate him.

"Earlene, have you still got Dallas Matherne on the books?" I asked.

"Oh, he's on the books, H. But we haven't heard from him since the inundation. I figure he must've looked for work elsewhere. Most of the guys stayed with Doucet, but a lot of fellas moved on."

"Matherne is the only one I'm interested in right now. I need to find out where he went and what he's up to. Think you can do that for me? See what you can turn up?"

"I'll ask around. Don't know how to locate these strays. I expect they'll all contact me come tax time. But maybe somebody's heard from Dallas."

"Well, just be careful who you ask. If he finds out I'm looking for him, he might dig in deeper."

"No worries. I'm pretty tight with one or two of these old fellas, and your daddy trusted them."

"Another thing, Earlene. See if you can find anything on Matherne's past. So far, I know he spent his early career on offshore rigs, probably born and raised right here in Louisiana. Why would a guy like that suddenly move to Tennessee for a maintenance job, then move back in just a few years? Doesn't add up. Think you can find out anything about that?"

"I can try, H. That's all I can tell you. Your daddy never mentioned it, and I expect he might've been the only one to know, if anyone."

"Also, I need you to see if Mr. Gremillion's secretary is still at DNR. See if she'll meet me, somewhere outside of her office or our office."

"Ok, I'll look into it."

"You're the best. I'll call you back tomorrow, around lunchtime?"

"OK, H. Just be careful! Your Aunt Ethel is worried sick!"

"I know. But I'm afraid I'd put her in danger if I went home, so it just has to be this way for a while. Try to make her see that, Earlene."

"I'll do my best," she said. "Just be careful, H."

Chapter 13
COINCIDENTAL MOLE

I spent the next morning at USL's library, virtually empty over the semester break except for a few serious grad students lurking behind the stacks in dank corners, creeping through narrow aisles of musty tomes, or hunched over carrels strewn with books and papers. I dug out a couple of dissertations by petroleum engineers, to see what I could learn about the industry and its history. In the basement, I scrolled for what seemed like hours through mind-numbing microfilm newspaper articles about the Calco-Aloco merger and the people involved. I learned that Calco Oil had gobbled up several smaller oil companies before and since its merger with Aloco, making it one of the largest international oil mega-corporations in the world.

Carl Haggerty's name kept appearing in articles as a high-powered D.C. attorney, an oil lobbyist, and a linchpin in the mergers. I wondered if Carl was related to Joseph Haggerty, whose office at DNR had purportedly provided the faulty geological map. I was pretty sure Father wouldn't have missed a connection like that, and if word spread, that knowledge could have provided ample motive for Father's murder.

The next afternoon, Placide and I drove to Baton Rouge for the meeting Earlene had arranged with Candace Soileau, Gremillion's former secretary, at the new River Center Library downtown.

I waited near the checkout counter until an attractive young lady entered, her short blonde wavy hair giving her a youthful androgynous look.

"Major Doucet?" she asked when she spotted me at the designated spot. "I'm Candace Soileau."

"Please, call me H," I said.

"No problem, H. And you can call me Candace."

"Thanks for meeting me. Earlene reserved a small meeting room for us to talk. Follow me."

When we had seated at the conference table, she said, "I'm not quite sure why I'm here."

"I've asked you because I'd like to better understand your office's recent tragedy."

Her smile dimmed. "Yes, H, we've had quite a shake-up. We're all still in shock, and no one's daring to talk about it above a whisper."

"Were you aware that Mr. Gremillion was supposed to meet my father the day before Father died?"

"Yes. I made that appointment."

"Were you also aware that he had an appointment to meet with me? And that he was on his way to that meeting when he was run off the bridge?"

"I had no idea! He never mentioned another meeting

to me. He was on his way to Houston for a meeting as far as I knew."

"Mr. Gremillion agreed to meet me in Henderson on his way to his Houston meeting. I suspect someone found out about our appointment and made sure he didn't keep it. Do you have any idea if the investigators have checked his phone for bugs—or yours, for that matter?"

"If they have, they haven't shared that tidbit with me!" She paused to let that possibility sink in for a few seconds, her eyes darting around the room. "I'm afraid I'm a little dumbfounded here. You seem convinced he was murdered."

"I hate to say it, but I think there's a good possibility that he wasn't just run off the road by a random drunk. And it's possible that whoever is responsible could work at DNR or even higher than that, though that's pure conjecture at this point."

She paused to think over that idea, then said, "I hope you know I don't have any idea what you're talking about."

"I didn't mean to suggest you did," I assured her. "But I've spent some time digging around, and the name Joseph Haggerty in DNR came up a few times. Do you know him?"

"Well, of course I know him! He asked me to come to work for him temporarily, shortly after Mr. Gremillion's death! His secretary is on leave for a couple months with a new baby due."

"And did you?"

"Of course. They hadn't hired a replacement for my boss yet, so I needed a job!"

"Fantastic! Do you have access to his records?"

"I have access to what he wants me to have. Of course, there are plenty of ways he could hide files that I *don't* have access to, as we probably both know. I wonder if the investigators know that someone inside the department might be implicated?"

"I can't answer that. I do know that the so-called 'investigators' have been less than helpful so far. I'm not even sure they're not in on it. That's why I'm trying to find my own channels."

"And you think you can confide in me?"

"I have no way of knowing that, obviously. But Father must have trusted your late boss, so that's what I'm going on. Besides, you're a lot less likely to be involved than the top tax bracket I've discovered with their greedy paws in it. Most of the players so far seem to be in upper administrative positions, and I'm pretty sure they're not interested in widening their circle to the working class. They have one or two hired pawns, but you don't fit the paradigm."

"I appreciate the vote of confidence," she said with a laugh.

"But we have to realize that your phone might be bugged by now, too. Even your home phone. Working for Haggerty puts you in even more danger now than I suspected. Look, Ms. Soileau, ...I mean Candace, ...I'm hesitant to call you at your house, particularly now that I know you're working for Haggerty. We'll have to be even more careful than I originally planned. Do you have a friend or relative where I could call you occasionally? At some designated time, of course? Someone you absolutely know you can trust? Preferably someone Haggerty doesn't know exists." I held out my pen, in hopes she could jot down a number for me.

She seemed to be conflicted as she thought for a

minute, but then she took the pen. I handed her my open Day-Timer. "This is an acquaintance that I doubt anyone knows about. I won't elaborate," she said.

"No need to, as long as you're sure you can trust him," I agreed, assuming the contact was male.

"I trust him with my life."

"Good. Pick a convenient time for me to call you, when you can be reasonably certain to be there."

"I suppose you can call around 8 PM on Sunday. We get together most Sunday evenings to grill something."

"Perfect. Thanks. But please don't breathe a word of this to anyone, even your friend. Just tell him I'm a long-lost relative or something. Think you can do that? I don't want him getting too curious."

"I guess so, H. I can tell him you're my cousin. He knows I have a big family in Lafayette, and a great aunt there who's extremely ill," she said. "Any idea what I should keep my eyes open for?"

"Anything out of the ordinary, particularly any records that come across your desk connecting Calco Oil or Sapphire Salt to DNR. Their motivation is greed, simple as that, so anything concerning finances and transactions might give us a clue. Also, any appointments Haggerty asks you to make for him could lead us somewhere. Only, for God's sake, be careful. Keep your ears open, of course, but just worry about files that come across your desk. Don't go snooping, whatever you do. We don't know who's working for Haggerty. I'm hoping to find out what was important enough to get my father and Gremillion killed. But keep in mind, if it was important enough to get them killed, there's no length these guys won't go to if they feel threatened."

"I'll keep my eyes open, but don't worry, I'm not about to go looking for trouble. I have my future to think of, and I'd like it to last several more years."

Chapter 14
COOKED BOOKS

When I called the office to check in the next morning, Earlene told me Mrs. Daigrepont had left a message for me to call her. Surprised and a little concerned, I hung up and dialed right away.

"I'm glad you called," Marlisa said. "I might actually have some information for you." She sounded upbeat, so that was a load off my mind.

"Great. Let's meet and talk about it."

"I have a couple errands to run, but you can come by my house a little later today if you like. Maybe in a couple hours or so?"

I jotted her address on my hand, then jogged down the levee and crammed myself into the tiny shower. I took just a moment or two longer than usual shaving and blow-drying my hair, convincing myself it was the polite thing to do. I slapped on some Brut, an extravagance I hadn't thought of lately. Placide didn't comment, but I noticed a double take when I slid into the passenger seat. Must be the Brut, I thought, feeling a little sheepish.

The sky was a clear, crisp blue, as oil field industry trucks and tankers roared by us on Highway 90. The rare kind of winter day in Louisiana when the humidity drops so low that the sky is lapis lazuli, and everything looks like it's just been scrubbed. Even the Canadian geese, here for the winter, seemed to soar with renewed zest in their precise V formation across the azure background, three shades deeper than our usual grayish-blue sky bleached out by 90% humidity. Or maybe it just looked brighter since I was on my way to see Marlisa.

Back in New Iberia, we crossed the bayou at Bridge Street and found Marlisa's small house on the corner under an ancient live oak. Placide promised to be in sight when I needed him.

Marlisa appeared at the door in bare feet, jeans, and a red USL T-shirt, her hair hiked up into a loose ponytail, with stray wisps falling on her cheeks and neck. She led me to the dinette set, where papers littered the width of the modest table.

"H, I've learned a few things about Armstrong since we spoke," she said.

"I'm all ears."

"For one thing, Sapphire is leveraged to the hilt. The business was failing, with no new contracts. The books are doctored so that Armstrong could lie about the company's losses. It looks to me like he's been selling off the company, piece by piece."

"Who would have guessed?" I said sardonically. "Where did that tidbit of information come from?"

"From my friend Christie. Yesterday she came by, all upset, with a manila folder of papers. She told me her husband, the Sapphire accountant, had discovered that the books don't add up, so he's worried. Millions of dollars have disappeared, and the numbers have been doctored to make the profits look much greater on paper than they actually are. Creditors are rolling in now wanting what's due, but the bulk of the money is probably in some offshore account somewhere. She's afraid they'll suspect her husband. Of course, I had to promise her I wouldn't mention a word of this to anyone, or she wouldn't have shown me any of this."

"My lips are sealed. I know Armstrong has some high-profile CPA on Wall Street. Armstrong's not about to trust a local young New Iberia accountant with his actual earnings. It'll take a full audit to get to the bottom of it, and by the time it gets to that point, everyone will know about the fraud. If Christie's husband's nose is clean, he shouldn't have anything to worry about. This just gives my suspicion some teeth," I said, looking up at her from one of the pages. "Thanks, Marlisa. This will really be useful."

"I didn't even think to offer you a glass of iced tea, H."

"That would hit the spot," I said, glad for the chance to visit a few minutes longer.

She returned with two tall glasses, ice clinking, and set one in front of me, searching my face for a reaction as I glanced through the pages.

"How did your friend manage to get her hands on all this?" I took a long sip and slouched back in the chair.

"After the building was damaged, her husband had to move his office into their home temporarily. He's been having trouble sleeping, so she bugged him until he finally told her what was bothering him. While he was bass fishing last weekend, she Xeroxed a copy of some of the pages and brought them to me because she's frightened for him. I guess she needed to confide in someone. And you're the only other person I can trust, so I decided I'd hand it over to you."

"I'm glad you know you can trust me. But it does put you in some danger if anyone learns you saw this. I'd get this back to Christie as soon as you can."

"Oh, these copies are for you. I don't even want this stuff in my house!"

"This could really be helpful. Thanks!"

"Christie never trusted Sapphire, either. I know Charles saw it, too, but he would never tell me how bad it was. He didn't want to worry me, but that worried me all the more. I just..." Her voice trailed off, and I knew she still had a hard time talking about Charles.

"I'm sorry this is bringing up bad memories, Marlisa," I said, reaching out to pat her hand that lay limp on top of a stack of papers.

"Christie feels the same as I do," she said, quickly composing herself, "and she's been worried sick about her husband, especially since this bombshell dropped." Marlisa didn't pull her hand away, so mine lingered a second or two longer than necessary.

"Well, try to stay in touch with her," I added, pulling my hand away finally.

"Oh, I will. She's my only ally. Besides you, that is. But she's afraid for her husband."

"As long as he didn't have prior knowledge, he won't be accountable. But he should report this to the MSHA, ASAP. Right now, they seem to think Sapphire is squeaky clean. I suspect some ally of Armstrong outside the company was cooking the books, someone who's in as deep as Armstrong is. Those books were cooked long before they ever got to Christie's husband. Armstrong pulled the same thing in Tennessee, so it's not surprising. Probably the same Wall Street CPA. So far, Armstrong has robbed two companies blind with impunity, so he's obviously got some connections in high places. I'd love to nail him.

"Thanks for getting me these," I continued, patting the folder and standing to leave. "At least it gives us some proof of what I've been suspecting all along. These records should prove a good motive for a planned inundation to get the insurance money. The inconvenient part for those responsible is the unfortunate loss of life. In my book, we're looking at murder. Eventually, someone will listen."

"I'm happy if I could help."

"I'll be in touch, Marlisa."

"I'm glad," she said as she stood on tiptoe and kissed me on the cheek.

Taken aback, I walked on air out to where Placide waited for me.

~

My investigation was taking much longer than I expected and becoming ever more complex. That afternoon, I reluctantly called my XO and asked for an emergency leave extension. "I believe I'm getting closer to proving my father was murdered, but I'm not getting any help from law enforcement," I told him. "I'm hoping to use some of the leave time I've been saving."

"I understand, Major. In my experience, not all law enforcement is above corruption. I'll go ahead and fill out the forms for the record. Do what you need to do but get back here as soon as you can."

"Will do, sir. Thanks for understanding."

Saturday morning, Placide and I decided to bundle up, pack the ice chest, and shove off for a weekend of trolling through our refuge in the swamp. Nothing could ease the agony of waiting like the endless expanse of sky and water; the croaking and cawing swamp life; the thick cypress groves keeping us hidden; the slosh of gentle waves on the side of the boat. Placide stood watch while fly-fishing, and I slouched back and skimmed through the papers Marlisa had given me.

I'm no accountant, but even I could spot some of these old-school tricks. The balance sheets were so doctored that accounting fraud lit up like casino neon. Revenues were accelerated and expenses were delayed. Assets simply vanished from the pages. The same non-recurring expenses were subtracted yearly. This was going to be an accountant's nightmare to unravel. But I knew enough to know it would prove to be incriminating evidence in court of a failing business, robbed blind before its final crumbling.

My mind was awash with corporate fraud, so I picked up a rod and joined Placide on the stern, snagging enough white crappie between us to fry a mess for supper and emptying my mind of the whole sordid affair for the rest of the day.

We reluctantly docked at our slip on Sunday evening, back to our reality, but more rested than I'd felt in weeks. I touched base with Candace from the levee phone at our agreed-upon time to see if she'd learned anything yet. It seemed my only dependable contacts were women. Or at least the only ones who hadn't ended up dead.

"I need to see you," she said, sounding urgent. We planned to meet for coffee at the Tiger Truck Stop in Grosse Tête, about fifteen miles east of Baton Rouge, the next morning before she went to work, though she said she would have only a few minutes.

"I was hoping you'd call, H," she said when she plopped down at my table in the corner of the diner.

"I've taken the liberty of ordering you some coffee. I hope that will be OK?" She nodded, then reached for some sugar packets. "Have you learned something?" I continued.

"Quite a bit. First of all, Carl is Joseph's brother; you were right. Carl was the lead attorney for the Calco-Aloco merger. They were on a conference call on Friday. And Joseph had a call from someone in the White House last Monday. He flew to Washington for two days right after that."

My pulse raced. "Any idea what the meeting was about?"

"I can't ask him directly, but he's worried about something, that much is clear. He had me book him a flight to Nassau tomorrow and a hotel for three days."

"The Bahamas?"

"Yes."

"Round trip?"

"Yes. He didn't book his wife on the flight. And right at Christmas, too! It sounded bogus to me."

"I agree. Where he's staying?"

"He's at the Sheraton British Colonial."

"Look, Candace, can you describe Joseph Haggerty to

me?" I asked, my mind racing.

"Better than that. I brought this trade publication. Haggerty's picture is on page seven. He's the third from the left with Treasury Secretary Arnold Huff and some other men at the Hall of Distinction Ceremony at LSU," she said, opening the slick magazine to a page with the corner bent down, and laying it on the table in front of me.

"So, Secretary Huff is involved, too. Nice work, Candace. No wonder Haggerty requested you! I'm impressed!"

"Thanks, but now I suspect it was more likely he hired me because he knew Gremillion had some goods on him and he wanted to be able to keep his eye on me. The picture is a little small, but maybe you can get an idea of what he looks like. See here?" she said, pointing to the picture of a short bald man. "He's nearly bald, large wire frame glasses."

"This is a big help," I said.

"There's one other thing, H."

"Oh?"

"A man named Dallas Matherne came in yesterday while Mr. Haggerty was out of the office. He asked me to tell Mr. Haggerty that he hadn't received his ticket."

"His ticket?"

"Yes. Then he handed me a number and asked me to have Haggerty call him."

"A number? This is fantastic!"

"The odd thing is, I was just heading out to go to lunch and he walked out with me and offered to buy me lunch. I couldn't tell if he was trying to flirt with me, or if maybe he was trying to pry information out of me. That's when I thought maybe I could get some information from *him*, so

I agreed."

"You went to lunch with him? Well, tell all!"

"I didn't learn much at first, but I decided he was flirting, so I played along. He started getting talkative when he ordered a second beer. He was angry, he said, because they were sending him away to Costa Rica. San José. When I asked why, he said they wanted to get rid of him just because he missed work one day."

"I think it was more complicated than he let on."

"I figured. He asked me if I'd meet him for a drink after work today. I said OK. That's why I wanted to see you, to see if there's anything you want me to try to ask him."

"Do I? Where to start? First, give me Matherne's number. Then, I guess, see if he'll tell you *who* is sending him to Costa Rica, and why. Be casual about it, though. We know Haggerty is involved, but didn't you say he mentioned 'they'?"

"Yes, 'they.' Here's the number he gave me. I'll see what I can find out this evening. One thing's for sure; he doesn't act like a married man. OK, H, I've got to get to work."

"This is fantastic, Candace." I wrote down the office number. "Let Earlene or me know if you learn anything more tonight. But please be careful!" I said, as she grabbed her bag and hurried to the door.

"I have a job for you," I told Placide on the ride back to Henderson. "I need a flight to Nassau, Bahamas, tomorrow, and a room at the Sheraton British Colonial until the day after Christmas. Remember to register me as Hank Lee. Oh, and you'll need to have Earlene get out some more cash for me. Also, please give Earlene this phone number today. It's Dallas Matherne's number, and I have a sneaky suspicion he might be leaving the states any day now."

Placide just glanced sideways at me, speechless.

That evening, I went over my notes so far. Could this really go all the way to the White House?

I arrived in Nassau late Tuesday afternoon, grabbed a cab for a wild ride down Bay Street, swerving in and out in heavy traffic. When I got out of the taxi, I was bathed by a balmy sea breeze and the charming British dialect of the dark-skinned natives who greeted me outside the hotel. Assailed by a passing thought of Midge and our quick get-away to the Outer Banks once on liberty, I immediately pushed that thought out, but if one had time to kill and wanted a romantic weekend, this seemed a likely place. That thought was followed immediately by thoughts of Marlisa's quick stolen kiss. She was every bit as dangerous as Midge, I warned myself as I quashed that thought, as well.

The hotel lobby sparkled like a lady of the evening. Twinkling garlands adorned every pillar and indoor palm tree, while canned Christmas carols and the scent of pine permeated the cavernous lobby. I passed several pairs of Christmas honeymooners, arm in arm, looking to me like mere children, as I carried my bag to my room on the third floor. I hung my sport coat and my few shirts and slacks in the closet; shoved my skivvies, bathing suit, and some shorts and T-shirts into a dresser drawer; and threw my Dopp kit on the bathroom counter. I unpacked the Minox I brought along, hopefully to snap some evidence.

I figured Haggerty was likely to frequent some of the

numerous watering holes at the hotel. An adult beverage and a bite to eat were in order for me as well after the long trip from New Orleans, with an hour and a half wait in Miami. I hadn't eaten anything but airline peanuts since Louisiana.

I leafed through the social directory in my room and decided on the Patio Bar and Grill, the most casual choice, probably the most likely spot for Haggerty to show up at this hour. After a quick shower, I pulled on some shorts and a Polo shirt, pocketed my camera, and headed down.

I wasn't positive it was Haggerty, but a short bald guy with large wire frame glasses sat at the bar talking to another man over one of those tall exotic island drinks with a paper parasol hanging out the side. Haggerty had no way of knowing me, so I had nothing to risk by getting close. I took a seat at a table behind a post and unfolded the morning paper. I was in a good spot to grab a clandestine pic.

I couldn't hear what they were saying, but I did catch Haggerty calling out, "See you tomorrow morning, Warren," to the one who had stood to leave.

It had to be Joseph Haggerty and Warren Armstrong. That was the only Warren I had heard about. Now I knew for certain that Joseph Haggerty was not only tied to big oil, he was also tied to the salt company. One company was as corrupt as the other. With such huge stakes, anyone who got close to the truth was disposable. Collateral damage.

Later that afternoon, with too much time to kill, I walked out to the beach and rented one of a long line of chaise lounges with awnings. I kicked off my topsiders while a steel drum played a calypso tune in the distance. Looked as though I'd have an evening to kill. The balmy breeze off the water made it feel more like Easter than Christmas. I put my hands behind my head and watched for thirty minutes or so as two young island boys in cutoffs recruited tourists, then dove for conch shells for them. One of the young boys saw me smiling in their direction and began playing peek-a-boo with me around the corner of the lifeguard stand. I finally motioned him over. "You can dive for a shell for me," I told him.

"Which shell you like, Mister?" he beamed. "You show me the one you like, and I'll get it for you. Five dollars."

I followed them out onto the pier, where dozens of multi-colored shells sparkled in filtered sunlight under three feet of water so clear you could see the bottom. "That one," I said, pointing to the most colorful shell I spotted.

"Sure, Mister," said the smallest of the two, who couldn't have been more than six or seven. He dove without a splash into the crystal blue. Within moments he surfaced, a large coral-colored conch shell held high over his head and a smile as wide as the shell itself. "Here, Mister. You like?"

"It's beautiful. Good job," I smiled, handing him a five after he hoisted himself easily onto the pier.

"Thanks." He grinned, stretching out the bill for a closer look, then tucking it into a zipper pouch pinned to the inside of his shorts. The two boys walked on, beaming as they looked for their next mark.

I tucked the shell under my arm and returned to the lounge chair. I opened the *Nassau Guardian* newspaper I'd picked up in the lobby. An article in section two caught my eye, about the oil exploration that Calco Oil had begun in the '70s and continued today, using new digital seismic survey technology to test the Great Carbonate Banks of the Bahamas for future oil drilling. I pondered whether these enterprising youngsters would have to face a future on the oil rigs a decade or so from now. How long would this water remain pristine once big oil got its hands on it? Hopefully, the Bahamians would be smart enough to resist a fate like Louisiana's, in the interest of their laid-back lifestyle and their tourist industry if nothing else.

Calypso music rang out from the beachfront bar as young scantily clad honeymooners scuffed through the sand looking for shells, or ran in and out of the waves, or sat sipping Fog Cutters in shared chaise lounges. A volleyball game was in full swing a little farther down the beach, complete with giggling young bikini-clad American wenches, which meant the young studs were nearby flexing and posing, too. Hopefully, this vibrant tourism industry could fend off the encroachment of big oil, I thought drowsily, drifting off.

I woke up as dusk was settling in brilliant pink and orange hues over the now calm ocean waves and the beach. Along with the twilight, a hush had settled over the day's festivities, interrupted only by the plaintive cries of gulls hovering low over the surf looking for dinner. The volleyball games were winding down and the laughs were more pensive now, as young couples began to disperse to plan their evening's activities and romance. This was not the place to visit alone, I thought. Anyway, it was time to get back to my room and shower. Maybe get a drink downstairs later to unwind.

When I walked into my room, the message light on my phone was blinking, so I called the front desk and got a callback message from Aunt Ethel's number. After the hotel operator placed the call, Placide picked up on the second ring.

"Placide?"

"Yessir, H," answered the familiar voice on the other end. "We have a little emergency here."

"Oh, no. What happened, Placide?"

"It's your Aunt. A couple of thugs have been nosing around here wanting to know where you were. She told them she didn't know nothing, but them folks didn't believe her. Roughed her up a little but didn't hurt her."

"What did they do to her?"

"Pushed her around, is all. Said if you didn't contact a certain number by noon tomorrow, they'd be back for more. And they told her if she called the law, she'd be dead. Louis is pretty upset, and Ethel just keeps on crying."

"Oh, crap. And I'm not there to help. What's the number?"

He read it off and added, "Don't worry. I'm going to stay out here at the house. They're hunting you down, though, that's for sure."

I told Placide that he was as much a target as I. "Don't worry," he responded. "I reckon I can take care of myself. Been doing it a lot of years. You just do what you have to do there."

"Thanks for the heads up. You be careful, too." I hung up, realizing the situation was becoming even more dire. I dialed the operator and placed the call to the number Placide had given me.

"Yes?" came the deep voice on the other end.

"This is Major Doucet."

"Doucet. One warning and only one. Stay the hell out

of business you don't belong in. One word that you or that giant bodyguard of your daddy's is still snoopin' around, and your aunt buys the farm. Hear?"

"I thought you were gunning for Placide and me."

"We decided to up the ante. Maybe that old lady will get your attention better."

"Who are you?"

"Someone you don't want to know. Now, do I have your word?"

"You have my word," I lied, anxious to get off the phone before they traced it.

I needed to get home ASAP, but I was stuck here for a few more days. Placide would be with Ethel and Louis, so they'd be OK. I showered and went back down to the Patio Bar to collect my thoughts while I had a quiet drink alone.

The next morning, I got a cup of coffee to go and read the paper in the hotel lobby. About 0800 hours, I watched as Haggerty and Armstrong exited the elevator and headed out front for a taxi. I grabbed the one behind them and told the driver to follow that car.

"Yes sir," the cabbie said, and we headed up Bay Street after them. When Haggerty's cab pulled in at the Coral Harbor Golf Course a half-hour later, I realized I'd have to let them go for now. I decided I'd do some Christmas shopping and try to beat them back to the Nineteenth Hole, where I figured they'd probably stop for drinks and lunch.

"Take me to the shopping district," I told my cabbie, and we headed back toward town. He agreed to pick me up at the same corner at 1100 hours. That gave me a few hours to browse the shops, pick up a couple of trinkets for

Aunt Ethel and Earlene, and grab a cup of joe at some beachside bistro before I went back to the clubhouse for lunch.

Chapter 15
ONE-WAY TICKET

I sat by the window at the Nineteenth Hole, absent-mindedly watching as several foursomes putted the eighteenth hole, shook hands, and walked in, grumbling about bunker shots and sand traps. Corporate execs taking liberal advantage of their expense accounts, by the looks. Some forty-five minutes and two glasses of iced tea and a BLT later, Haggerty and Armstrong showed up on eighteen in their pastel Arnold Palmer golf shirts and crisp chinos. A young guy, dressed incongruously in cut-offs and a Nike T-shirt, was tagging along. The young guy sank his putt first, followed by the other two. Then the three paraded in, slapping each other on the back and making excuses for missed shots.

The threesome sat a couple of tables over from me, close enough for me to get a shot of them with my camera. I kept my eyes on a few duffers on eighteen, but when I heard them deep in conversation, I pulled out my Minox. Haggerty's back was to me, but it would still be easy to identify him now that he'd removed his golf hat and looked out the window. I snapped a pic, as though I was aiming at the putter on 18, but I had the threesome in my sight.

I saw Armstrong hand the young guy an envelope. A payoff for services rendered? I snapped a shot of that exchange. Must be Matherne, I thought. He raised his voice in anger, but I couldn't make out what he said.

"Calm down, Dallas," Haggerty said. "Keep your nose clean and you'll see your wife soon enough." At that, Matherne rose and stomped out of the club in a snit.

A few minutes later, when I passed their table on the way to the front, I heard Armstrong tell Haggerty, "Yeah, Deslatte vouched for him. He was friends with his daddy."

I hopped in a cab out front and said, "Take me to the Sheraton."

"Yes, sir." We bounced along in the vintage Bel Air, past resort hotels, souvenir shops, and plenty of honeymooners connected at the hip as they crept from shop to shop. I wondered cynically how many of those young cloud-walkers would still be clinging so fondly to one another a year from now.

I dialed Aunt Ethel's number from the hotel lobby pay phone and plunked in a few dollars in change. Placide picked up on the third ring.

"Any sign of our predators?" I asked.

"No, Sir, H. I guess they think you're layin' low like you promised since they haven't seen you or me around."

"How's Aunt Ethel doing?"

"Oh, she's holding her own. She's pretty tough, considering all your daddy put her through with his scrapes."

"You got that right! Maybe we'll just stay out of sight, out of mind for a while. Let them think I've gone back to the base. OK, Placide, you have my itinerary, right?"

"I'll be at the airport."

"Good man. You hang in over there."

I took the three flights of stairs to my room and changed into trunks and a pullover. It would be a long time before I made it back to the Bahamas, if ever, so I decided to soak up some more rays while I had the opportunity. I grabbed a hotel towel, suntan lotion, my camera, and my Day-Timer, threw on some shades and a ball cap, then scuffed down the hall in my flip-flops.

The young shell divers were still hustling honeymooners when I rented my chaise for the day, so I walked over to say hello. The older boy looked up, didn't recognize me or else thought I'd be good for a double-dip, and asked, "Conch shell, Mister? Five dollars."

"No, kids. One's enough," I laughed. "Just came by to say hello. How's business?" They both beamed, nodding in unison like two bobble-head dolls.

I high-fived them. "Keep up the good work," I said. After all, they were budding capitalists, making a living off the tourist dollar.

I settled back in the chaise and opened the Day-Timer. 'Dallas Matherne, driller, mole,' I wrote. Having been a former Ideal Tractor employee, had he 'advanced' to being Sapphire's mole in Doucet Drilling? Or was he Calco Oil's mole? Or Haggerty's? They were all conspiring. But why? What purpose could Matherne have served? And why did he miss work that critical day? Was the inundation planned for that particular day? If so, he had to figure he'd be investigated after calling in sick. That royal fuck up would focus the bright light of suspicion on him immediately. On the other hand, that white-collar gang had enough money to make him disappear, one way or the other, and a plane ticket clearly beat "the other."

The perfect crime, or so they must have thought. My brain was scrambled from trying to piece it all together. In frustration, I finally just stuck the Day-Timer behind the small of my back and closed my eyes, letting the balmy sun and breeze have their way with me until I drifted into another nap on the beach.

What seemed like just moments later, I was jerked awake, steel drums ringing out their island calypso beat from the beachside bar nearby. Dusk was already settling in, and the beach was nearly vacant. It took a moment to shake out the cobwebs and realize that Dallas Matherne standing over my chaise lounge with a gun, saying, "OK, Doucet, now it's your turn," had all been a scattered dream. I gathered my thoughts and my things and headed upstairs to catch the news, maybe order room service.

Wide-eyed an hour before my wake-up call on Christmas morning, I went out for an early walk by the surf. The sun was just beginning to lighten the eastern sky, but the hour hadn't deterred the two little conch shell salesmen. There they were on the pier with a large cardboard box full of shells. As the larger boy dove off the pier, the younger boy tossed the shells out to him, which he then planted randomly near the pier, in preparation for unsuspecting customers. What little con artists. I had to laugh, but I couldn't help marveling at their ingenuity. They were collecting their shells every night, planting them early every morning before the rich Americans arrived on the beach. Tomorrow's conspirators, I chuckled. At the same time, I couldn't help recalling my own privileged Christmases spent around a gaudy ten-foot pine tree in Aunt Ethel's parlor among brightly wrapped boxes of hastily purchased and overly extravagant toys, soon to be lost, broken, or neglected. The contrast unsettled me.

I wandered up the beach a little way, people-watching, as one does. The beach was nearly empty this early: the little con artists planting their shells for the benefit of gullible tourists; a couple of bronzed girls in bikinis finding early spots for a day of competitive tanning; a wizened old man with his metal detector occasionally picking up a dime or a quarter; the tiny plovers with their rapid sprints and stops finding breakfast along the shore. The hushed early morning hour that would soon be brought to an end by the throngs of sun worshippers with umbrellas, coolers, beach balls, volley balls in tow. Youngsters would soon be running and squealing in and out of waves, anxious mothers hollering not to go so deep. Honeymooners would curl up on beach blankets and grope each other, order piña coladas from the roving waiter.

When the sun sat like a sunny-side-up egg on the eastern horizon, I headed out front for a taxi. "Over here, Chief," called the cabbie at the front of the queue. After bumping along Bay Street in a '57 Chevy, he dropped me off at the airport right at 0700 hours. I handed him a good bit extra, which he answered with bright eyes, a tip of his hat, and a wide grin. "Yes Sir, Chief! Thank you, Sir!"

I picked up a *Miami Herald* at the news stand and found a bench near departures to park myself on. Within thirty minutes, Dallas Matherne arrived, carrying two decent-sized bags up to the Bahamasair counter. I folded my paper and slipped into the queue a couple of places behind him, snapping a pic when he got to the counter.

"One way, San José, Costa Rica?" the preoccupied young lady behind the counter asked when it was Dallas's turn to lift his bags to the scale.

"Correct."

"I.D., sir?"

He pulled his wallet out of his hip pocket.

"Passport and Visa?"

He reached in his breast pocket and pulled out the documents rubber-banded to the envelope I had seen last night. I wondered how much the going rate was for complicity in a dozen deaths. It must have been a big chunk. Had to leave his life in the states, whatever that consisted of. I snapped another pic, then exited the line.

Disgusted by the cesspool of murderous thieves, I took a cab back to the hotel and retraced my steps to the Patio Bar and Grill for some grapefruit juice and a few handfuls of peanuts.

Since today, Christmas Day, was my last in this tourist mecca, a lonely place when you're all alone, I picked up a historic walking tour map and strolled the city, stopping at some high points. I jogged up the Queen's Staircase, dropped a couple dollars in the reggae guitar player's cup. The sun and breeze were magnificent, the islanders were jolly and welcoming. A light lunch of conch fritters and a Kalik beer at an outdoor patio topped off the day nicely. The city was bustling because tomorrow was their main festival, Junkanoo, based on a century-old slave festival, to begin at 0100 hours the morning after Christmas!

The Junkanoo street parade woke me the next morning, the islanders dancing in bright masks and elaborate costumes, accompanied by the rhythm of drums, whistles, and cowbells. After a cup of joe, I made my way down to the street, where I saw my favorite little conch shell divers enjoying the parade, decked out in their own homemade crepe paper costumes. "Happy Christmas, boys," I said, handing each a five-dollar bill. They responded with wide grins and their own little junkanoo dance. Now my trip was complete. Time to pack my gear and head to the airport.

Chapter 16
BLACK EYED PEAS

I pressed my forehead to the airplane window to watch the Lilliputian world below. Old Man River, twisting like a garden hose, was dotted with toy barges; HO gauge trains snaked their way to and from storage docks, where thousands of miniature Lego containers waited to travel north and west; tiny Erector Set refineries pumped gray and yellow smoke into the void between earth and plane. My waltz through white-collar conspiracies on exotic tropical islands had taken its toll. I was ready to get back into the gritty world of the oil industry that kept paradise afloat.

"Happy Holidays, H," Placide said, taking my outstretched hand.

"Thanks, Placide. Same to you." I clapped my other hand on his substantial upper arm. "Great to be back. Aunt Ethel still doing OK?"

"Yes, H. No more threats. Maybe they believed your promise."

"Dream on. No, they're just waiting to see what we do next." After he grabbed my bag, I said, "Let's stop for a bite. Airline pretzels and coffee are just a tease. Then I need to stop at Lakeside Center to pick up a late Christmas present for Ethel."

Knocking off two birds with one stone, as the saying goes, Placide drove to the mall, where we could fulfill all our desires, so long as they were just eating and shopping.

After we got our heaping catfish plates, I asked Placide, "Do you recognize the name Deslatte?"

"There's a Lance Deslatte. Bought a shale processing plant near Morgan City several years back. Shady character. That's a whole 'nother long story."

"Yeah, that's the one. I saw him bullshitting Earlene at the wake. How 'bout you give me the short version."

"Rumor has it he borrowed $500 million from a bank in Houston for expansion of his plant, but he didn't do no expansion. Put $400 mill of the loan in his own pocket. He'd pay his bills to suppliers for a couple small orders, establish credit, then place a huge order and default on his payment. Your daddy's supply officer wised up quick and wouldn't deliver to Deslatte until after his check cleared."

"And this guy's still in business?"

"Far's I know. Word is, he pays off Governor Mansur to keep his nose clean with the EPA. Pays off just enough on his debts every month to stay out of jail somehow. He also operates a hazardous waste dump on the same site. He offers his creditors free waste disposal when they start puttin' the heat on for past due accounts."

"How do you know all this, Placide?"

"Through one of our suppliers, but it ain't any secret. Your daddy got invited to the supplier's deer camp a few times. Of course, your daddy didn't go noplace without his bodyguard, so I heard some stuff. Always got my ears open even if I don't say no whole lot. Deslatte even offered your daddy some hush money one time. He learned soon enough he couldn't buy off a Doucet. Your daddy tried to turn Deslatte in once, but it didn't go nowhere. Deslatte always knows who to pay off. That's old stuff, though. What does it have to do with Oka Chito?"

"I may be out in left field, but I believe this Deslatte guy and Warren Armstrong are in bed together. I don't know why, yet, but I'm getting closer. His name was mentioned regarding Matherne. If I'm right, just trying to turn Deslatte in could have been enough motive to off Father. Might help if we could put a mole in his operation."

After lunch, we walked over to D. H. Holmes, where I picked up a likely-looking nest of imported mixing bowls for Aunt Ethel and a box of assorted teas and biscotti for Earlene. An LSU ball cap and sweatshirt for Uncle Louis and my late Christmas shopping was done for another year. I figured I'd just stick some cash in an envelope for Placide.

I tossed my shopping bags on the back seat, and we headed to New Iberia. Now that my aunt had been dragged into this mess, I decided I'd better move back home so I'd be there to take the heat if those thugs tried to rough her up again. My attempt to protect Ethel and Louis by getting lost in the swamp had failed.

Aunt Ethel greeted me in the yard, all flailing arms and smooches. "Oh, Aitchie, I'm glad you're home, *cher*," she said between wet cheek kisses. "You had us so worried, boy."

"You'd think I was gone a year!" I laughed, enduring the gush of affection.

Uncle Louis, less thrilled to see me, continued taking the Christmas lights off the last wicker reindeer in the front yard. I remembered those decorations from when I was a kid. In fact, Vic and I had broken one of them trying to ride it like a horse. I saw that it still wore the wire Louis had used to re-attach its back legs, though I thought it best not to remind him. I began rolling up the lights for another year in the attic. Louis worked on silently for a few minutes; then he stopped what he was doing, stood motionless looking at the ground, and said, "Please don't put Ethel's life in jeopardy no more, H."

"Yes, sir," I said, keeping my eyes glued on the string of lights I was winding.

~

On New Year's Eve afternoon, after a few crisis-free days laying low, Earlene came by with a plate of homemade Christmas cookies. Ethel sent her home with brownies, candy, and more cookies, the traditional passing of the baton. Earlene seemed to like the box of assorted teas, the biscotti, and the trinkets I'd picked up in Nassau. "My lands, where is this boy going next?" Aunt Ethel complained when I also gave her a few of the same Nassau souvenirs and the conch shell I'd purchased from the two budding capitalists. But I could tell she was glad I didn't forget her.

As I walked Earlene to the car, I gave her a heads-up that Deslatte had something to do with Matherne.

"Were you able to get in touch with Dallas before he

left?" I asked her.

"I tried, but his wife told me he wasn't home, and she didn't know where he was."

"I learned that Matherne's already been sent to Costa Rica," I informed her. "I also learned that he has some connection with Deslatte, I think through Matherne's father. I figure Deslatte, and maybe Matherne, must have had some stock to sell off before the inundation, too. That seems to be the modus operandi of these thugs. Money before human life. So, they're both implicated in the inundation and the deaths. Looks to me like the disaster was intentional, Ethel."

"My God! Intentional? Deslatte was already trying to get me to invest in some new venture when he spoke to me at your daddy's wake," she told me. "I let him know all the funds are tied up right now."

"I figured as much. He probably came into a hefty sum recently from a lucrative stock selloff that's burning a hole in his pocket. He'll be investing in some new scheme soon if he hasn't already.

"See if you can think of someone daring and trustworthy enough for some covert snooping that we can get hired on at Deslatte's processing plant," I continued. "Someone Father would have trusted implicitly. Besides Placide, that is... Oh, and I also need someone to come out and stay with Ethel and Louis around the clock, Monday through Friday. I can't risk having them get hurt, and Placide and I can't be here every second."

"I'll be thinking, H," she said. "Your aunt and uncle shouldn't be a problem. But finding someone Deslatte doesn't pinpoint and getting him hired might be a challenge."

"I'll come by the office after New Year's. We can talk more about it then. I just want to keep Ethel and Louis safe and out of as much of this mess as possible."

"I couldn't agree more. You're putting a lot of pressure on them both," she said. "But I understand, H. Maybe I can come up with a name or two between now and then."

Victor managed to drag himself out to the house long enough for a late morning New Year's toast. Before he took off, he cornered me. "Look, big brother, I know you're avoiding me. But we need to get together and work out the details of my company."

"Vic, I get it. I've been a little busy the last few days. If you want to talk about details, why don't you have your attorney contact Earlene? She'll put you in touch with Father's attorney, and those two can hash it out any way Father wanted it. I'll agree to whatever they work out."

There was a time I was afraid Vic had been in on the inundation plot, hoping to take over the drilling company. But the fact that Vic pissed off everyone he had dealings with made that unlikely. He was too involved in spending his daddy's money on cars, women, and gambling to have an organized plan in his head. And I was confident the billionaire class wouldn't have trusted Vic to pull off their insane plots anyway. But boy did they screw up when they trusted Matherne!

Thankfully, Vic didn't stick around long. Probably had a silicone-titted bimbo waiting at his condo to help him bring in 1981 with a bang, so to speak. At least he had the decency not to bring her to the house. He knew Ethel might have run her off if he had. Vic was in a big hurry to leave, but not without snarling, "Watch your back, redbone," on his way past Placide.

I was relieved not to have any more drop-ins, family or otherwise. I told Placide we'd be fine if he wanted to visit his family, but he said he didn't know if he had any left.

"Well, I guess you know, you have a family now," I assured him. He had been staying in the bedroom with the bath adjoining my room since Ethel got roughed up, so his stuff was already there.

At Ethel's request, she, Louis, Placide, and I met in the parlor the next morning for our late family Christmas exchange by the artificial tree that had replaced live trees after Vic and I grew up. But there was no escaping the ritual in this household, even if you missed Christmas day. I guess I wouldn't have it any other way, truth be known. It just wouldn't be home otherwise. It wouldn't be Aunt Ethel, anyway.

Ethel gave me a new wallet to replace the beat-up one she had seen me carrying and a new Day-Timer for 1981. She gave Placide some XL socks and a 3X plaid flannel shirt. He beamed at both our gifts, particularly the envelope stuffed with money I handed him. All we had to suffer through yet was the traditional New Year's dinner for good luck in the coming year. Clearly, we hadn't eaten enough black-eyed peas last New Year's.

Aunt Ethel carted her new mixing bowls to the kitchen. Uncle Louis put on his new ball cap and sweatshirt, pulled on a jacket, and escaped to the yard for a smoke break, described instead as "a look around the back forty," while he waited for the Orange Bowl to come on. I followed Ethel to see if I could help in the kitchen. She had me dice some peppers, celery, and onions, the Holy Trinity, probably the only task she trusted me not to screw up.

"Aitchie, I don't know what kind of business you've got yourself mixed up in, but you're putting us all in danger, hear?" she scolded as she seasoned the large pot of black-eyed peas.

"Aunt Ethel, I can't begin to tell you how sorry I am about all this," I said, my eyes watering from the onions. "I'm just trying to clear your brother's name. I never believed he committed suicide, and every threat we get convinces me more."

"Yes, but Aitchie, you need to let the police do their job. Those men scared the devil out of me and Louis. And your Uncle Louis's heart ain't all that strong. Do you have any idea how awful he felt, watching them hoodlums push me around, and him not able to do anything?"

"I feel awful about that, too. But don't you see, Ethel? The cops aren't doing a thing. In fact, they've already closed the case on Father's so-called suicide. I promise to make sure no one ever hurts you again. But don't you think we owe it to Father to continue his fight? Wouldn't he do the same for us?"

"I hate when you put it that way, 'Tee. You're a hard man to argue with, just like your daddy. But I'm worried about you. Plus, I sure don't want to see your uncle have a heart attack over this. Wouldn't losing him defeat your purpose?"

"I couldn't agree more, Ethel. In fact, Earlene is finding someone to come out here and stay with you and Louis around the clock, so you don't have to worry about anyone ever hurting you again. We're not going to let you stay alone out here for now."

"I don't want some stranger here, Aitchie," she

whined, shaking her head miserably as she slid the onions I'd cut into a frying pan.

"I'm sure it won't be for too long. I'm getting really close, Ethel, so I'm hoping this will all be a bad memory soon. Just try to think of it as one of the hired hands you used to have around all the time," I said, trying to reassure her. "It will give you someone else to feed all that food you whip up before dawn every morning." I attempted a laugh, but it fell flat. "And, whoever it is, I'm sure he wouldn't mind giving Louis a hand out back when there are chores. Try to think of it like that. Louis could use some help with this old place, Lord knows. I'd never forgive myself if anything happened to you or Louis." I opted not to tell her about all the deaths I already felt responsible for.

Ethel remained sullen the rest of the day, but she served up her traditional southern New Year's dinner: ham, black-eyed peas, cabbage, corn bread dressing, all the fixin's necessary for a lucky 1981. She had set a place for Vic, in case he returned, but of course, he never arrived. She finished saying grace with "...And Dear Lord, please let Aitchie finish with whatever he's got himself into before anybody else gets hurt. In Jesus's name, Amen," and Louis chimed in, "OK, dig in, everyone." Then the four of us stuffed ourselves to oblivion in relative silence. After dinner, three of us planted ourselves in front of the TV for the Orange Bowl. After LSU's loss to Florida State earlier that year, Louis felt vindicated when Watts's pass to Valora for a two-point conversion gave Oklahoma its one-point victory over Florida in the last minute of the game. It was good to see Louis smiling again, even though Ethel had chosen not to join us in front of the TV.

Chapter 17
TAKIN' CARE OF BUSINESS

"Sid Ardoin might be willing to help y'all with Deslatte," Earlene told me when I got to the office Monday morning. "He's one of our best derrickmen. Know him, H?"

"Name rings a bell. I think I met him at the wake. Can we trust him?"

"Your daddy did. Sid was in charge of the night shift mud operation the night of the inundation. Stuck with it till the end. He doesn't have much use for Victor, but I guess that's no flaw," she said.

"Can't fault the guy for that. What's his beef with Vic?"

"It seems Vic got a little frisky with Sid's wife at the honky-tonk. Sid pushed him around a little. Upset your daddy at first, until he found out why. Then he just tried to hush it up...like every other scrape that boy got himself into."

"Sounds like Father. Sounds like Vic, too, I guess. Well, I can't hold it against Sid. Go ahead and get in touch with him."

"Done. I already called him this morning. He's been working in one of our jobs offshore since the inundation, but he got home for New Year's. In fact, he's on his way over here as we speak."

"You're a jewel, Earlene!" I said, grabbing her shoulders impetuously and giving her a peck on the cheek. "No wonder Father was crazy about you."

"Goodness, H. Aren't you the frisky one this morning?" she said, giggling.

"How about Ethel and Louis?" I continued. "Find anyone to stay out there?"

"I took care of that, too. Eric Arcenaux is passing by Ethel's this morning." She looked at her watch. "In fact, he should be there by now. I called Ethel to set it up, so she's expecting him. I'm sure she'll like him once she gets to know him. He was a mechanic on the rig. Good friends with Sid. In fact, Sid recommended I contact Eric. Real polite fella, and always cheerful, but scrappy enough no one's going to mess with him. He said he'd be glad to help Louis with his chores while he's there, too, to keep himself busy."

"Fantastic! I think I met him at the wake, too. How'd Ethel take it?" I asked.

"She griped some, but I think she's OK with it now that I explained it. Lord knows, they have enough rooms out there. It's not like he'll be underfoot. I just told her to have Louis put him to work because he'd rather be busy than sitting around. That perked her up some."

Ten minutes later, I led Sid past the glass cubicles, where a few curious heads popped up, some calling "Hey" to Sid as we passed. I took him to the conference room at the end of the hall. I recognized him right away as the man leaving Morton's office on one of my visits to MSHA. About a foot shorter than I, he looked uncomfortable wearing a sports shirt and slacks instead of coveralls, his muscular thighs and upper arms like pot roasts, nearly splitting the seams, his gait and demeanor reminded me of a man with a Napoleon complex, his face like beef jerky from years in the sun. He looked like he'd be able to hold his own, all right.

"We spoke at Father's wake, didn't we?" I asked, gesturing him to a chair at the conference table and taking the chair next to him.

"Yes sir, we spoke. Surprised I didn't meet you before that."

"Afraid I haven't been around much the last few years," I said. "I believe I saw you at Mr. Morton's office, too. What brought you there, if you don't mind my asking?"

"Morton was askin' me about that night of the inundation. Questioned all us guys individually, leastways the ones that hasn't scattered. I just figured he wanted to see if our stories matched up. Told him the truth, that's all I could do. Never heard nothin' about what come of it, though."

"No, I don't really expect any of us will," I said. "But at least it sounds like he's investigating. I have my doubts about him, though. Anyway, Sid, Earlene tells me my father trusted you, and he didn't dole trust out wholesale."

"Thank you, sir. I did my best. I liked your daddy, too. He was a fair man. Hard-nosed, but fair. *Yie, yie*, I hated to hear what happened to him. Damn shame," he said, looking down at his lap. "I'm awful sorry."

"Thanks, Sid. Yeah, hard-nosed is no lie. Listen, Sid. The reason we called you here today, I'm asking you to go way out on a limb to try to clear Father's name. Might be a way you can avenge your buddies' deaths, too."

"What's the deal?"

"I can't lie to you, it's a big job and it's dangerous. But there's a respectable bonus and a promotion in it if you agree to it." I kept my eyes on him for a reaction.

When he nodded, I went on to explain the plan I'd concocted. Sid's job was to get himself hired by Deslatte, see what dirt he could find out about the operation with a little low-level snooping. "You'll be jumping into the middle of a hornet's nest," I warned him. No sense mincing words, I thought. "I'd have done it myself, but Doucet is a dirty word in some circles."

"Major Doucet, I should tell you, I had a little run-in with your brother once."

"Yeah, I know all about that. Had a few run-ins with Victor myself over the years. But that could actually help you get your foot in the door. If Deslatte thinks you can't take it with Vic anymore, now that Father's gone, I figure he'll jump at the chance to get you away from Doucet Drilling. If you're willing, why don't you bring your résumé by here tomorrow? We'll get Earlene to update it a little and shoot it off to Deslatte.

"I need to make sure you understand what I'm saying here," I continued. "There are people out there hell-bent on making sausage meat out of me. Understand? And I know for a fact they won't stop at anyone else who gets in their way."

"Yes, sir. I get it."

"If one word leaks out that I put you up to this, ...well, your life will be in at least as much danger as mine. You've got to let everyone there think the same thing—that you've had enough of Victor Doucet and you need to get away from Doucet Drilling before your beef with him escalates. Think you can do that?"

"No problem. I owe it to the guys we lost out there. Besides, I've got nine lives."

He sounded as feisty as he looked, a positive sign. "That's good. Just don't get complacent about those nine lives." I felt redundant, but I didn't want to be responsible for any more loss of life.

I sat back down for a minute or two after he left to think things through. It occurred to me that, like Father, I was beginning to add people to my own inner circle. Had to be, I reasoned. And I felt good about Sid. I just hoped he didn't end up dead.

When Placide and I drove over the levee at Henderson swamp later that afternoon to move out of our temporary digs, Placide noticed from a distance that some of the chairs on his aft deck had been overturned and a window was broken. He backed down off the levee and parked on the backside. "Wait here, H," he said, pulling his snubnose .38 out of his ankle holster. He reached under the seat and tossed a .45 Ruger across the floorboards to me. "I don't expect you're packin' your heat." He was right.

"You got an arsenal under there?" I asked. He didn't respond but slid out from behind the wheel and was over the levee like a shot.

I untucked my shirt and stuck the .45 in my belt. I jogged about 20 feet farther down the levee, sidled down to the *batture*, and crept across to the cypress tree closest to my boat. I could see that the glass in my cabin door had also been broken, but when I slinked aboard and peered in the window, I didn't see anyone inside. I slipped in the door and had a look around. The place was a mess. Cabinets were trashed, files were scattered, clothes were strewn everywhere, but whoever had been there was gone. Luckily, my .44 was locked safely in my briefcase at Aunt Ethel's.

I went back out on the dock in time to see Placide sucker punch some skinny-ass punk on his aft deck. A second wiry little shit with a durag tied around his head jumped on Placide from behind and straddled him like a bull. Placide spun around like King Kong, grabbing both the guy's arms that were wrapped around his neck and slamming him backwards onto the deck floor.

I ran down the dock and onto the boat just as the first guy got his bearings and came up swinging, but he was no match for Placide. Meanwhile, I came up behind the guy on his back, struggling to get up. I poked the .45 in the back of his head. "Don't even try," I said. He sneered up at me and sat back down.

Placide yanked the other one up and stuck the .38 in his temple. "Sit," I told them both, nodding toward the overturned deck chairs.

They looked to me like common punks, coke heads probably, glaring at us through hate-filled eyes. They both had stringy brown hair to their shoulders, tattoos from their wrists all the way up both arms, and an attitude as long as their hair. They smelled of marijuana and sweat. They picked up two of the deck chairs, and glared ferociously at me as they sat down, arms folded defiantly across their guts. "Who are you assholes working for?" I asked them.

"We don't work for no one," the skinnier of the two said, the one with the durag tied around his forehead. "We just saw no one was comin' around here for a few days..."

"So, you cased the joint and thought you'd help yourselves," I said. "Sweet. And you chose our two boats to ransack why?"

Meanwhile, a Henderson police car with flashing red lights and sirens came up over the levee. 'Tee Jack must have seen all the excitement and called them. "We caught this swamp scum after they broke into both our boats," I told the boys in blue while they looked at my fake I.D. "Don't know if they've hit any other boats. Looks like they may have just hit ours."

"Now why on God's earth would you think they'd target you guys in particular?" the barrel-chested sergeant with a face that looked like raw hamburger asked while the other cop was cuffing the guys and hauling them to the car.

"No reason I can think of, sir," I said, innocent as a child.

"Look, I recognize you, Doucet. I don't know what you're pulling with the alias. I'm a busy man, so I'm going to look the other way this time, just as long as you get your asses on back to New Iberia, or wherever you belong. We don't want no trouble here in Henderson."

"Yes, sir, thank you, sir. We already planned to leave. We'll get out of Henderson within the hour," I assured him. Our hideout was busted wide open now anyway.

After the pigs filled out their report, they hauled the two thugs away for questioning and probably a day or two in the slammer and a slap on the wrist.

'Tee Jack came down the levee to where Placide and I stood. He had been watching from a distance after his phone call. "Be damned," he said as the cops drove off, lifting his ball cap to scratch his head, then setting it farther back on his crown. "I don't like to see no trouble down here, me. Nothin' like this ever happened here before."

"Common teenage cokeheads, I'm guessing, just looking for a little drug money," I lied. They might've been junkies, but I figured they were probably hired by some of the upper crust scum we were shaking out of the woodwork. "I hope this and our deposits cover the damage," I said, pulling out a few Jacksons that I figured would soften the blow and more than cover the windows they broke to get in. "We've both been gone for several days. They said they were eyeing the place while we were away. Has anyone come around asking a lot of questions?"

"Matter of fact, my wife did mention a couple of strangers in business suits asking a bunch of questions the other day about a guy named Doucet and a giant redbone. She told them she didn't know nobody by that name or that description. Told me she just didn't trust those guys."

"Well, don't worry, we won't cause you any more trouble," I assured him, hoping to avoid further explanation. I thanked him, then headed back to my boat to pack and load up all the stuff I'd accumulated as Placide turned to start packing his gear.

An icy breeze was stirring up the cove, swaying the docked boats as I stepped aboard. A lonely egret flapped its wings and lifted away to find more privacy. I started packing, throwing some of my food and equipment into a box and some grocery bags I'd saved. We could drop them off at the homeless shelter. I'd take the coffee, Tony Chachere's and olive oil, and a few other things to Ethel's house, see if she could use any of it. I was going to miss the swamp, I thought, with one last backward glance as we drove over the levee for the last time. My only peace since I'd been back in Louisiana had been anchored somewhere out in a cypress grove with a fishing line in the water.

Aunt Ethel looked stunned when we hauled our stash into the kitchen that afternoon. She was not one to eat anything out of a can unless she did the canning herself. But, like all depression survivors, I knew she was even less someone to waste food, so, as I predicted, she said she'd find a way to "use up" the canned peaches and green beans and tomatoes in some casseroles and cobblers. "It might come in handy since you're going to have three extra mouths to feed for a while, Placide, me, and Eric Arcenaux," I told her. That seemed to perk her up, or at least shut her up.

While Placide and I unpacked the food and helped Ethel find a place for everything in the pantry, Uncle Louis and Eric walked in the kitchen door after some bush hogging out back. Louis was still laughing about something Arcenaux had said. When Ethel asked him what was so funny, he said, "Oh, Eric's a cut-up, him. Called the inundation a Cajun Mt. St. Helens. Know why? Because instead of blowing, it sucked!" That sent Louis into a fit of laughter all over again, as Eric beamed mischievously. Looked to me as if Louis and Eric were getting along just fine. I was pretty sure Ethel wouldn't deny Louis a little pleasure, so maybe this was going to work out after all.

I remembered Arcenaux, but Placide introduced us anyway.

"Howdy, Eric. Yeah, we met at the wake," I said, giving his hand a shake.

Arcenaux was a brawny guy, solid muscle, like everyone else who had worked for Father. He looked like he could snap a small tree over his knee, bust a bull in the head with his fist to the detriment of the bull. I wouldn't want to tangle with him, that's sure.

"Looks like you can rest easy, Ethel," I joked, marveling at the size of Eric's upper arms. Though she would never have admitted it, I figured she'd like having some company around besides Louis. And I knew Louis would appreciate the brawn and the sense of humor this guy brought with him. This side of beef would make her and Louis both feel safe.

When we'd unloaded the groceries, we carried our bags upstairs. Eric followed along to show us where he'd bunked, just across the hall from the two rooms Placide and I used over New Year's. It was beginning to feel like my old college dorm days up there, but without toga parties or beer bashes in the offing.

"So far, it's been quiet, quiet," Arcenaux told us after we dumped our bags and met back in the wide upstairs hallway.

"Beats hell out of the alternative," I said. "How are you getting along with Ethel and Louis?"

"Oh, we're doin' fine. Louis put me to work out back soon as I got here, so he'll keep me busy out there. And Miss Ethel cooked up some powerful gumbo for lunch. I even got a giggle out of her. Hell, it's a nice little break from offshore for me, too."

"Great. If you can make Ethel smile once in a while, you'll be her best pal." I filled him in on some of our earlier excitement at the dock. "So, we'll be staying out here too, now. We'll be able to relieve you on weekends."

After dinner, the three of us pulled together a penny-ante game in the upstairs hall with Placide's Elvis cards. Uncle Louis probably would have enjoyed it, but we didn't dare invite him. Aunt Ethel would have sworn I'd "be the death" of her if she'd caught wind of it.

"By the way, what do you know about Dallas Matherne?" I asked him while Placide dealt. His smile faded.

"We were all pissed off when he called in sick and left us short-handed. Big-time gambler, Matherne. He'd lose his shirt then come crawlin' to the guys with his tail between his legs when his rent come due. I fell for it early on. Never got paid back, though, so I didn't make that mistake again. I don't think none of the other guys did either. Old man Doucet didn't think much of him either. Just a matter of time before he was history, I reckon."

"That's just about what I suspected," I said.

"If it hadn't been for Matherne, the day shift guys might be on the right side of the dirt today," Eric said. "I had no use for the guy, myself. I doubt if anyone else does either, especially after that stunt. I'd be glad to testify against him if it comes to that. I'm pretty sure Sid Ardoin would too, and some of the others."

He was still pretty shaken up, so I didn't want to pressure him on the subject. And I suspected a sizable gambling debt and a penchant for the ladies would have made Matherne an obvious choice for some con men with unlimited funds and a load of dirty work to get done.

The next morning, the three of us helped Uncle Louis mend the old fence out near where I'd helped Louis dig that post hole.

Arcenaux kept Louis laughing with his Cajun jokes. "One time ole Boudreaux and Thibodeaux went duck hunting in Boudreaux's *bateau*," he said. "Boudreaux brought his retriever along, and when Boudreaux shot a duck, he sent that dog after it. But that ole dog walked right on top of the water, trip, trip trip, picked up that duck, and walked back to the boat, trip, trip, trip. Surprised, ole Thibodeaux said, 'Boudreaux, yer dog can walk on water?!' Boudreaux replied, '*Mais oui,* and I can't tell you how embarrass' I am. I never could taught that dog how to swim."

We all had a good laugh; then Louis joined right in with a few of his own corny jokes, looking younger than I'd seen him this trip.

After we finished in "the back forty," I sent Arcenaux home to visit his family for a day or two since Placide and I were stuck twiddling our thumbs at Ethel's for now, waiting to see what Sid Ardoin could come up with.

We didn't have to wait long. As I suspected, Deslatte jumped at the chance to hire someone away from Doucet Drilling. Sid had convinced Deslatte he couldn't work for Doucet with Vic at the helm. It was an easy sell.

Deslatte hired Sid as an operator trainee on the night shift, in good stead to access all units since he would eventually have to learn the ropes in each. No stranger to working nights, he knew those guys notoriously slept or drummed up a poker game. He told Earlene, "I'll have *beaucoup de temps* to get the goods once I get through a short training period."

I knew they'd stalk him like a Cooper's hawk over a field mouse, at least until Deslatte was sure Sid could be trusted. We assumed they'd bug his phone, so we added a few new lines to the code Placide and I used. He would call his wife Louisa in New Iberia, always from a payphone, routinely on Wednesday afternoon at 1500 hours, or any other time, of course, if he had an emergency. "I might be a little late Saturday morning," meant, "Have H meet me at Maybelle's at noon Saturday." In the event of an emergency, "I'll run by the Farmers' Market on the way home," meant, "I need H to get down here ASAP." Our designated rendezvous place in Patterson was J & R's Seafood on Main Street. His only other options in an immediate emergency were either to get the hell out of Dodge STAT and call when he was safe or to call 911. Now it was just a waiting game.

~

I called Candace Soileau at her boyfriend's house on schedule that Sunday. "I'm glad you called. I may have something," she said. "Can you meet me on my lunch hour tomorrow?" I agreed to meet her at Nino's in a strip mall in Baton Rouge at noon.

She walked in just after 1200 hours, blue eyes peering out from under a spiky fringe of blonde bangs. She looked like an oblivious teenager with her tousled, clipped hair until she matter-of-factly set several pages of information from her briefcase onto the white tablecloth of our small corner table. "I made these copies, so they're yours," she said quietly. "I think you'll find this information useful." A gross understatement. Among other things, she had somehow managed to get her hands on a list of Louisiana's latest major stockholders in Calco.

When the waiter brought our pasta dishes, Candace scooped the pages up out of his way, but not before I had learned that none other than Governor Mansur and Secretary of the Treasury Huff were among the major stockholders in Calco Oil. The Haggerty brothers, Armstrong, and Deslatte, also appeared high on the list. They had all been major stockholders in Sapphire Salt, too, until they sold out before the inundation. Calco Oil was the largest company contracted with Deslatte Shale Processors. DNR was monitoring Deslatte's operations, but with Governor Mansur's help and Joseph Haggerty's conflict of interest, all the reports were coming back squeaky clean.

My guess was that Father had found out they had sold Sapphire stock and replaced it with Calco stock, and he was trying to let Gremillion know. Or maybe it was the other way around. No way to tell since both Father and Gremillion had met their maker at the hands of these thugs. And if the authorities had found any evidence to that effect in either Father's or Gremillion's files, they must have confiscated or destroyed it and vowed to eliminate anyone who got wind of it. The politicians were all in collusion, every last one of them, up to and including DNR, the governor, and the White House.

"How did you get your hands on this?" I asked in disbelief.

"Mr. Haggerty asked me to find everything I could

related to the inundation. I expect he's building his defense. I'm sure he never dreamed I'd find all this or know what it meant if I did find it.

"This might be useful, too," she added, pulling out a file folder of copied letters with Carl Haggerty's name on the letterhead of a powerful D.C. law firm, proving Carl, Joseph Haggerty's brother, was the D.C. lobbyist and fixer. If a hedge fund needed insider information, Carl Haggerty was the one to ferret it out. Carl had a hell of a lot of clout in D.C. and a hell of a lot of interest in shutting down investigation of the inundation.

"Look, Candace, I hate to tell you, but this information puts you in grave danger if Haggerty ever gets wind you found it and passed it along. I'd better not contact you anymore. Here are my numbers, in case you need to contact me." It was essential that Haggerty didn't know I had possession of enough evidence to put him away for a long time, and more essential that he didn't find out who ratted him out.

As she was leaving, I urged Candace to seriously consider resigning. "In fact, I'll put in a good word with Earlene at Doucet. I'm afraid it's too risky for you to stay on with Haggerty now."

"I'll think about it," she said.

"Think hard! You're in danger." I let her leave a few minutes ahead of me. I didn't want anyone to make the connection, especially after this bombshell.

I had a crapload of information now on payoffs, insider trading, corruption, and fraud, but I still couldn't definitively tie anyone to the inundation or to Father's death. Or to at least two other deaths and a couple of failed attempts so far on my life. Not conclusively, anyway, and I knew any other way would just get me an escort to the curb. Still just circumstantial.

They could extradite Matherne if they believed me, but I had no doubt that the state and local officials were on the dole, too, most likely taking campaign funds or public works dollars for hush money at the very least. Had to be, or this thing would have busted open long ago, possibly years ago. Father might even still be alive. It was time to talk to Earlene, see what she'd learned from our attorneys, and also have her try to locate Dallas Matherne's wife, even though I knew that might wake a sleeping giant. I called from a payphone before I left the little strip mall.

"I tried to contact Mrs. Matherne again yesterday, but that number's no longer in service," Earlene said. "Matherne worked closely on the night shift with Ted Romero, so I called him. His wife directed me to Sarah Beth Matherne's parents, where Sarah Beth's been staying since shortly after Dallas's disappearance. I made you an appointment with her for tomorrow morning, 9:00, here at the office," she said.

"Super. How did you get her to agree?"

"I just told her you had some news on Dallas to share. So, I hope you have some token to give her."

"I'll have a token, all right. Also, Earlene, I've got some more research for you to do. See what you can find out about Warren Armstrong's dealings with Ideal Tractor and Sapphire Salt. I'm suspecting there's some insider trading, at the very least. Also, see what you can find out about Joseph Haggerty at DNR and his brother Carl Haggerty. Carl is a lawyer and lobbyist in DC. They're all implicated."

I got to the office early the next morning and helped myself to some joe in the break room. A few minutes after 0900 hours, Earlene informed me Sarah Beth Matherne was waiting in the conference room.

"I'm Major Doucet. Thank you for coming," I said when I entered.

She bristled immediately. "I want to know where my husband is, Major Doucet."

"Whoa, Ma'am. Believe me, I'm not involved. All I can tell you is that he is out of the country under a new identity. But it was none of my doing. I'm afraid I don't know any more than that. I just happened to learn about it while I was investigating my father's death. I have no idea where he's been sent," I said, only fibbing slightly. "My investigation has put my life in danger, so, I've got to ask you to please not alert anyone that we spoke."

"Wasn't your father's death a suicide?"

"I have every reason to believe it was murder."

"Murder! Major Doucet, my husband was not involved in no murder, I can tell you that!"

"Not directly, I realize. Possibly indirectly."

"No way. Not Dallas."

"Mrs. Matherne, I didn't come here to accuse him of anything. I came here mainly to warn you that you might be in danger. These men your husband was working for are ruthless, and anyone who slows them down tends to end up in the obit column. If you hear from Dallas, you need to do whatever he says and not make waves, for your own safety and for his. If Dallas follows orders and you don't cause a scene, there's no reason to believe they won't keep their word to reunite you two and give you a new identity. That is, if you want that."

"A new identity?" she asked, a shocked look on her face. "Right now, I don't know what I want," she said, pulling her lips into a tight frown as tears started to form in her eyes. "This is all a terrible shock. I didn't have no idea Dallas was mixed up in something dangerous."

"He hadn't acted at all strange lately?" I asked.

"Well...," she thought a few seconds, her eyes aimed up and to the left, before she continued. "I just figured work was getting to him. Put a strain on our marriage, him stressed out all the time and taking it out on me."

"What I need to tell you isn't easy, and it isn't pretty, but I think, as Dallas's wife, you have a right to know some things that no one has bothered to let you in on. Bear with me," I said, then began my story, leaving out the goriest details leading up to where we sat this morning.

"You see, Mrs. Matherne," I added by way of summing up, "I have reason to believe that it was your husband's job to make sure the inundation occurred, with the promise of a large bonus. Unfortunately, if he ever shows his face in the U.S., he could be indicted, even if the brains of the conspiracy get off scot-free. I'm not sure if he was blackmailed or acted out of desperation. But either way, he was just a disposable pawn in the scheme, whether he knew it or not.

"But the main reason I'm here is to ask you a few questions. And if you're willing to help me get the brains of the scheme, I'll do everything I can to reunite you and your husband. The alternative is, they get off scot-free and you may never see Dallas again. So, I sincerely hope you'll try to help me. It would help us both."

She dabbed at her cheeks and eyes with a napkin. "OK, I'll try," she agreed. "But I really don't know anything about what Dallas was doing or why he even decided to come back to Louisiana. We were doing fine up there in Tennessee, where I'm from. I never wanted to come down here, but Dallas just had to have this job, for some reason I never understood. But then he got a nice raise, so that kept us here. My folks even followed us down here after my daddy retired, but they don't want to be here either. They've been talking about moving me back up to Tennessee with them."

"That sounds like a good idea, considering the danger you're in here," I said. "Look, I'm trying to find out about a map. Your husband came to the rig about the same time Calco Oil merged with Aloco Oil. Mysteriously, that's the same time a new geological map showed up. The map came from DNR, and I believe it was a fake and that Dallas was responsible for making sure Calco followed it. All the Aloco people were replaced by Calco people, and my father's drilling company was contracted to take over drill operations. Dallas was a mole in Doucet Drilling, I'm pretty sure, placed there to make sure the new map was followed. His so-called 'raise' was more likely a payoff by a third party. I've sifted through his employment records, and Father never gave him any raise. Unfortunately, the bogus map they introduced led to drilling directly into the salt mine. I believe that was the intended outcome and that Dallas knew it and made sure it came off as planned."

"I don't believe Dallas could have done anything like that!" she exclaimed. "He had his faults, but he wasn't a crook! Anyway, that merger was a long time ago, two, three years."

"I've heard Dallas had some gambling debts." Might as well spit it out, I thought. "If a man is desperate enough, sometimes he'll resort to behavior completely out of character to get his neck out of a jam. But if he was feeling some guilt about what he was doing, it might have been the reason he called in sick the night the rig went down. Or he might just have wanted to save himself from drowning like the others. Try to think back. Remember anything at all? If he was blackmailed, even the least significant sounding detail could help exonerate him." Personally, I had not an ounce of sympathy for the scumbag, but I didn't want Mrs. Matherne to know that.

She let out a long sigh that gave me hope she was ready to open up. "Well, Dallas had to travel to Baton Rouge on business one time when we first moved down here. Seemed nervous about the trip. He never told me what it was all about. Came back here all secretive and kept his briefcase locked. Before that, he didn't hide anything from me. After that, he jumped on me for the least little thing. If I asked what was wrong, we'd get in a fight. I accused him of having an affair, even threatened to divorce him. That's what my daddy hoped for. He never had no use for Dallas, and especially after Dallas dragged me down here to Louisiana. That and the fact Daddy told me he knew Dallas was a big flirt. He caught him flirting with some girl in a bar one night when we still lived in Tennessee."

"I couldn't say whether he's having an affair or not, Mrs. Matherne. But he did know the danger of what he was doing, and the danger to you as well. My question is whether he was blackmailed. Either way, he was hired to do the dirty work so the big guns could keep their noses clean and reap the serious profits. Whatever they gave Dallas was probably a pittance in comparison. But I'm pretty sure he could clear his name if he'd agree to turn state's witness and cooperate. You might put that bug in his ear if you happen to hear from him. Just so you don't tell him where you got the idea. Do you recall anything anyone might have had on your husband? Any shady past dealings? Anything that could be used to blackmail him?"

"Not unless he had an affair. I know he had started gambling again, but I never thought it was serious!" she added.

"I'm afraid his gambling got a little more serious than he let on to you. Anyway, if he can prove he was blackmailed, his chances in court are fairly good. I'd like to bring down the brains of the outfit, though, and Dallas might be able to help do that." I decided to dig deeper. "Do you remember anything else he did that seemed suspicious to you?"

"Only that he bought a bunch of stock in Sapphire Salt before we moved here. We had to take out a loan to do it. I was afraid, but he told me he got a tip on it. It went up just like he said it would. He sold it for a bundle right before the inundation. That's what I'm living on now. I thought he was mighty lucky to sell it then!"

"I'm afraid it wasn't luck," I said, my suspicions confirmed.

"This can't be happening," she said. "He must have been blackmailed." She kept her voice lowered, but I could tell she was running out of patience.

"I'm sorry to be the one to break this to you," I said. Poor guy probably got himself roped into something bigger than he realized, and with a load of gambling debts, a deal with the devil would have been a tempting option. "I'd like you to contact me if you happen to hear anything from him or about him, OK?" I wrote Earlene's and my aunt's numbers on my notepad. "Tell him I might be able to help him if he'd call me. And seriously, I'd consider moving back to Tennessee! You'd be much safer there than here, I have no doubt, at least until this is settled. And promise me this conversation is just between us. In return, I'll do everything in my power to clear Dallas's name, or at least get him off light. He wasn't the brains behind it, that's sure. Just a pawn trying to make a little money to keep his head above water after he got too deep in debt." I thought he might have to go into the witness protection program if he turned state's evidence, but I decided not to drop that bombshell.

"OK, Major Doucet, I promise," she agreed, appealing to me with her eyes. "I'm counting on you to help him."

"I'll do the best I can. Try to get him to call me."

"Thank you, Major Doucet," she said weakly, rising to leave.

Chapter 18
SHOWDOWN

After Sarah Beth Matherne left, Earlene stepped in the conference room. "I've got some good news, H."

"High time for some good news! Lay it on me."

She took a seat opposite me. "Our attorneys' FOIA request was a success, H. We've discovered that Armstrong owns a hedge fund, and Huff is on the board."

"Jesus, Earlene."

"Oh, it gets much worse than that. The hedge fund purchased Ideal Tractor, after its bankruptcy when the price was low. Sapphire Salt was a different story. Their production was down, too, but Huff had hired Wheless Engineering and Consulting to estimate their salt mining reserves before he got his cabinet position. They discovered that the salt cavern had been mined too close to the outer edge of the dome, Probably thanks to Huff's time as CEO, leaving only a thin wall of salt between the cavity and the surrounding rock and dirt. The consultants predicted the salt mine would have collapsed anyway, probably within a few months. So, when Armstrong took over, he and Huff took an ax to both companies' operating expenses, rewarding investors in their own hedge fund rather than investing in either company."

"My God. It's no wonder they're willing to commit murder to keep this story from leaking," I said.

"Together, they loaded Sapphire Salt with large amounts of debt, laid off dozens of employees. Then, using false accounting reports, they sold company holdings and put the profits in an investment trust, which Armstrong's hedge fund owns, of course."

"No wonder they wanted to sabotage the salt mine. With no compunction about losing lives, apparently."

"There's more: Our attorneys have discovered that under Huff and Armstrong, Sapphire has loaded the investment trust with millions in rent, further enriching investors. Then, Sapphire transferred pension responsibility to the federal Pension Benefit Guaranty Corporation, the PBGC. And get this, H! As 'coincidence' would have it, Treasury Secretary Huff is on the Board of Directors overseeing the PBGC. As a board member, Huff would have participated in decisions regarding underfunding both Sapphire's and Ideal's pension programs. They've managed to steal much or all of the pensions from all the guys they laid off and all the families of the casualties."

"Good Lord! This is unbelievable! Greed has no limit."

"Exactly. And all the billionaires involved sold off their stock and collected their millions before orchestrating the failure. So not only did they strip employees of their pensions, they left employees with huge losses on their stocks. Sapphire's creditors are now accusing Secretary

Huff of assisting Armstrong in transferring millions of company assets to the major stockholders."

"Of course."

"Hopefully, we can include Deslatte, the Haggerty brothers, Gov. Mansur, along with Armstrong and Secretary Huff, and any other wealthy investor who profited from the scheme."

"You've outdone yourself again, Earlene. I don't even know what to say, besides thanks."

"No thanks needed, H. Your daddy always had the best attorneys money could buy. And your investigation convinced them to keep digging. We'll all be happy if we can nab these rich murdering bastards."

Those were words that I knew for a fact had never come out of Earlene's mouth before.

I hadn't had time to digest all that info yet when I got a call at Aunt Ethel's that afternoon from Louisa Ardoin, Sid's wife. "Major Doucet, Sid plans to stop by the Farmers' Market in Patterson on the way home," she said. That was our code for "You need to get down here right away," so Placide and I wasted no time.

When we got as far as Centerville, I rang Sid's apartment from a payphone. "Fifteen minutes," I told him.

Sid was already drinking a Coke at a corner table when we arrived. When I joined him, he handed me a manila folder, thick with copied documents. "My man!" I marveled, leafing through the stack of a dozen or more pages. "How the hell did you get all this so fast?"

"Made friends with one of the janitors, ole Landrieu from Crowley, my hometown. You put a couple ole Cajuns together, you won't get no shortage of bullshit. While he was talking one night about how things ain't the same back home, I watched him punch the code in at Deslatte's private office. I'm pretty good with numbers, me, so I remembered 'em. Had pretty free access after that. Then I just had to copy these and return the originals."

"Way to go, Sid," I said. "Of course, you realize Deslatte has security cameras all over that plant. You're in even more danger now that you broke into his office!"

"Oh, I didn't do nothin' until I found out where the security cameras was. I turned 'em off before I broke in, then turned 'em back on. What, you think this ole Cajun was born last night?"

"Perfect! But if they happen to check the clocks on those cameras, you're still in a lot of danger. We could have all the evidence we need right here. Can you give me a rundown?"

"That whole operation down here is a sham," Sid said. "Didn't take me long to figure that out. Supposed to be recycling, but I smelled a rat right away, and I do mean smelled. At night's when they start their dirty work. There's a whole team comes in and the valves are opened wide, the incinerators are cranked up balls to the wall, and out blows more smoke than St. Helens. They're real sneaky about it, too. Wear white lab coats and call themselves safety inspectors. They're breakin' more EPA regulations than some whole states combined. And Deslatte uses his 'recycling services' in trade to pay off his biggest suppliers when someone starts puttin' the heat on him for past due accounts."

"Sounds about right," I said, leafing through the pages.

"Yeah. That name 'Deslatte Shale Processors and Recycling' just covers up Deslatte's hazardous waste disposal business," he continued.

"I've heard about that. Did you get any details?"

"Yeah. After he runs the waste through a 'filtering press' to 'process' it, he claims he recycles the resulting product into cement, but there ain't much cement coming out of there. A few pallets here and there for show. He's burning off what he can at night and piling up what's left of the waste in a huge toxic sludge pit way out back, behind a wall, and far away from the plant.

"Ole Landrieu told me about a camera set up on the bridge over Highway 90 monitoring traffic so Deslatte'll know when the EPA is about to show up at the gate," he continued. "Of course, all the higher-ups are gettin' kickbacks to use the facility, so the governor turns a blind eye. Or he might even be in on it. Deslatte's charging refineries fifty bucks a barrel, supposedly to process their waste in that filtering press, but it don't get filtered, and it just ends up in the pit."

"How did you ever manage to get all this information?"

"Learned a lot of that by listening to Landrieu and some other ole fellas during our breaks. Everybody down here knows what's goin' on, and they ain't shy about talking about it, leastways when the bosses ain't around. Landrieu's been there fifteen years, and he tells it like it is. Knows the operation like the back of his hand. Pay's good and he's too old to go back on the rigs, he says. He showed me the sludge pit, and then I found this proof in Deslatte's files." Sid pulled out a document with lists of chemicals that had supposedly been "recycled."

It looked like Deslatte's record-keeping was going to backfire on him, because now we had the evidence we needed.

"Of course, I don't know what all them numbers mean," Sid continued, "but I thought some of it might be useful. There's copies of some letters in there, too. Looks like Deslatte bought Calco Oil stock low, before the Aloco merger, then sold high before the I-ran revolution caused the market to crash in '79. After the crash, employees with stock options lost their ass. See? It's all in here. There's copies of letters advising some powerful folks when to sell. Look at them names! Deslatte and Armstrong, they're in cahoots. And I'm guessing they ain't alone. Deslatte bragged about the pile of money he made selling his Sapphire stock right before the inundation. He invested all that money into Armstrong's hedge fund. See here?"

"Yep. Same thing the rest of them have done," I said. "My question now is, was Dallas Matherne a player or a pawn? He and a bunch of upper administration muckety mucks all profited on stock sales the same way as Deslatte. Did you see his name anywhere?"

"Don't know nothin' about Matherne," Ardoin said, "but if he was a pawn, someone must have told him when to sell. I sure didn't know when to sell my few shares. Took a bath, me."

"A lot of folks did," I said. "Anybody who wasn't aware of the planned inundation. I also need to find out who those two goons are in the black Blazer. They tried to flip my car once and ran a DNR guy right off the Atchafalaya Bridge. I figure they're the same ones who killed Father, or more likely, paid some cheap hitmen to do it for 'em. I'm guessing they're with the federal government in some capacity. But I need evidence."

"Any sign of them two lately?"

"Within the last week or so. Placide said he's spotted them stalking us, but they know from past experience what a marksman Placide is, so they haven't dared mess with us, yet anyway. I don't go anywhere without Placide," I said. "If they know I'm here talking to you right now, they'll start keeping tabs on you, too, if they haven't already. Or if they ever figure out that someone broke into Deslatte's office. Just stay below the radar, Sid. But for now, you need to pack up and get your ass back up to New Iberia, right away. Do not pass Go."

"I know how to watch my back, me," he said.

"Just don't get overconfident. These guys lack anything resembling a conscience. Their only God is money. Human life is disposable if it gets in the way of money."

"I gotcha."

"OK, thanks for all your help, Sid. You've put some of the missing pieces in place. Looks like we've got enough evidence here to get some feds on Deslatte's case," I said, patting the envelope that I'd stuffed the reports back into. "Now you just need to concentrate on getting the hell out of there. Go back to your apartment just long enough to grab your stuff. We'll let Earlene mail them your resignation and contact your landlord. It's too risky now to even think about going back to the plant.

"Placide and I will head out in a few minutes," I said. "Just keep your eyes on the rearview from now on, even after you're back home safe. And contact Earlene as soon as you get there. I'll give her a heads up."

"Will do, H."

As it turned out, Sid didn't even have time to get to his apartment. Those two goons had either followed us or followed him to Patterson. That camera over Highway 90 might have alerted them. From his vantage point by the front window, Placide spotted the Blazer pulling out of a parking spot down the block and wedging itself in a couple of cars behind Sid as he was driving back out Bernard to 90. I would have alerted the police, but I figured the Patterson police could be in on the scam too. So Placide and I fell in several vehicles behind the Blazer.

Sure enough, a mile or two down 90, we watched as the Blazer slid up beside Ardoin's pickup and knocked it toward the shoulder. These guys weren't much on originality. But Ardoin was ready for them. He must have seen them coming. He slammed on his brakes, spun his car around behind the Blazer, and peeled out across the barrier and in the opposite direction, prompting Placide to speed up. When the Blazer tried to make its own U-turn, Placide screeched sideways in front of it to block it, hollering to me, "Hit the floor, H." Cars doing 60 slammed on their brakes, skidding to a stop behind us. Cars behind them slammed into what became a screeching, crashing pileup of twisted metal.

Shots pinged off the body of the Torino as Placide ducked his head below the dashboard, handed me the .45 from under the seat, and pulled the .38 special out of his ankle holster, then lifted his head to fire a few rounds. I poked my head up to fire off several rounds, then dropped down. Just then the window on my side shattered, blasting bits of glass into my right cheek and raining glass on my back and neck when I hunched below the dash. A bullet grazed my right shoulder in a lightning flash of searing pain. I was glad to have an ace marksman on my side, though I was in a sitting duck position, bullets pinging and whamming against the passenger door of the Torino, my shooting arm useless now.

"You got the driver, H," Placide called, ducking below the dash himself to reload. "He's slumped on the wheel." Placide rose up and shot once over my head, then ducked again. Another hail of bullets hit the passenger door. Placide rose again and took another shot, followed by yet another shower of bullets. Placide rose and fired once more. This time, silence.

We waited.

More silence.

It was over almost as quickly as it had begun, even though the firestorm had seemed endless at the time. When I heard sirens, I raised my head from under the dash, where I was busy saving my ass, and saw Placide nod his OK.

When the cops arrived, they found two men in the Blazer, the driver with one bullet hole in his temple and the passenger with one in his forehead and another one in his neck. There was no question we were being shot at. The Torino had a dozen or more bullet holes in the body, a smashed windshield, as well as the window on the passenger side where my face should have been, and two flat tires. I felt lucky to be alive. I held my right upper arm while blood ran out of the shoulder wound and drenched my shirt. More blood ran down my cheek and neck from embedded glass, so Placide took over and talked calmly to the police.

Some EMTs arrived, bandaged my shoulder, and confirmed that it was just a graze. They were able to remove several shards of glass from my face and bandage it. "Don't worry, scars shouldn't be too unsightly," one of them told me, as if he thought I needed assurance of that.

It took several hours of rerouted traffic for a handful of wreckers to drag all the twisted and mangled cars off the road. Sid, Placide, and I were all escorted downtown for a police report that took the rest of the afternoon. And what a story we had to tell.

With the information I had now, along with everything Earlene had found, I could go all the way to the top, bring down a long list of billionaire politicians and corporate execs.

Chapter 19
WHITE-COLLAR CRIME

With evidence now of corporate fraud, insider trading, and yes, even murder, I called the FBI office in Lafayette and made an appointment for the next day.

Placide and I stopped at our office before my meeting to get any further reports from Earlene. She informed me that the two guys in the Blazer were indeed rogue Secret Service agents. I knew someone had to have put them up to it. Secretary Huff's name came immediately to mind.

I loaded up all the paperwork our attorneys had provided to add to the evidence I already had. When Placide and I walked into the FBI building on Versailles, we were ushered into an interview room and introduced to a young agent named Bascomb.

"You say you have evidence of a federal crime, Major Doucet?"

"Yes sir. I'm afraid I've jumped in over my head. The crimes I've discovered go all the way to the top. And my life is currently in danger."

"By 'to the top,' how high are we talking here?"

"I'm talking about all the way to the White House, sir. I have paperwork, photos, as well as crimes I've witnessed first-hand."

"Well, Major, I'm all ears." He hit a buzzer on his phone. "I'm calling in my stenographer. I'll want to get this in writing... Ah, here she is. Come in, Margaret. This is Major Doucet."

Margaret took a seat at a small table with a stenotype machine. And I had plenty for her to type. I started with the inundation and all the people killed in that tragedy.

"Yes, I'm aware of that disaster, of course," Agent Bascomb said.

"My father owned the drilling company."

"Oh, I'm sorry. Of course, Doucet Drilling. I hadn't made the connection. I believe it was reported that Harvey Doucet committed suicide after that tragedy."

"It wasn't suicide, sir. That's what the police reported, then promptly closed the case. But I know better."

"Oh?"

"That's why I took an extended leave from the Air Force. I knew, as a Catholic, Father would never commit suicide. I wanted to prove it was murder. But in the process, I've learned so much more than I even hoped or wanted to learn."

"By all means, continue, Major."

I moved on to the discrepancy I'd found in the maps of the drill site and where the faulty map came from; the Secret Service agents who ran me off the road and ran Gremillion to his death in the swamp, and finally ended up dead themselves yesterday.

"Yes. We've got the reports of the bridge incident. And

yesterday's incident. And you were the shooter?"

"Yes sir, Placide and I." I described that whole incident, to which Agent Bascomb interjected, "Good God, Major. Go on."

I described the "alleged" suicide of Dawkins after I had snooped at Ideal Tractor in Memphis, and of Armstrong's ties to Treasury Secretary Huff. I told him about Father's car being blown up, and that I was supposed to be in it at the time. I handed him the police report from Tennessee; copies of files the attorneys had obtained from their FOIA request; copies of accounting documents Marlisa had provided, thanks to Christie's husband; copies Candace Soileau had made of Joseph Haggerty's file; the clandestine photos I had snapped of Armstrong, Haggerty, and Matherne; and the other files and notes Earlene and I had dug up. I told him about the implications of Deslatte's shale processing plant and toxic waste dump, the complicity of Governor Mansur and Secretary Huff. And, of course, I told him about Armstrong's hedge fund with Secretary Huff on its board, the theft of profits and pensions, and the stock selloffs.

Agent Bascomb looked dumbfounded throughout much of my narrative. When I finally finished, about an hour later, he said, "Well, Major, that's some story! I do want to caution you from any continued investigation. But I'd also like to thank you for being a responsible citizen. Rest assured, we'll take over from here and fully investigate these allegations. If what you provided us is proved, you may be responsible for pulling down a large conspiracy network. But for now, I think you can get back to your important job in the Air Force."

"How long might it take before I hear something?"

"Well, Major, with such high-level players implicated, I believe this will be fairly high priority. We should have some answers in a couple of months. Trials and appeals could go on for years, though. Sign these notes, please, and we'll be in touch."

Placide and I didn't waste any time getting back to New Iberia. I called Marlisa right away. "Marlisa, can you meet me for a drink? I have some amazing news," I said.

"Oh, great! I can't wait to hear some good news for a change. Provost's?"

"Yes."

"I can be there in an hour."

When she arrived, I ordered us each a glass of chardonnay. "I've come to the end of the investigation," I told her. "The FBI is taking over from here, so we'll just have to wait for their investigation now."

"That's fantastic, H! I guess this means you'll be going back to North Carolina." She looked a little woebegone. "I have to admit, H, I hate to see you go."

"I'll miss you, too. You've been my rock through all this. Maybe you can come visit me once in a while?"

"Yes, I'd like that."

"And I'll come visit you whenever I get leave. I've used up most of what I had saved up, but I'll earn some more. Would you like me to visit you?"

"I'd like nothing more."

When I walked her to the car, she gave me more than a peck on the cheek this time. I saw Placide wink at me from the car when we finally ended our embrace.

Then I called Earlene and filled her in.

"I'm glad you had the wherewithal to never give up, H. I hope we'll see you soon."

"I have to admit, I never thought I'd miss Louisiana after I escaped. Now I can't wait to come back. I'm glad Father set up contingency plans with LeBlanc, so I can go back knowing the company's in good hands, with you and Marc at the helm."

"Yes, don't worry, H. Marc knows the ropes, so he slid right into the position with minimal transition. He's already got another new drilling contract, thanks to Léon Savois."

"Wonderful. Let him know how pleased I am to have him there. And take care of yourself, Earlene. You're indispensable, you know."

"Thanks, I will, and I'll keep up with Ethel and Louis, too. You can rest easy and go finish your commitment to Uncle Sam."

Next, I called my XO and asked him to get me a military hop from England Air Force base in Alexandria, Louisiana, back to Seymour Johnson, ASAP. The long nightmare was finally over, for me anyway.

Epilogue
JUSTICE

Four Years Later

Over the last few years, Marlisa had come to grips with her loss, and she and I had become an item. We visited back and forth a few times over those years. I had secured single housing on the base, so Marlisa had a place to stay, right by my side, when she visited. We had evolved from friends to confidants, and finally, to lovers.

Midge, only an abstract memory now, had met the man of her dreams and was settled comfortably in a Charlotte home with two cats and two kids. I couldn't have been happier that she found someone who apparently lacked my neuroses. Maybe I'd even lost some of my own neuroses. What is life, after all, if not a test? A means of shaping us into what we become. Granted, a tough test, at times. But had events not transpired as they had, as tragic as many of them were, I would never have met this vision that was Marlisa. I knew Charles would always remain in her heart, but she was beginning to have enough room left over in there for me as well.

I learned that Marlisa had been the one who sent the two yellow roses to Father's funeral. She had sent a similar pair of roses to each of the funerals following the inundation. Charles's coffin had been draped with a spray of yellow roses, and she wanted the two yellow roses to give her a connection with the others who had lost loved ones.

She told me, "Yellow roses symbolize remembrance and the promise of a new beginning." I hoped she'd be willing to share that beginning with me.

The whole town of New Iberia had been following the various trials, attending court whenever possible, hoping to avenge the needless death of loved ones, friends, or mere acquaintances after our town's worst man-made tragedy ever. As we were leaving an Appeals hearing in Baton Rouge, Léon Savois introduced me to his son, Jamie, a strapping youth of twelve now, nearly as tall as his father, who could have ended up another statistic four years ago. "You remember my father and mother?" Léon asked me when Auguste and Angelle walked over to them. He patted his father on the back.

"Of course. Nice to see you again," I said, shaking both their hands. Angelle's eyes sparkled with pride as her grandson put his arm around her prodigious waist.

Léon informed me about the new drilling contract in the Gulf that he and Marc LeBlanc had agreed on, and it looked like they'd continue working together on future projects. Léon's father was one of several witnesses who had been called to testify about the catastrophic environmental degradation of Lake Chevreuil since the inundation. Of course, Auguste, who said on the stand that he had always despised "that damn jack-up stuck right there in the middle of my fishin' lake," and that now, "They ain't no more fish in there to catch," had no qualms about saying exactly what he thought under oath, a characteristic of many a Cajun creeping up on 80. His candor, spoken often in the local franglais, had caused an occasional ripple of laughter to lighten the mood in the courtroom and a sporadic rap of the gavel for order.

Léon had been subpoenaed to testify on Doucet Drilling's behalf, and along with other character witnesses, like Placide, Earlene, Sid Ardoin, and Eric Arcenaux, had managed to clear Doucet Drilling's name of complicity in the scheme. And Candace Soileau, who had taken my advice and come to work for Doucet, had also testified in defense of Doucet, as well as confirming Joseph Haggerty's complicity in supplying the faulty map.

Jack and Mable Brouillette also came over to say hello. If Mable still felt any resentment toward Marlisa, she kept it at bay when she saw Marlisa's arm in mine. Jack and some other salt miners had testified in more than one trial on the intentionally destructive practices at the salt mine even before Armstrong took over. It was finally determined that the company had intentionally allowed the mine to deteriorate, knowing it would soon collapse anyway. Or rather, assisted in its deterioration. Its imminent destruction was originally planned by then CEO Huff, before Armstrong ever arrived on the scene to join him and to clean up on insider trading, accounting fraud, racketeering, and bogus insurance claims.

By now I had begun to understand how Father, in his grief after losing Mother, could just bury himself in work instead of family. It seemed the more I searched for clues to his murder, the more I understood that his icy demeanor, previously a mystery to me, had really been a defense mechanism in a corrupt world. Besides being a cynic, he was a romantic and an idealist. But born in an era when men were supposed to be tough, he never dared to let down his guard and show it. I could relate. I guess I had become just like him. I think I even figured out why he had so overtly favored Victor. My closer resemblance to Mother would have been a constant reminder of his loss and unarticulated grief. With all his bravado, he simply couldn't bear the pain. Nor could he admit his weakness to anyone, not even to himself. Finally, my angst had turned to empathy. Father had lived a lonely and tragic life that ended in a lonely and tragic death.

Thanks to Marlisa, I was finally erasing some of the stench I had picked up working on the case. Now I could see how snubbing my nose at the business and joining the Air Force would have been a personal affront to Father. The business was his life after Mother died. And fighting all the fraud, an inevitable accompaniment to corporate greed, had ended that life. I was proud that instead of joining the corruption, he had kept up the good fight until the end. He was a stoic, a rare breed, and deserved a better legacy than the ungrateful son I had become.

Not surprisingly, Victor's trial joined the throng of court trials. Not his first rodeo, of course. I had sometimes considered whether he might have been involved in the insider trading leading up to the inundation. But he'd been too preoccupied with completely egocentric concerns to have a clue of what was going on in Father's world. Besides, none of the big fish would have trusted him enough to include him in their intricate insider trading scheme. No, Victor's problems were on a much smaller scale and involved immediate gratification at any cost. It seems he had finally had a run-in with another irate husband, unfortunately a man he also owed a huge gambling debt to, and ended up doing some time for aggravated assault.

Fortunately for the business, Father had come to his senses and written Vic out of ownership of Doucet Drilling but left him enough money to live comfortably without ever having to lift a finger again, which was probably a stroke of genius on Father's part, though it left Victor with too much time to get into scrapes and too much money to lose at the craps table. Vic had tried to contest the will for a few months, but soon realized he had come out of it well-set, stopped doling out his inheritance to attorneys, and stopped going around the office to hassle those who remained. Sadly, he no longer considered me family. His resentment, despite his nest egg, was still too great.

But I had begun to see through Victor's resentment to his vulnerabilities and insecurities. Hell, hadn't I harbored my own resentment for years? After all, we shared not only DNA, but also the same unfortunate experience of living in a shattered family with surrogate parents, who, despite being the next best things to parents, could never quite replace in our minds our real mother, nor the father who had virtually deserted us. Victor and I had merely acquired contrasting coping mechanisms: Victor plied himself with material goods and fast women to replace the lack of love; I simply escaped New Iberia at my first opportunity, dragging all my animosity with me. Neither option could have proved successful. I couldn't fault Victor anymore. I could only blame all our flaws on a circumstantially dysfunctional family and an indifferent universe.

I vowed that one of my long-term goals would be to mend our shattered fences if Vic ever decided he was ready for us to make amends. So far, the prospect loomed far in the distance, like looking through the wrong end of a telescope. But after my experiences of the last four years, I was the first to admit that one never knows what the future might hold. I hoped that one day Vic would realize we were the only family left and let go of his animosity instead of his money for a change.

I had returned to Seymour-Johnson to finish my last few years in the Air Force. The moment I hit my twenty years, I took my retirement and, instead of becoming CEO of Doucet Drilling, I took a job as a safety engineer with OSHA. Instead of delving into big oil, I would instead be striving to keep big oil and other Louisiana industries in line with safety and health procedures. I vowed not to cut anyone any slack, including Doucet Drilling.

Doucet Drilling had kept Marc LeBlanc on as permanent CEO. I was on the board as part-owner, my main goal keeping anything resembling our past experience from ever happening again.

Thankfully, Earlene stayed on as office manager and efficiency expert. And no words can describe how valuable Placide still was to the company. If not for Placide, I wouldn't be here to tell the story. Always vigilant, always faithful, he was the family I never really had. And I guess we were also the family he never had. He was a man of few words, but we had made a fiercely loyal team. I no longer needed a bodyguard, but he remained my closest friend and confidant.

I could only imagine how long it would have taken Vic to get rid of those two gems, Placide and Earlene, if Father had not finally seen the light. I was sorry I hadn't gotten to know Father after he realized what his indulgence had caused Vic to become, though he would probably never have admitted it anyway. His disappointment would have been both profound and repressed. Father would have been proud of his team: Earlene, Placide, and Marc. Hopefully, he would have eventually forgiven me for not entering the business.

Uncle Louis had met his maker peacefully a couple of years ago at Christmas. His weak heart finally just gave up. Aunt Ethel found him in bed Christmas Eve morning after she had risen early and prepared him a peach cobbler. At least, she liked thinking, he died peacefully in his bed. Isn't that how we'd all like to go, after all?

I had already returned to the airbase by then, so I wasn't home to console her that morning. But she had the presence of mind to call Placide, who was there like a shot, Earlene told me. He had kept his small apartment nearby in New Iberia so he could keep an eye on them, still insisting they were the only family he knew. Eric Arcenaux, whom Louis had taken a liking to, gave Placide a break by keeping an eye on Ethel and Louis sometimes during his two weeks off every month. Arcenaux had continued giving Louis a hand in the "back forty," especially with any heavy work. He also kept up with Ethel after Louis was gone and gave her a reason to keep making those cobblers.

Not that Aunt Ethel wasn't as strong as an ox. She still rose early, to "take care" of the old place, she said. She could still wield a paintbrush or a screwdriver as well as a spatula. And she still told me I'd be the death of her whenever she got the chance, of course. But I figured it would take more than her nephew's reckless antics to bring that tough old bird down.

I had immediately taken a few days' liberty and returned to Louisiana for the funeral, where I found two yellow roses in a bud vase. That's when Marlisa told me the story of the roses and finally considered a more lasting relationship.

Of course, Aunt Ethel also loved Marlisa. Who wouldn't? So, she finally stayed off my case about settling down. I guess she saw hope for me yet. She hadn't stopped begging for "little Doucets" one day, though, and I knew she never would until I provided some. She wasn't waiting for Vic, that's for sure. Any Doucets he sired would likely not bear the name, legally anyway.

I had encouraged Marlisa to finish the degree program she had abandoned when she married Charles. She was now a Louisiana history teacher at Catholic High in New Iberia. She had helped me brush up on my dance steps, so you might see the two of us doing the Cajun waltz on any given night at one of the many Cajun hotspots and festivals within a fifty-mile radius of New Iberia.

More often than not, the outcomes of the trials that still trailed on in appeals after four years shocked and disappointed all of us. It seemed the higher up the economic scale and the worse the crime, the lighter the sentence.

Luckily for Dallas Matherne, after his extradition from Costa Rica, he had turned state's evidence at Sarah Beth's prodding. And what a story he had to tell. His testimony of a large monetary gain for ensuring that the bogus map was followed implicated the masterminds of the plot. After serving his two-year sentence, he was placed in the witness protection program, essentially for being a rat, but Sarah Beth had refused to join him for the same reason.

Sarah Beth had long since wised up, divorced Dallas, and instead of moving back to Tennessee with her parents, had, for the last three months, been Mrs. Sid Ardoin, Sid's first marriage having dissolved after another of his wife's indiscretions at the honky-tonk. Marc LeBlanc had promoted Sid to Project Manager at Doucet, a wise choice in my view.

The various trials had gradually brought the intricate web of crime and corruption to light. As the agriculture and oil businesses were approaching free-fall during the oil crisis, this cabal of corporate execs, lobbyists, and politicians had concocted the scheme to walk away with millions each.

After the FBI investigation, plus the documents we had provided and the FOIA documents, federal prosecutors empaneled the Grand Jury, who issued indictments to Treasury Secretary Huff, Louisiana Governor Mansur, Warren Armstrong, Carl and Joseph Haggerty, and a few of the other major stockholders, for conspiracy to commit fraud, racketeering, and insider trading. Of course, the federal investigations and trials of Carl Haggerty and Huff in DC had dragged on, and some appeals were ongoing, but those defendants were spitting in the wind. All they could hope for now were pardons from a sympathetic president down the road.

Sid Ardoin's testimony of Deslatte's insider trading, illegal toxic waste dumping, and fraudulent conveyance, on top of his other charges, had already netted Deslatte five years up the river and a sizable fine for polluting, considering the destruction to the environment and lives his business had caused. He had sold his business at enough profit to live comfortably, but he'd never be a multi-millionaire again. The EPA had monitored cleanup of the toxic sludge pit. We could only hope they would continue to monitor the facility more closely under the new owner. And I'd be visiting them periodically in my new OSHA capacity, just to make sure there was no backsliding.

The new, altered map, along with the new drilling company, new oil company, and all new employees, was the coup that kept the correct map a secret, with Haggerty's help in DNR. Then came the planned inundation of the failing salt mine with Matherne as a mole in Doucet Drilling to make sure it came off without a hitch, at least for the major players, following massive stock selloffs. Top all that off by paying a few dozen officials exorbitant bribes, and the plan seemed fool-proof. And if a few people got killed in the bargain, it was apparently worth the sacrifice. I was proud to be the one to punch a hole in their overinflated egos, though the sentences were a joke.

Armstrong was finally sentenced to a million-dollar fine and ten years in a white-collar prison, with possibility for parole in five. "A slap on the wrist and a tennis complex with a couple of guards," I whispered to Placide when we heard that verdict.

Oh, there were some hefty fines involved to divvy up among victims' families, but not even a drop in the bucket compared to what their crimes netted them in profit or what the families had lost in property, pensions, and lives of loved ones.

The two dirty Special Agents in the Chevy Blazer that Placide and I shot, it turns out, had been appointed and probably well paid by Treasury Secretary Huff. Of course, they were unable to testify, indisposed as they were. I suspected some time would be added to Huff's sentence at his sentence hearing, considering the extreme measures he had taken to keep his crimes from being discovered.

I had furnished prosecutors with contact information for Jake Richard, the oilfield worker who had witnessed the thugs trying to flip my car four years ago. His testimony sealed their complicity in the fraud from the beginning of the ordeal to its sordid end on Highway 90 in Patterson. And Placide testified that the same vehicle had reportedly ended Gremillion's life in the Atchafalaya Basin. As it turns out, those two thugs in the Blazer had also paid dearly with theirs.

As for the cowboy with expensive boots in the blue pickup, he had simply faded back into the vast sea of scum, likely somewhere in Tennessee, probably awaiting another opportunity as a hired killer. Dawkins's "suicide" had never been solved, but I figured the cowboy was the hired killer behind it. At least Captain Gordon in Memphis hadn't given up on finding him, so there was slim hope. But Gordon was pretty sure the blue truck had been repainted and sent to Mexico by now, so all he had left to go on were alligator boots and a beer gut, a pretty common sight in a place like Memphis. Placide had flown up there to look at some mugshots but didn't recognize any of them. It was likely it would take another crime for that scum to rise to the surface. Only then would we learn for sure who hired him, but I hadn't given up hope that he'd eventually hang himself. Thugs usually do. Even something as simple as a traffic ticket would dredge him up.

Fortunately, Placide's and my self-defense pleas held up, based on the indisputable evidence of the bullet holes in the Torino, photos of my wounded shoulder and glass shard cuts in my face, in addition to testimony by several eyewitnesses who had landed in the pile-up of twisted metal on the scene.

Nothing much had changed otherwise. Governor Mansur was re-elected by the good people of Louisiana despite his awaiting appeal on various charges. President Stanton had wisely removed Secretary Huff immediately from his cabinet position while Huff awaited his appeal.

Father's name was cleared of any suspicion of involvement in the inundation after the facts came out. And prosecutors were able to pin the sleeping pill overdose on the two special agents. Aunt Ethel finally thanked me for clearing Father's name, despite her misgivings about my involvement in the investigation. A devout Catholic, she was relieved to know she'd be seeing Father again when she joined Louis in heaven, where she was sure Father would be waiting, notwithstanding the errors he had made as a mere mortal. I was convinced that Father had discovered the selloff and the inundation scheme, and those high-level thugs were paid to shut him up, just as they had wanted to shut me up. Until we put a crimp in their style, they had pulled off what they thought was the perfect crime.

Mostly, I was relieved that it was all over. On one hand, it seemed as though I had lost four years of my life. On the other, I had gained more in that four years than in my entire previous life. Oh, I was still a cynic, especially when it came to the corporate oligarchy that was whittling away at what we call democracy, including big oil, with its continued destruction of Louisiana, thanks to tax breaks, subsidies, and lax regulations. But I finally realized that, like Marlisa, and like Father for that matter, I was becoming a romantic. I just hadn't been dealt a hand before that allowed me to realize any inherent goodness in people.

Oh, the bad apples would still be there, of course, festering away and trying to rot the rest of the apples. Greed would continue to result in an exponentially widening gap between rich and poor. The justice system would continue to reward corporate greed with lighter sentences than the underclass. Unregulated and rampant pollution would continue to erode the very core of civilization.

But the strong ones, the basically good ones, could keep the rot of corruption from touching them. Marlisa was just such a person. The others I had surrounded myself with had the same trait. We would stick together to ward off the stench of greedy players like Armstrong, Deslatte, the Haggertys, Mansur, and Huff. Their greed would reap its own reward in a lonely life, a complete absence of trust in anyone or belief in the inherent good of their fellow man, and more money than they could possibly spend in a lifetime. Hell, if you live in stench, you can only smell stench. I had had my fill of stench.

Marlisa and I stood hand in hand in front of the Appeals Court in Baton Rouge after another of Joseph Haggerty's unsuccessful appeals. Besides Haggerty's part in supplying the faulty map, Sid Ardoin's records from Deslattes's Shale Processing Plant had implicated Haggerty in the fraud and insider trading for unloading Sapphire stock, and for his connections to his brother Carl's fraud in DC. This was his last shot before his turn up the river.

After we said our goodbyes to Placide, Sid, and the others outside the courthouse, I asked Marlisa to accompany me to The Village Restaurant, a favorite hangout of politicians in downtown Baton Rouge, for dinner over a bottle of Chardonnay. The tiny velvet ring box was burning a hole in the pocket of my khakis. Tonight was the night I'd pop the question, and I had a feeling this might be the night she would say yes. I was already picturing a honeymoon in Nassau, where I hoped to introduce her to two young friends of mine, probably nearly Jamie's age now, and have them dive for a conch shell for her, if they were still budding capitalists. I wasn't about to let this vision get away, no matter how long it took.

Afterword

Pillars of Salt is a fictional account of an actual disaster occurring on November 20, 1980, at Lake Peigneur and Jefferson Island, a mile north of Delcambre and nine miles west of New Iberia, Louisiana. Exploratory drilling by an oil rig in the lake accidentally punctured a salt mine at the 1300-foot level. The lake water simply melted the salt dome, creating a massive whirlpool and a vast cavern that swallowed the rig, a tugboat, eleven barges, several flatbed trucks, and 65 acres of Jefferson Island, including houses and trees. The onrush of water caused the Delcambre Canal to reverse, pulling water from the Gulf of Mexico, filling the lake with saltwater, and leaving shrimp boats stranded in the canal on dry land. For several days, the rush of water created the highest waterfall ever in Louisiana, 164 feet.

Miraculously, no people were killed in the actual disaster, though three dogs were lost. The late Léonce Viator, Jr. (d. 2014) and his nephew were fishing in the lake and narrowly escaped to shore. He mentioned in a video that he wouldn't be fishing in that lake anymore.

Any evidence to identify the cause of the disaster was lost in the lake or destroyed. An interesting eight-minute video of the disaster, including a few words by Mr. Viator, can be found at: https://wccourt.com/2017/11/20/in-re-louisianas-disappearing-lake/

My book begins with the disaster and leads to an entirely fictional account of what *could* have happened.

About Atmosphere Press

Atmosphere Press is an independent, full-service publisher for excellent books in all genres and for all audiences. Learn more about what we do at atmospherepress.com.

We encourage you to check out some of Atmosphere's latest releases, which are available at Amazon.com and via order from your local bookstore:

Saints and Martyrs: A Novel, by Aaron Roe

When I Am Ashes, a novel by Amber Rose

Melancholy Vision: A Revolution Series Novel, by L.C. Hamilton

The Recoleta Stories, by Bryon Esmond Butler

Voodoo Hideaway, a novel by Vance Cariaga

Hart Street and Main, a novel by Tabitha Sprunger

The Weed Lady, a novel by Shea R. Embry

A Book of Life, a novel by David Ellis

It Was Called a Home, a novel by Brian Nisun

Grace, a novel by Nancy Allen

Shifted, a novel by KristaLyn A. Vetovich

Because the Sky is a Thousand Soft Hurts, stories by Elizabeth Kirschner

About the Author

Author J.A. Adams is retired in Northern Colorado after teaching English for sixteen years at Louisiana State University. This debut novel grew out of observing and becoming enamored with the Cajun culture during those years.